A Devon Deception

Best wishes

Julia

A
Devon
Deception

Julian Mitchell

Matador
9 Priory Business Park,
Wistow Road, Kibworth Beauchamp,
Leicestershire. LE8 0RX
Tel: 0116 279 2299
Email: books@troubador.co.uk
Web: www.troubador.co.uk/matador
Twitter: @matadorbooks

ISBN 978 1800460 607

British Library Cataloguing in Publication Data.
A catalogue record for this book is available from the British Library.

Printed and bound in Great Britain by 4edge Limited
Typeset in 11pt Century Gothic by Troubador Publishing Ltd, Leicester, UK

Matador is an imprint of Troubador Publishing Ltd

Once again, my grateful thanks to Len, Debbie and Eoin not just for their editing skills, but also for their support and encouragement.

ONE

"You're too bloody close!" the driver shouted loudly to himself directing his fury at the person behind. The headlights of the following vehicle were so close to the back of his twelve-year-old Land Rover that he couldn't see them in his rear view mirror, just the reflected glare through his back window. Driving down the narrow lane, Dan Morris, a freelance investigative journalist, was a little late for his rendezvous at Oceans Restaurant on Bolberry Down overlooking Bigbury Bay. He had arranged to meet his partner, Karen White. The restaurant was set back a few hundred metres from the rugged coast.

He was late returning from a parish council meeting where a planning application had been discussed. Travelling rather faster than conditions would safely allow, due to his lateness, he reasoned that he was relatively safe as the darkness meant he would be alerted to any approaching vehicle by its headlights; he hadn't bargained for the dazzling lights from behind.

Driving too fast was one thing, but being tailgated at speed was quite another. As far as he could tell it was the same car that had been behind him through the lanes that was now taking much closer order.

Early spring snow had fallen during the day – unusual, but not that rare an occurrence – and the fields surrounding the single-track road reflected white in the peripheral bright flare from the main beam of his headlights. Fortunately it had not settled on the road, which glistened with a black sheen suggesting it was turning to ice. As the road was a dead end, only leading to the restaurant where he was to meet his girlfriend, he was bracing himself for the inevitable altercation with the stupid driver behind as he could only be going to the same place. Although Morris was usually mild-mannered, he would find it difficult to be rational and even-tempered when confronting the person who had driven so cretinously.

He slowed as he approached the cattle grid at the end of the road and prepared for the right-angle turn that would take him up the track to the restaurant. He was thankful that the tailgater had dropped back about two cars' lengths; he assumed, wrongly, this was to match his reduction in speed as he negotiated the sharp turn. As the Land Rover slowed the car behind accelerated.

There was a sickening thud and his head jerked back forcibly against the headrest. In normal conditions the result of the impact would have been less severe and he would have been able to regain some semblance of control. Also if the road had continued in a straight line it might have afforded better grip, but the tarmac stopped at the cattle grid. Unfortunately, after the right-angle turn to the restaurant the continuation of the road turned to snow-covered gravel, that then gave way to an icy grass-covered steep slope down to the cliffs beyond.

Although Morris yanked the steering wheel down to his right and literally stood on the brake pedal, his backside lifting clear of the seat, the direction of travel was set. The brakes locked and his car didn't deviate from its course as it careered over the gravel, sledging over the snow and inexorably hurtling towards the cliff edge and the jagged rocks below.

If the slope had been shorter he would not have had time to react. Miraculously he managed to undo his seatbelt when realising there was nothing he could do to stop or change course. Remarkably, considering the perilous circumstances, in one smooth motion he opened the door and threw himself clear as the car careered forward, relentlessly heading towards the precipice.

It plummeted out of sight and from a sudden brief burst of light he knew it had ignited on impact with the rocks below. What he didn't know was that the burst of light was from the initial flare as the petrol tank exploded before the flames had been quickly extinguished by a huge wave crashing over the stricken vehicle.

Due to his momentum, he too was slithering out of control over the snow headfirst down the slope. His mind was in overdrive as he recalled the terrain from past walks and he knew that the cliff edge was approaching fast: shortly he too would be plunging headlong into the darkness, the sea spray, the rocks and certain death.

As the cliff edge neared and his impetus slowed a little he could just make out the ragged outline of something in his path. As he grasped the weather-beaten gorse bush the pain in his hand was excruciating from the spines, but he knew far greater albeit momentary pain awaited him if he released his grip. He was so close to the edge, he could hear the waves below crashing onto the rocks. The act of grabbing the bush had changed his position from head first to feet first down the slope. He was now lying on his front looking back up from where he began his unwelcome slippery descent.

The headlights of the shunter vehicle at the top of the slope picked out the ruts made in the snow by his own car as it had careered out of control down the slope. Even in the immediate aftermath of his harrowing ordeal, Morris rationalised this was no accident. This was a deliberate attempt on his life and if the assailant had seen him jump from his vehicle he may well be coming down the slope to confirm his kill or to finish the job.

He could just make out the shadowy figure silhouetted against the main beam of his car. Fortunately, as the ground sloped away down to the cliff, the main thrust of light shone over the top of the saviour gorse bush.

As Dan Morris looked up he could still see the macabre figure walk between the two beams and momentarily stand between them, no doubt peering seaward to satisfy himself that the rammed car had plummeted over the edge. Then he could see the figure start heading down in his direction.

He started shivering from shock and from lying in the freezing snow; he was powerless to defend himself and awaited his fate.

He reluctantly glanced back up the steep incline to find the silhouette had disappeared. Then the headlights picked out the figure getting to his feet from where he must have slipped in the treacherous conditions. The freezing snow that had proved so perilous was now to save him.

The black shape then moved back across the headlights and appeared to stoop down to collect something. In a few moments he reversed and the tail lights gradually disappeared from view back up the approach road.

Still in shock, with gorse spines piercing his hand, Morris dragged his aching body up the slope, initially on all fours; he was immune to the pain all over his body and the cold crisp snow beneath his knees and hands.

He was physically and mentally struggling after the attack to come to terms with what had just happened to him, or to comprehend why. Little did he know that this attempt on his life would not be the last.

TWO

Crimes in South Devon were like London buses: you could wait for ages then three would come along at once! The crimes being dealt with by detectives were seldom all concluded at the same time, only in exceptional circumstances. Neither did other criminal investigations neatly replace them. Normally crime detection was not that well ordered, but this was such a time.

Detective Inspector Richard King (he was never called Dick) and his small team of detectives had recently successfully concluded investigations into cases centred on and around Dartmoor National Park. Cases that included the disappearance of a young woman from Haytor – a prominent rocky outcrop on the east side of the park – and the numerous thefts of vehicles and machinery, predominantly from farms, which eventually had led to the successful prosecutions of the perpetrators. A barn fire lit up the criminal triumvirate of cases.

There was no doubting that King's already formidable reputation had been enhanced by these high-profile cases, though privately he chastised himself for not apprehending the farm thieves at an earlier stage, which would have saved further victims financial loss and in one case pain and suffering.

In his leisure time – what little he had – he loved art and was a great admirer of the Plymouth-based artist Robert Lenkiewicz, who despite his name was born in London. The renowned and idiosyncratic painter fascinated the inspector. He actually owned one of his self-portraits, personally given to him by the great man after he had apprehended someone trying to deface the famous wall mural he had painted in 1972 at the Barbican – not quite an old-fashioned Banksy, although price comparison on the artworks would have been similar.

King was of average height and average build, but they were all that was average about this career copper. Although he had supreme confidence in his own ability as a detective, his ego was so small it was practically non-existent. He was highly competent in his job, but he had no interest in promotion as he accepted his career grade had been reached: he was quite content with his rank and role. This was a self-limiting progression. A personal decision due in part to his philosophy that in work people can, possibly driven by misplaced ambition, rise to the level of their own incompetence. By remaining as an inspector he felt in control. What's more he liked what he did and didn't want to become a more senior officer and be further away from hands-on police work.

Having lost his wife to a brain tumour two years previously, he immersed himself in his job, finding solace in the many case successes and the interaction with his close colleagues, particularly those of a lower rank than his own.

He had developed a habit of sucking a sherbet lemon while pondering his next move in any investigation. The sweets were his way of coping with his nicotine addiction: he had reluctantly quit the dreaded weed in 2007 following the introduction of the law that banned smoking in enclosed places – so his lungs were fine, but his teeth needed more attention than before.

In his job DI King was only influenced by facts and he had supreme confidence in his own judgement of people and events; he was seldom proved wrong. He had a very close working relationship with his detective sergeant, Lucy Harris, and both would have liked an even closer connection away from work, but the senior detective's loyalty to the memory of his dead wife remained too strong; that and his professionalism prevented him from acting on his latent emotions.

Detective Sergeant Harris was competent and confident at her job having received an excellent grounding as a police constable for seven years before becoming a detective. She was attractive with short-cropped blond hair and loved outdoor activities, principally mountain bike riding over the rugged terrain that Dartmoor offered. She had a very good working relationship with her boss, Inspector King, and although not formally appointed, he undoubtedly was her mentor. Harris was very ambitious and realised that the experience she was gaining from him was priceless. She had aspirations to be an inspector just like him.

Her main policing attributes were her quickness to grasp facts and her ability to succinctly record scene-of-crime details. She was also very adept at planning, which was crucial in a complex investigation. This last quality manifested itself in her making arrangements to gather information from witnesses or suspects without wasting valuable time.

Not being married or with a partner, fantasies can often develop in a boss/subordinate relationship and she dreamed of having Richard King as more than just a working colleague. She was unaware that her feelings were reciprocated – though so far not acted upon.

King's other loyal detective in his small team was Sam Dyson. Diminutive in stature she was growing in confidence in her work, although occasionally lacking a little self-belief, understandable when comparing herself to the charismatic inspector.

In her work she was diligence personified as in any investigation that required extensive searches of data she was thorough and tenacious. She too was ambitious, but knew she had much to learn before being considered for promotion to sergeant.

The inspector was absolutely delighted to welcome a new member to the team, under his direct control, in the form of Detective Constable Alex Hammond. His great-grandparents were part of the so-called Windrush Generation (named after the ship that had transported them) who had come to Britain between1948 and 1970 from the

Caribbean to help rebuild post-war England. His grandparents sold fruit and vegetables wholesale, but Alex's father, rather than continue in that family business, became one of the first black officers in the Met Police; Alex was to follow in his father's footsteps. After attending Exeter University, he had the necessary degree to apply for direct entry into the police as a detective.

A few months previously he had been temporarily seconded from Exeter Police to King's team to help with its burgconing workload. After that consummate secondment he had returned to his home station, but was so impressed with King and the other detectives in Plymouth that he had requested a permanent transfer, which had been granted. A promising career beckoned for DC Hammond and at six foot six inches tall and weighing sixteen stone, comprising mostly muscle, he was a welcome addition should the toam encounter any villains who would not go quietly!

While on duty in Exeter city centre after a home team football match – that Exeter City had lost – he had intervened when a gang of six so-called supporters had set upon a solitary fan from the opposing team. The ringleader of the yobs may have regretted the racial slur he had aimed at Hammond, but his memory was a little confused after his arrest and hospitalisation. His sheer size and evident muscle tone normally acted as a deterrent to would-be attackers, unless alcohol had given them misplaced bravado. He was due to return in a week's time, when he had finished a case he was involved in as the arresting officer, that had reached Exeter Crown Court.

The only staffing concern for the inspector was the appointment of his new boss following the departure of Superintendent Edwards on promotion. His successor was Detective Chief Inspector Brian Roberts who was being temporarily promoted to superintendent and transferred from Exeter Police. King had no problem with someone receiving temporary promotion or becoming his boss. What he did have a problem with was his personal knowledge of the officer, as they had previously worked together about ten years before with Tavistock Police.

The balding, overweight senior officer had risen steadily through the ranks. His promotion, albeit temporary, had followed because obviously he was good at his job, but his interpersonal skills were somewhat lacking in his relationships with work colleagues, particularly those of a lower rank to his own.

When he and King had worked together they had nearly come to blows over the treatment of a junior constable who was bullied by Roberts, then an inspector, to the point of breakdown. People change, King thought without really convincing himself, as he knew that people with that sort of personality flaw probably got worse as their power and influence increased. He was already sharpening his protective instinct, particularly towards the inexperienced Detective Constable Dyson, but was more than aware he had to show respect to his new boss. Deep down he knew he was an utter bastard and doubted that the intervening years would have mellowed him. Indeed, higher rank may have made him worse.

Little did any of the detectives know that this latest crop of cases would stretch far beyond the county border of Devon, involving skulduggery as well as threatening the lives of several people, including one of their own.

THREE

When a corpse has been exposed to seawater for a lengthy period, it can become hideously bloated. The naked man, whose body had been washed ashore in Hope Cove, a South Devon beach, was no exception. All of the emergency services had been alerted to the grisly find, including the RNLI. These brave people didn't have far to travel as the body was a stone's throw from their lifeboat station; sadly today they wouldn't be rescuing this man. Inevitably, as the emergency services arrived after discovery of the body, it would be the police that would take centre stage.

Richard King was to lead the investigation and he had already contacted the first response police officers and told them what to do and what not to do. He wanted people kept away from the area, which was now a potential crime scene. He also instructed that if the tide was coming in, photographs should be taken of the body before it was moved by the officers out of reach of the rising water level; rather unnecessarily he had asked that the body be left where it was if the tide was going out.

He and his detective sergeant and constable were travelling the twenty-six miles from Plymouth central police station in the same car; a journey that would take drivers forty-five minutes was reduced to half an hour thanks to an escort of flashing blue lights and two-tone siren. Speed was of the essence as the potential crime scene could soon be washed away.

They travelled more or less in silence with King sucking on his trademark sherbet lemon and in reflective mood. It was only recently that other cases had been concluded and he was still troubled by the murder of a young woman in the prime of her short life. That regret apart, he was very happy with his detective team and particularly pleased that DC Alex Hammond would be rejoining them as a permanent posting following his hitherto short-term secondment.

Hope Cove, with its newly acquired human jetsam, comprises two beaches, Inner Hope and Outer Hope, and holds the dubious honour of being the only place in England where Spaniards made landfall during the reign of the first Queen Elizabeth.

As he got older, King enjoyed driving less and less and was happy to be chauffeured by DC Dyson. He liked all of his detectives to be involved at the start of a potential murder investigation as at some point they might be needed. If a case was later considered an accident or suicide then he would reassign them to other tasks.

The inspector had given his initial instructions to the on-site police and now wanted a more accurate assessment of tide times. Sergeant Harris, thorough as ever, provided more precise information.

"Sir, I've checked the tide information and we are having neap tides today as the Sun and Moon are in line with each other, which means smaller tide movement. This afternoon's high tide will be at just after four o'clock so I estimate the tide will reach the body again in about an hour." This new information gave a greater sense of urgency to the task in hand.

It appeared that the earlier ebb had deposited the corpse at high tide, which at least gave a starting point for the investigation as to the time it had been washed ashore. Harris had already checked this information and told her boss that the earlier high tide had been at about half past three earlier that morning. However, shrewd as always, King did not automatically accept that the body had drifted in on the tide. He needed to be sure it hadn't merely been dumped on the shore, so attention might have to be given to any sightings of it being deposited on the beach.

All three detectives ducked under the POLICE LINE DO NOT CROSS cordon tape that was strung across the entrance to the beach. A police pathologist, Doctor John Gleeson, was kneeling by the dead man and taking photographs of different parts of the body and surrounding sand.

"Hi, John. Initial thoughts?" King and the pathologist were work colleagues of many years' standing and had a mutual respect that didn't quite extend to friendship.

"Hello, Richard. Male between thirty-five and forty years old. Approximately 177 centimetres or about five foot ten inches tall. I'd estimate about fourteen stone in weight or eighty-nine kilograms, so about ten kilos overweight or one and a half stone according to Body Mass Index. A smoker, judging by the nicotine on his fingers. Suffered a blow to the back of his head with a round object, bigger than a baseball bat, but not that sort of shape; by that I mean not tapering. The blow was of sufficient weight or delivered with sufficient force to fracture the base of his skull."

"What about time of death?" King enquired of his colleague.

"That's not easy to establish. The postmortem may give the approximate time of death, but due to the effect of the seawater that will only be accurate to plus or minus two hours.

"I should be able to tell if he was dead before he entered the water or drowned. When I open him up it should reveal how much seawater is in his stomach and how much is in his lungs. The more water in the stomach the greater the probability the man drowned. When drowning the body reacts by sealing the airway to the lungs hence the stomach water is key. I could go on, but I'll include the clinical diagnosis in my report.

"As to the bloating, I have seen many drowning cases. If someone has been in the water a while, they bloat as they fill with gas; their eyes can pop out and the tongue protrudes grossly. The longer they're in the water, the softer the tissue becomes. On the other hand, we have had people who have drowned and, despite having been immediately brought out of the water, and in some cases hospitalised, looked normal; sometimes, a little foam comes out of the mouth from the water in the lungs. I think judging by his bloated appearance this fella may have drowned within the last twenty-four hours.

"He is wearing a jade ring on the little finger of his left hand; symbolically this represents harmony and is supposed to bring good luck. The gemstone is etched with the initial letters 'MC'. The only other observation I would make at this stage, before I have a closer look back at the lab, is that I don't think he was short of money, not just because of the jade."

King looked quizzically at the pathologist who appeared to be making an observation outside the field of his expertise.

"Why do you say that?"

"I recognise the watch he's wearing. It's a Rolex Submariner gold watch. I happen to own one that I bought second hand. Buying new you wouldn't get much change out of twenty-five grand."

"Thanks, John. Please let me know when you've finished the postmortem. Obviously, I'd like to match his prints against our database."

With that he and his detectives quickly walked around the beach in different directions; King was an occasional miracle worker, but he was no Canute. They were looking for anything else that might give a clue to the dead man's identity. After ten minutes Lucy Harris called her boss over to where she was standing. As he approached she was taking a blue latex glove from her pocket and reaching down to the sand. She picked up what appeared to be a small black leather rectangular box with a green strip of leather sewn on it from end to end. The salt water had begun to break down the stitching, but the word 'Moro' could still be read.

"Well spotted, Lucy. We'll have to get that forensically tested. Whether it's linked to the dead man or not is something else we'll have to check out. We may be clutching at straws, but we have precious little else to go on."

After another half an hour the detectives had combed the rest of the diminishing beach and watched as the body was removed before the sea could reclaim it. Feeling slightly cheated by the elements, they moved above the high tide line. The inspector took out a sherbet lemon from his ever-present sweet bag and after a short time addressed Harris and Dyson.

"Finding out what happened to the missing woman on our last case was very difficult as we didn't have a body or any clues as to what had happened to her. In this case, even though we have a body and, possibly, some evidence, I think it will prove as difficult to solve. If the blow to the back of the head is not as a result of a fall, which John Gleeson should be able to confirm, this is a murder investigation. No rest for the wicked, I suppose."

Sergeant Harris understood the sentiments of King's comment, but would have preferred an alternative word to wicked. Her mobile rang. King regarded his mobile as an unnecessary intrusion, often leaving it switched off, so contact tended to be with his sergeant.

"Sir, it's the acting superintendent for you." The inspector hid his irritation as he took the mobile.

"King here, sir."

"Ah, Dickie, I couldn't reach your mobile so rang your sergeant."

"Poor signal out this way." Which didn't explain why his boss could make contact with his sergeant's phone.

"You're out at Hope Cove, aren't you?" He didn't wait for a reply. "I'd like you and your team to take on another case. Happened not far from where you are now. That's why I'm ringing."

"What's the case, sir, and when did it happen?"

"Last night. The uniform officers attended and dealt with it, but having spoken to the victim, they think it could be attempted murder. Car run off the road."

"Last night? It's now mid-afternoon, sir. I like to be at a crime scene early before anything is disturbed."

"Look, Dickie, just get on with it before the trail gets even colder. I've sent a copy of the incident report electronically to your sergeant. The area has been taped off and the uniform boys will fill you in with what happened. Report to me first thing in the morning back at the station on both the cases." He rang off.

King handed the phone back to his sergeant and put a sherbet lemon into his mouth. Two things irritated the inspector: firstly the delay in getting him involved in what could be a serious crime and secondly the way in which his superior addressed him. What's more he was aware that Roberts knew it irritated him and yet he continued to use the unwelcome epithet. He suppressed his annoyance; he was a master at masking his emotions. Harris sensed he was annoyed and understood some of the reasons for his antipathy towards his new boss. Soothed by his sweet, after a short time he spoke to her: "Acting Superintendent Roberts has given us another case to deal with. Possible attempted murder last night just around the headland at Bolberry Down. As we are out this way, let's leave our uniformed colleagues to do house-to-house stuff here, although I'm not hopeful that anyone will have seen anything, and take a look at the crime scene around the corner."

Turning to his detective constable, he asked her to stay at Hope Cove to help the other officers and report to him first thing in the morning. King and Harris got into their car and headed for Bolberry Down.

FOUR

The battery-powered lights on a spike, which could be bought from any garden centre, that night were acting as improvised landing lights. They twinkled in the dusk as the Cessna 206 wobbled from side to side in the brisk breeze as the pilot throttled back and prepared to land.

Bolt Head Airfield was an unmanned grass airstrip situated on the promontory of Bolt Head. The so-called 'farm strip' runway, being over 600 metres in length, could easily accommodate the small aircraft. The airfield was commissioned as an RAF airstrip in the autumn of 1940 and was to become an important strategic site for missions across the Channel, a situation which did not escape the notice of the Luftwaffe.

The brave men of yesteryear were far removed from the people using the airstrip this night.

The welcoming party consisted of two men, dressed in black, who had placed the eight battery-powered lights, four on each side of the twenty-four-metre-wide landing strip, and approximately twenty paces apart. Their brand new Nissan Navara

4x4 pick-up truck was parked at the end of the field, partially obscured from any prying eyes by a high unruly hedge. Its desire to remain hidden was also helped by its colour, inconspicuous black, although the makers simply called it metallic black.

The men had quickly positioned the makeshift landing zone just before the light aircraft had started its descent about half a mile short of the landing strip.

After the expected slightly bumpy landing it taxied to a halt at the far end of the airfield. Time was now of the essence as, although there were no populated buildings abutting the field, it was bordered by a tarmacked road, which led to a farm, and the arrival could easily have been observed or at least heard in the semi-darkness.

Although the pilot knew it would only take a few minutes to unload his cargo and be airborne again, he switched off the plane's engine and doused its lights in an effort to avoid detection. One of the men on the ground opened the aircraft's rear door, not even giving a monosyllabic greeting, while the other, without using head or side lights, drove the 4x4 close to the plane and made ready for the transfer. The inside of the Cessna had been modified and only the front two of its six seats remained. The rest of the cabin and baggage areas had been filled with individually shrink-wrapped shoebox-size packages that had been further wrapped tightly in polythene bundles of six with improvised handles for easy transportation. The street value of each bundle could be calculated at a cost of approximately £25,000. The twelve bundles were quickly removed and neatly stacked, most in the cavernous boot of the Navara and the remaining bundles were placed on the back seat.

The eight lights were quickly switched off and collected on foot and stashed in the rear foot wells. It didn't matter if their language was not the same as no words were exchanged between the three men during this slick operation as the 4x4 quietly pulled away from the aircraft and, still without lights, headed for the field's exit.

The pilot restarted the plane's engine and, as quietly as possible, taxied towards the other end of the airfield for two reasons: firstly, to take off into the wind to aid lift and, secondly, in order to use its full length. When it reached the end, it was swung around and lined up in readiness to become airborne. In the fading light his only guide was the slightly longer grass on either side of his avenue to the sky.

As he revved the engine ready to give it maximum thrust, it was only then he switched on the single spotlight at the front of the plane; this improved his visibility at the front, but only a matter of thirty metres ahead, and even then with very little peripheral light. At maximum revolutions of the engine he released the brakes allowing the Cessna's thrust to surge through the considerably lighter aircraft, relieved as it was of its cargo, to quickly accelerate to near take-off speed; it would be another hundred metres before it would be fully airborne.

Because the field was still used by aircraft, livestock were kept in adjoining fields and never allowed to graze on its plentiful grass. Sadly for the pilot not all walkers obey the Country Code and the last to cross the airfield had inadvertently failed to properly secure the gate between the juxtaposed fields. Attracted by the more plentiful fodder, some of the herd of beef cattle from the adjacent land wandered through the open gate. There was absolutely no need for any of these cattle to cross the close-mown grass as there was ample grazing on the side from which they had entered. Logical thinking wasn't part of bovine reasoning.

One of them that had been eating blissfully on its new pasture became spooked by the revving of the plane's engine and rather than running in the opposite direction, inexplicably headed across the by now partially illuminated runway.

The pilot saw the beast too late to take evasive action, which in any event, at the speed he was travelling, may have had serious consequences. He knew he had to act fast. It took a few seconds for him to react between spotting the unwelcome intrusion and deciding how best to avoid a collision. If he reduced the plane's thrust he would probably have hit the frightened animal anyway. Deciding to try and fly over it, he yanked back hard on the joystick in an effort to gain sufficient height. This seemed like a successful manoeuvre, but just when he thought he had completely cleared the intruder, one of the plane's wheels made solid contact with the rump of the animal. Due to rapid acceleration the plane hit it with such force that the pilot thought the undercarriage must have been significantly damaged as it sent the beast spiralling down the improvised runway.

He struggled to keep control of his aircraft as it continued to gain height, as the impact had significantly altered its trajectory. As he fought to regain control he could just make out below him the coastline and at one point thought he might have to ditch into the sea. Fortunately, there was no damage to the controls, though he knew that landing at his remote destination – an airfield in northern Spain – could prove to be difficult with the suspected damage to the underside of his plane. He wouldn't know just how bad it was until he attempted to land.

Meanwhile the men in the Navara were completely oblivious to what had happened back at the airfield and by now they were heading due north through the Devon lanes towards their drugs store to feed the rapacious County Lines gangs operating in many small towns across Devon. This consignment wasn't going far. It would take them about an hour to get to their destination. Their base, virtually in the middle of Dartmoor, would afford easy access to all the towns and cities in and bordering the national park.

*

As the damaged Cessna approached the northern Spanish airport of Oviedo, not far from Gigon, the pilot did not want to alert the emergency airport services, such as they were, as he would have to explain where and how he had sustained the damage. As he hadn't lodged a flight plan when he left, for obvious reasons, it might have aroused the unwanted suspicion of the authorities if he made a fuss on his return. Rather, he would trust to luck and land unobserved at a far corner of the airport, close to his car, which he had left in a lane well away from the small terminal building. He had been well paid for his clandestine mission.

He reflected he had already been lucky as at one point he considered ditching in the Channel; unfortunately for him his luck was about to run out.

He approached the remote landing strip, only illuminated by perimeter street lights, and gingerly reduced speed and height. As he touched down in a dead straight line with the centre of the runway, marked by a faded white line on the tarmac, the twisted undercarriage was now set to take the fuselage at an oblique angle to the pilot's intended course. This sudden dichotomy of travel flipped the plane so its wing was now scraping the ground causing sparks to fly. Although it was low on fuel after its flight, what was left ignited.

The fire was still blazing when the airport fire tender arrived at the scene and the flames quickly succumbed to the extinguishing foam. The white retardant eventually revealed the blackened upturned shell of the Cessna. The firefighters could just make out the outline of the incinerated pilot hanging upside down in the cockpit. Even if he had been able to release himself from his restraining harness, it may not have saved his life.

The air accident report prepared some weeks later attributed his death to pilot error as he had chosen to land on an isolated and poorly lit part of the airport. The twisted undercarriage was assumed to have received its damage on landing impact. The report concluded that had he been closer to the terminal, the firefighters' quicker response may have extinguished the flames far earlier. The fact that the illegal drugs trade had claimed another victim went unreported.

FIVE

Bolberry-on-Sea is a quintessentially English South Devon coastal village situated at the mouth of the River Avon. Its population of less than 500 souls is swelled in the summer months by half as many again due to the often absent second homeowners returning, and tourists occupying otherwise empty houses.

Numbers also increased at this time of year by occupation of the two static caravan sites at Warren Point just around the headland to the west. The picturesque village comprises a church, petrol garage, village stores (with post office incorporated), a village school – under threat of closure due to low numbers of children attending – a butcher, a hair salon, café, water sports centre, beach shop (summer months only) and a pub, the Duke of Cornwall (simply referred to as the Duke), which boosts its business doubling as a bed and breakfast.

Not everyone in the village appreciated the temporary influx of people or, indeed, the usually absent second homeowners who returned during their summer vacation and Bank Holidays. Neither were these particular residents in favour of any futuristic houses being built that would consume yet more of the village's precious coast and, to some, be a further blot on the landscape.

Furthermore some villagers feared that any new dwellings would likely as not be bought by rich business people from the big cities as a summer retreat, thus adding nothing to the village community. For some residents, and some parish councillors, the current outline planning application before the council for twenty-five executive homes fell exactly in that category.

However, the apparently more enlightened members of the community, particularly those running businesses, welcomed any increase in people as potential customers. Their philosophy was short-term growth in population was better than no growth at all and non-permanent residents still spent money when they were in situ. The business community also thought the village resident numbers permanently increasing was a good thing; if this was with wealthy people so much the better.

As in any community, particularly a village, its high-profile members were an eclectic group taking their designated responsibilities and contribution to village life seriously. Most served on the Bolberry-on-Sea Parish Council, some as genuine do-gooders, some out of self-interest, some out of their own self-importance and one due to his calling.

The Reverend Robert Brown, vicar of the picturesque parish church, falls in the last category and also in the first. A mild-mannered individual, unmarried, who sees good in all people, a character trait that is very appropriate for someone who found his vocation in life at an early age. His stipend is not great, but he doesn't have to pay any rent. It provides a comfortable living for the vicar as well as providing a modest amount for his curate.

Like most vicars in charge of rural communities, he looks after the churches in several parishes. As well as St Paul's in Bolberry-on-Sea, he preaches at St James the Less in Kingston, at All Hallows church in nearby Ringmore, St George's in Modbury and St Andrew's in Aveton Gifford. His 'home' church is St Paul's as he lives in Bolberry-on-Sea village. The reverend is always pleased to welcome people to his services or simply to have them look around the impressive building; signs are prominently displayed encouraging donations. Visitors could marvel at its ornate stained glass windows, elaborate wood carvings and gruesome gargoyles that spew out water when it rains.

Being responsible for five churches and surrounding parishes is no easy task. Saturday is the only day he is not involved in church work unless required at the bedside of an unfortunate parishioner.

The vicar is supported by his curate, Lucas Peverell, who helps out at services in the five churches. His duties include distributing and retrieving hymn books, assisting the reverend during Holy Communion and collecting monetary donations at services. His main job is working at the local garage in the village, mainly dealing with booking cars in for service and other associated paperwork, including the VAT returns.

He is not at all mechanically minded so doesn't get involved with the manual work of the garage, but can tidy up after the skilled labour provided by the owners. He rents a flat in the village, from Colonel Davenport, the parish council chairman. Peverell is not at all happy that the colonel has recently increased his rent by £25, even though the monthly amount still represents good value accommodation.

He can often be seen riding his scrambler motorcycle around the countryside to carry out his religious duties and stopping off at pubs in the various parishes. He is a rugby fan and twice a month travels to Sandy Park to watch Exeter, but never if they are playing on a Sunday, partly because of his ecclesiastical duties and also because he has to place greater reliance on buses, as opposed to trains, to get to the game.

Mike Farthing is Peverell's boss as joint owner of the local garage selling the only petrol for miles around. He inherited the garage on the death of his father ten years ago and has made very little improvement to it since then; the fabric of the building is, to say the least, tired. He is the wrong side of sixty and retirement beckons, but with no pension provision he will be dependent on proceeds of the sale of his business to give him a reasonable lifestyle in his old age.

His equity was halved five years before as the business needed a cash injection to stay solvent and he sold a half-share to his long-standing mechanic. Farthing looks younger than his years and is very attracted to Abigail Croft, a retired headmistress, who lives in the village, and often dreams of them spending the rest of their lives together – at her place not his. She is aware of his infatuation, but regards their friendship as purely platonic.

Farthing's Bolberry Garage services and repairs any vehicle with the aid of his miserable mechanic – and now business partner – Jim Preston; his 'glass' is always half empty. Unlike his co-owner, he doesn't serve on the parish council, which he often described as an overblown talking shop. Preston lives alone in a small, rather dilapidated cottage on the outskirts of Bolberry-on-Sea. He was born in the village, went to school in the village, worked in the village, at his present job, and seldom leaves the village, even though he has a passport and money to travel. Never been married, never been in love, never lived life. The only occasion he left the village for any length of time was when he was in the services, returning after demobilisation. His simple pleasures in life are a few pints at his local pub and smoking a packet a day of small Hamlet cigars.

He is a creature of habit going to the local Duke of Cornwall pub every night and sitting in the same chair, quaffing the same number of pints – five – and drinking the same brew. His short and stocky stature seems to fit his demeanour. The landlord at the pub, Dave Smith, jokes that Jim is very well balanced as he's got a chip on each shoulder; Preston doesn't find it funny.

Another councillor is a traditional local butcher, Gavin Harkness, who has served the village and surrounding area for over twenty years. His shop,

Pleased To Meat You, is sourced by local farmers and he is proud of all his many meat cuts, particularly his Devon lamb. Being a mild-mannered individual his affable disposition was assured until someone started extolling the benefits of veganism; then he wasn't quite so affable. His wife, Maria Harkness, helps out in the shop and has a more tolerant view of people's dietary preferences.

The local hair salon by the sea, aptly titled Making Waves, is unisex and the owner, Dawn Proud, is keen to cater for the needs of people who live locally as well as any visitor in need of a cut and blow dry or trim. Proud is a councillor and at council meetings rarely enters into discussions, such exchanges usually being dominated by a few outspoken colleagues. Nevertheless, she is a shrewd judge of issues and when she does speak her contributions always add value.

Her (rumoured) partner, Sandra Coppola, had come to England from Naples six months ago seeking work and approached Dawn Proud as she said she had some experience in hairdressing. As it turned out she was more adept at sweeping up hair rather than dressing it. She was renting a flat in the village, but latterly had taken a room in her employer's house. Her work pays for her stay, although as they became close, the rent to her boss/partner/lover has been waived. She is not yet twenty, vivacious and loves exploring the coastal paths and driving around the South Devon countryside – always alone – in a car borrowed from her lover.

One of the more bombastic councillors runs the

village stores. Ted Bayliss and his partner, Jane Ferris, have served the community for the last seventeen years and manage to earn enough from their shop to support themselves, but only thanks to the incorporated local post office, which provides a regular income. He is a rather brusque individual with a gruff voice, which can often be heard at council meetings; negativity is his default position. Jane Ferris by contrast tries to see the best in any proposals under discussion at council meetings and in life generally; she is never swayed by her rather pompous partner.

The Duke of Cornwall is the village pub and the landlord, Dave Smith, always has a warm and friendly welcome for locals and visitors alike; small in stature, but big on personality, he is a larger than life character always ready with a tale or a joke. He serves on the council and has done so for the last twenty-five years. At the last six council elections (held every four years) he has topped the poll. His income from his lively pub is bolstered by the four rooms he uses as bed and breakfast, his guests being grateful for the discount if they eat and drink in the Duke.

Other council members without piety or profit as their motivators are Doug Grant, a rather brash car dealer with a showroom in Exeter, who spends most of his leisure time at Bigbury Golf Club, which is less than ten minutes' drive from his home; Abigail Croft, the retired headmistress, who likes her village just as it is; and Scott Osborne, a young teacher who lives in the village and teaches at Kingsbridge Community College, which is ten miles away. At only twenty-three he is the youngest councillor by some margin. He cycles to work and back, a journey that takes him forty-five minutes.

Kirsten Massey, a local artist and spinster of the village, scrapes a living from selling her seascape paintings at galleries in towns around Devon. She rents a two-up two-down cottage in the village from Colonel Davenport, so has the same landlord as the curate; unlike him, she didn't begrudge the modest increase in her rent. She also serves on the parish council and her motivation for doing so is to get social interaction.

Last, but not least, is the aforementioned Maxwell Davenport, a retired army colonel who presides at parish council monthly meetings as its chairman. He refers to himself (as do the minutes of council meetings) as Colonel Davenport, choosing to omit 'retired'. He is not particularly popular with the other councillors, but is respected as he keeps meetings in order, not allowing any waffle, and is prepared to carry out onerous duties that are not necessarily a chairman's responsibilities; other councillors neither have the time or inclination to do them. He lives alone and is evidently a man of considerable means. No one is quite sure why he is so wealthy, but most favour inheritance. A very tall, dapper man with a full head of hair, he still retains his military bearing, projecting a commanding presence befitting his ex-army rank.

He collects his copy of the *Financial Times* from the village store, which is obtained especially for him – the only copy ordered by the shop – to keep a check on his numerous financial investments.

As chairman, Davenport is assisted in his role by the clerk to the council, George Barton. His job is to arrange meetings, record minutes, issue correspondence and deal with the financial aspects of the council. He also offers advice on procedural matters, albeit rather reluctantly for fear of giving the wrong advice. This is a salaried post earning him close to £12,000 per annum. He can advise the councillors, but doesn't have voting rights.

The Bolberry-on-Sea Parish Council, as the lowest tier of local government, manages and maintains the infrastructure of public facilities on behalf of the community they serve, dealing with issues that arise; litter and dog fouling are regular agenda items.

These rather mundane, but important, tasks were about to take a much lower priority as the councillors, and indeed the wider community, were about to become embroiled with an issue that would set councillor against councillor and lead to recriminations and criminality.

SIX

King and Harris duly arrived at the site of the attempted murder at Bolberry Down at about 3.30 that afternoon and were immediately approached by a uniformed police constable as he recognised his detective colleagues. The inspector knew him as PC Collins and didn't see the need for formal introductions.

"So what have we got, constable?" The diligent officer gave his account, occasionally referring to the notes he had taken.

King waited patiently for him to finish his detailed report before asking a question.

"Presumably when the police arrived last night, realising this is potentially a crime scene, the area where the ramming occurred was secured? It was cordoned off then, not this morning?"

"Four officers attended last night in two cars, sir, me and three others. Our shift didn't finish until eight o'clock and after listening to the victim's account, myself and a colleague drove back to the entrance to the restaurant drive where we are now. Using flashlights we could see the tracks of Mr

Morris's vehicle heading for the cliff edge. We taped along the coast side of the footpath that runs in both directions ensuring the actual point where the incident had occurred would not be disturbed."

King and Harris were impressed with the PC's report and that the taping had been done on the night of the incident.

The conscientious constable continued: "Although at that time of night we knew it was very unlikely that anyone would intrude on the crime scene, we wanted to deter any early morning walkers. We also had to think of our own safety as the ground was very treacherous and one of my colleagues slipped over as he was walking down the slope towards the cliff edge to see if the vehicle was on the rocks below."

"Was any inspection made of the scene last night?" King enquired.

"Only a cursory inspection, sir. As it happens I was back on duty at first light, about 8.15, with other officers. Unfortunately, by then the snow had melted. The four of us walked in a line from the top of the slope down to the brambles and cliff edge looking for anything that may help in the investigation."

"I appreciate the darkness and the ground conditions were slippery, but didn't it occur to you that the crime scene could possibly change by morning? I'm referring, of course, to the snow melting and with it potential evidence such as a footprint from the assailant."

"Sorry, sir. I didn't want a lot of people walking over the area in the dark. I thought it best to do a full examination in daylight."

King was not happy. Harris made a mental note of the learning point. The experienced detective inspector saw little point in making the PC feel worse than he already did.

"What's done is done, but we'll never know if the site has been compromised by the delay. What did the daylight search reveal? Anything?" King wanted to know more about the stricken car. "What about Mr Morris's car? Has any attempt been made to recover it?"

"It was recovered earlier this morning, sir, and has been taken to Plymouth for forensic examination."

The inspector guessed as much, as tyre tracks, wider than that of a car, were visible close to the cliff edge, he assumed made by the recovery vehicle.

The constable continued: "We very quickly located part of a broken number plate that was partially covered in mud, which we assume was from the vehicle that rammed Mr Morris's car. When it was recovered from the rocks I could see it had a tow ball fitted and I suspected that's what did the damage to the number plate as it appeared to be about that height." At that point he produced a polythene evidence bag with the middle section of a car's registration plate. Harris took the bag from the constable and examined it through its clear plastic cover before she spoke.

"I'll take it to Forensics, sir. They may be able to help, but there's not much to go on."

The constable finally added: "We also retrieved a mobile phone halfway down the slope, which we later established belonged to Mr Morris. It must have fallen out of his pocket as he jumped clear. Unfortunately, there were no tyre tracks left by the ramming vehicle and the officers couldn't find any other evidence."

Although the inspector was a little irritated by the lack of immediate action following what after all was probably the scene of an attempted murder, he was gracious towards the constable.

"Thank you, PC Collins, for a very detailed account. If you could let my sergeant have Mr Morris's address and contact details, we'll pay him a visit."

King and Harris slowly walked down to the cliff edge, following what they thought must have been the path that Morris's car had unwillingly taken, and both looked around for anything that may have been missed by the other searchers; they found nothing. They passed what they thought must be the gorse bush that had saved his life as it was slightly flattened. King left Harris to walk over the flattened brambles and look over the sheer drop to the jagged rocks below. His fearless image didn't extend to heights. On her return she told him of the compressed unruly bushes indicating where the car had plunged over the cliff edge.

He had seen enough: "Let's have a word with the manager of Oceans Restaurant, if he's in, to see what he can remember of last night's events."

He was on duty and over a coffee he told them what had happened and Harris noted his comments. He described Morris's dishevelled state and how, using the restaurant's first aid kit, his girlfriend had cleaned his bloodied right hand and picked out some thorns. They thanked him and then walked back to their car.

"Okay, sergeant. What have we got?"

Harris, unfazed, didn't hesitate in responding.

"Looks like attempted murder, sir, but we can't rule out road rage until we've spoken with Mr Morris. If it was the latter, he may be unaware of what he did to upset the other driver. If the former, what we don't have is any clue as to motive. That may become clear after our interview with the victim. As to evidence, anything Mr Morris can give us as to possible suspects wanting to do him harm would be useful, the broken piece of a number plate and anything Forensics can come up with from the wrecked car."

"That neatly sums it up, sergeant. If you could fix an interview with Mr Morris at his home address in Plymouth for, let's say, five o'clock later today; even better if his girlfriend was there too."

SEVEN

I t was the evening of the extraordinary planning meeting held in the Bolberry-on-Sea village hall attended by parish and two district councillors together with members of the public. When it ended shortly before eight o'clock, some of the parish councillors and a few of the public that had attended retired to the Duke of Cornwall pub close by.

When the attendees entered the Duke there were only three customers in the pub: Jim Preston, the local mechanic; Phil, an ever-present regular who always occupied his usual stool at the end of the bar; and the Reverend Brown's curate, Lucas Peverell, who was sat near the gents' toilet nursing a pint of lager, while looking intently at his mobile phone. Preston sat well away from them sending out 'Don't talk to me' signals. He sat reading the local paper for most of the evening and although he was within earshot of the councillors he paid them little heed.

The landlord, Dave Smith, immediately went straight behind the bar to help Jake, his trusty barman, to serve the meeting attendees who were more than ready for a drink. Despite the obvious factions at the meeting and evident rancour, people didn't divide into 'for' and 'against' groups, but were prepared to debate the points raised earlier. While Dave Smith was pulling Doug Grant's pint he engaged him in conversation with others listening in: "I don't know if you can help me, Doug? I've spent all afternoon on the *Telegraph* crossword and there is just one clue I can't get."

Grant wanted to be helpful and asked, "What's the clue then, Dave?"

"Postman's bag."

"How many letters?"

"Bloody hundreds!" was the landlord's reply, followed by much laughter from him and the impromptu audience. This provided some light relief after the general downbeat mood of the meeting and Dave Smith wasn't finished there. He served Gavin Harkness, the local butcher, next and he wanted a pint of Doom Bar – a local brew – and a dry white wine spritzer for his wife, Maria. The publican handed him his change for the two drinks and joked: "I had a dyslexic Yorkshireman in earlier."

Harkness waited for the punchline. "He was wearing a cat flap." This drew a wry smile from the normally straight-faced butcher.

When everyone had been served, the jovial landlord joined the others on their side of the bar. Over half of the parish councillors had come in for a drink. Noticeable absentees were the chairman, Colonel Davenport (retired), the Reverend Robert Brown, Scott Osbourne, the PE teacher, and Kirsten Massey who wasn't at the meeting.

The co-owner of the garage, Mike Farthing, ordered a drink for Abigail Croft, himself and also paid for a pint for Preston, his business partner; Peverell, who also worked at the garage, didn't get the same treatment as he had a full pint. Jake, the helpful barman, promptly delivered Preston's drink and he looked quizzically at him. Jake pointed at Mike Farthing. No smile, no thank you just the glass raised an inch almost in grudging acknowledgement of receipt.

Inevitably when everybody had been served the conversation turned to the proposed development of executive houses. Some repetition from what had been said at the meeting was inevitable, but this time delivered in an uninhibited manner. Abigail Croft was the first to voice her opinion and reiterate what she'd said at the meeting, which was a form of overt lobbying: "Our beautiful coastline is not just about the waves crashing against the rocks, it's also about what you see when you look up. If you're on the coast path and look inland you can see that hideous caravan park, and now what they're proposing will mean even more of our attractive fields are to be defaced."

Mike Farthing, looking rather smarter than when in his work attire, was quick to add his support.

"I agree with Abby. It won't enhance the scenery, won't be good for the environment and these houses will be way outside the price range of local buyers. You mark my words, they'll be snapped up by non-locals as second homes."

When he finished speaking he looked at Abigail Croft for her approval and she smiled. With that they both moved away to a nearby table, not in a childish huff, rather they just wanted to sit down. They were still close enough to hear other people's views, but it would take a very compelling reason for them to change their own.

Gavin Harkness was the next to put forward his view.

"Listen, there are twenty-five houses proposed. That's probably around fifty adults coming into our village, possibly more if the family moves in with grown-up children. Potentially it's also thirty to forty primary school-aged children. Now we know our village school is in danger of closing because it simply doesn't have enough kids to make it viable. So these families could be the saviour of Bolberry-on-Sea Primary School, which will obviously benefit the existing residents as well as the new arrivals." Doug Grant wasn't convinced.

"That's all very well, Gavin, but some of us haven't got kids, therefore there's no real benefit for us. Also, I'm not persuaded by the developers offering to build us a new community hall. As I said at the meeting, to me that's an out an' out bribe. Councillors shouldn't be taken in by that sweetener."

"Hear! Hear!" Mike Farthing offered from the background in support of what Grant had said and again looked at Abigail Croft for approval.

The village stores and post office owner, Ted Bayliss, wanted to counter that verbal support: "That's a rather selfish attitude, Doug. What I think is that since the recession it's been increasingly difficult to make any sort of profit from our shop or the post office. Both are important amenities for the village and without more people using them, I fear the post office may have to close and then running a shop will not be financially viable. Having new people come into the village may just save both."

Dave Smith had been quiet for some time, which was unusual for him; his dependable barman, Jake, served some other customers who had just come in the pub allowing the landlord to have his say.

"Well, it's a no-brainer for me. Do you know something? Nearly one thousand pubs closed in Great Britain last year. A thousand! At one point a pub was closing at the rate of one every twelve hours! Twelve hours! I don't want the Duke to be added to that statistic. I make a reasonable living when the village fills up in the summer months. However, the reality is that from October to March customers don't tend to come in, except my regulars, partly because, as we know, the population reduces to normal levels once the holiday season is over. Also it starts raining!

"So picking up on Gavin's point, if seventy odd adults moved into the village – I mean odd in number – those that like to drink and have a chat may come to the Duke because they don't have to drive and are guaranteed a friendly welcome. The extra income could be the difference between me staying open all year round, just opening during the summer months or closing for good. So being honest, I'm in favour of the development because it'll help me keep my pub open for the villagers to enjoy all year round. Mind you if I'm really struggling I'll borrow enough money to get completely out of debt!" The light-hearted tongue-in-cheek ending to his heartfelt view didn't dilute the message.

Dawn Proud, the local hairdresser, agreed with the other councillors who spoke in favour of the planning proposals. She hoped that a high percentage of the people who would move into the village, if the development was approved, would use her unisex salon rather than driving for half an hour to Kingsbridge or elsewhere to get their hair done.

Eventually the conversation moved away from new homes, and people started talking in smaller groups. Abigail Croft and Mike Farthing were deep in conversation and he seemed far more animated than when he was serving customers at his garage.

While this conversation was going on, the miserable mechanic came up for another drink and, without speaking, simply put the price of his pint on the bar. Jake, in his usual efficient manner, had anticipated Preston's request. Preston didn't bother returning the gesture by buying Mike Farthing a drink as he thought he might have to buy one for his lady friend; his pockets were very deep. As he walked back to his seat and paper he sat down and muttered under his breath: "Bloody claptrap!" referring to all the views being openly expressed in the bar. He looked totally disinterested about what had been said, whereas, in fact, he had been listening intently and had heard every word.

EIGHT

Detectives King and Harris arrived at Dan Morris's apartment overlooking Sutton Harbour in Plymouth. The door was answered by a young woman who responded to being shown their warrant cards by introducing herself as Karen White, girlfriend of the journalist. Having been rather shaken by the attempt on her boyfriend's life, she had taken the day off from her job as a planning officer at South Hams District Council based in Totnes.

"Is Mr Morris at home?" King enquired.

"Yes, he's in the shower at the moment."

"Is he able to answer some questions about the incident yesterday?"

"Certainly. It'll take more than that to shut Dan up. He hates criminals and corruption in equal measure." She was trying to appear stoical on his behalf, but the detectives sensed an underlying unease over what had happened. Just then he appeared fully dressed with his blond hair looking darker than it actually was due to its wetness.

"Hi, I'm Dan. Thanks for coming round."

After King introduced himself and Sergeant Harris he wanted to get him to shed some light on the events of the previous evening. Karen White was perched on the arm of Morris's chair.

"I have read a record of an interview you gave to a police constable last night. So we don't need to go over that unless you have thought of something since?"

"No. In my trade I'm pretty adept at remembering things, so I think my statement can stand as recorded."

King nodded his appreciation as his sergeant prepared to take notes of the questions and answers that would follow.

"Well, Mr Morris, have you any idea why this happened to you?" King could have asked whether he thought this was road rage, bad driving or a premeditated attack. He hadn't asked those questions as he preferred witnesses to think for themselves rather than latching onto one or other theory.

"I'd been to a meeting at Bolberry-on-Sea village hall, which went on longer than expected. As I'd arranged to meet Karen I was in a bit of a rush myself. I was surprised when the car behind was keeping pace with me. I thought at first that it was just someone in a hurry to get past or a combination of that and bad driving. Now I'm not so sure. As I slowed to take the bend leading to the restaurant, he accelerated. The more I think about it this guy was determined to do me harm and at worst kill me. When I was clinging to the gorse bush and looking back up the slope I thought he was coming to finish me off. Now, since I've had time to reflect there is another explanation, namely that he may have realised what he'd done and was seeing if he could help me. There again because of the ferocity with which he rammed my car, I am fairly convinced he did it deliberately. Whether it was premeditated, I'm not sure. Perhaps I had inadvertently upset him with my driving, but I really can't think how. Apart from driving too fast because I was late, but that didn't warrant what he did to me."

When interviewing witnesses, King encouraged his sergeant to ask questions.

"Mr Morris, I believe you are an investigative journalist. I would imagine you can make enemies when digging for a story? What are you currently working on?"

"Last year I completed an investigation about drug dealing in London that led me to Bristol. I had a piece published in *The Daily Telegraph* and the police acted on my report. As a sequel to that investigation, I'm now working on exposing the so-called County Lines gangs. As police officers you, or your colleagues involved in drug detection, are probably very aware what these gangs are doing. Nowhere is safe from these scumbags. They bring misery to thousands of people while they get fat on the profits as the users slip further and further down the slippery slope of addiction, thieving to feed their habit so innocent people become a statistic of burglary or robbery. The police simply don't have the resources to catch the users and abusers let alone the drug barons. I'm sure you know that better than I do?"

The detectives didn't answer. Morris hadn't finished yet.

"Recently, when a notorious drug boss was convicted a couple of years back, he had amassed a personal fortune of over £20 million. He was given fifteen years in jail, of which he'll serve half, and probably still have much of his ill-gotten gains to continue where he left off, despite the confiscation of a large chunk of his fortune under the Proceeds of Crime Act."

This was turning into a diatribe and the journalist wouldn't be apologising as that's exactly what it was: a bitter verbal attack on these career criminals.

Having asked the question Harris was loathe to interrupt the journalist as he was actually answering what she had asked. She continued scribbling as the verbal onslaught showed no signs of abating.

"So, as you know, the drug gangs from the big cities expand their operations to smaller towns, often using violence to drive out local dealers who are no angels either. The big gangs often exploit children and vulnerable people to sell their drugs. Drugs that come mainly from European countries and are delivered not through Dover or other main ports, but right into the smaller towns and cities by land, sea and air.

"So far my investigations have led me from London to Bristol and now to my home city of Plymouth. I suspect the drugs are being brought in by boat to sheltered coves around the Devon and Cornwall coast and maybe even flown into remote airfields after dark."

As he briefly paused, Harris asked the inevitable follow-up question.

"So, is it possible you've upset one of these drug criminals and they want you off their case?"

Morris paused again and shuddered at the question as if someone had walked over his grave.

"It's possible, but I haven't exactly broadcast the subject of my latest work, although I have been asking around and paid for some information. I could have struck a nerve somewhere or an informant might have become a double agent, if you get my drift." King wanted to pursue the line of questioning.

"They may not have wanted you dead, rather to scare you off so you would stop poking around. So, the people you've talked to are directly involved in the drugs trade, as pushers or users?"

"Users mainly. Dealers are closer to the drug bosses, and allegiances with them are stronger and transgressions would receive severe punishment. Talking to me for money would be too risky for both of us. I did speak to a few dealers in Bristol on my last investigation, without repercussions. But here in Plymouth making contact with a few users – would that be sufficient to incite murder?"

"I can't answer that question, Mr Morris. It may be a user you spoke with wanted to ingratiate himself or herself to a pusher and seek a reward for the information. You may be posing a threat to their dealing; I know from past experience that these people are fiercely protective and ruthless.

"If what happened to you last night was not down to bad driving or road rage then I intend to pursue it as attempted murder."

Karen White had listened in silence to what had been said and looked straight at her boyfriend.

"You had better tell them about the damage to your car, Dan."

The detectives simultaneously looked at the girlfriend and then their expectant eyes swivelled away from her back to the journalist.

"What Karen is referring to is last week when I was in Plymouth I left my car in a small car park in the dock area of the city and caught a bus to Barne Barton. I wanted to have a chat with a few people about the drug scene and I let it be known that I was prepared to pay for any useful information. Didn't get that much, but it helped. Anyway, when I got back to my car the two rear tyres had been slashed. I put it down to vandalism and I still think it could have been."

King nodded more in acknowledgement of what he had said rather than agreement. He looked at Harris to see if she had any further questions. She hadn't, so it was left to him to continue with the interview.

"Can you let us have the names of any users or pushers plus the names of any people you suspect are higher up the chain?"

For the first time during the interview Dan Morris did not have a ready reply.

King nudged: "Problem with that request?"

"I'm a journalist, inspector, and I make money from my undercover work. If I start blabbing to the police, my informants will suddenly stop speaking to me; then my story and income could be lost."

The slightly irritated detective did not have the hesitancy of the interviewee when replying: "Look, Mr Morris, isn't it better to lose income than your life? Much as I respect your motives and your desire to protect your sources, let me remind you that an attempt was made on your life last night. You have your job and I have mine. I'm trying to solve an attempted murder case and prevent the villains from successfully completing their desired outcome, namely wanting you dead."

The journalist looked directly at King, but remained silent. The inspector had received the silent message loud and clear.

"Okay, I see where you're coming from, but I would urge you to give us some names before it's too late."

Karen White shuddered at these words and tightly gripped her boyfriend's arm in an obvious attempt to get him to reconsider; he remained silent.

"Just one last thing for both of you: can you think of anything else from last night that may have been triggered by our chat today?" He asked more in hope than expectation. Both gave the question serious thought and Morris closed his eyes as if trying to visualise what had happened to him the previous evening.

"Four spotlights!" the journalist blurted out still with his eyes closed. "The vehicle that rammed me had a bar over the cabin and there were four spotlights on it. When I was lying in the snow, had I been in the direct glare of them I probably wouldn't have been able to see anything, but I wasn't. I was lying below their intense beams, but there were definitely four of them."

Sergeant Harris noted this new information. The inspector was not entirely happy with the interview and didn't thank the recalcitrant journalist. Instead he wanted to warn him to be vigilant and fully aware of the seriousness of his position. He turned and spoke as Harris opened the door for them to leave.

"Let me give you some advice, Mr Morris, and it equally applies to you, Ms White; it's up to you whether or not you heed it. I don't want to unduly alarm you as this is purely a precaution. As we are treating this as attempted murder, it means someone or some people possibly wish to do you harm. I would advise you to break your normal routines. The places you go, the things you do, the times you do them, the transport you use, the places you eat, the places you shop or any activity in your life that is routine. Anything that may create a pattern of behaviour that someone could use to place you at a specific place at a specific time. Also, try not to be alone when you are out, particularly after dark." With that the detectives left, leaving two very worried people looking at each other in frightened silence.

NINE

Doug Grant, a car sales owner living in Bolberry-on-Sea and a member of its parish council, was a much-travelled man. He had always wanted to cross the Grand Canyon in Arizona on a tightrope. He knew that the part called Marble Canyon was one of the narrowest points at only 550 metres wide and he had always wanted to fulfil this item from his bucket list; he was about to get his wish. As a boy he had always been fascinated by the German-American high wire artists, the Flying Wallendas. Funambulism requires great balance and even greater courage and he felt he had both in spades.

The high walkway consisted of a galvanised steel wire anchored at both ends across the yawning gap. He had no harness or other safety equipment and merely carried an eight-metre-long balancing pole attached at its mid-point to a loop around his neck to take its weight; it also had a quick release mechanism.

He gingerly took his first step with the ground only a metre beneath the wire before it dropped away to the Colorado River 1,000 metres below. As he started out on his perilous crossing his nervous perspiration was cooled by a gentle breeze for which he was initially grateful; his gratitude for it was misplaced and short-lived.

He made slow, but surefooted progress for the first hundred metres. As he gingerly reached the middle of the chasm, he noticed that the gentle breeze was developing into something far stronger; something he had not foreseen as the usually reliable weather forecast was wrong. There was no turning back. He edged tentatively forward, but became increasingly concerned at the strengthening wind. He had barely passed the mid-point of his epic walk when the wire started to sway alarmingly. This movement was hardly noticeable initially, but as he went further over the giant gash that scarred the landscape it began to increase. At first the oscillation could have been measured in millimetres, but with the increasing wind speed the means of measurement changed to centimetres.

Undaunted, he continued to edge forward with the wire running exactly under the middle of his leading left foot; his back foot was at right angles to it. As he slid his foot forward it veered fractionally to his right due to the movement of the wire. This subtle variation was not detectable by the human eye, but Doug Grant knew he was in trouble.

He tried in vain to readjust his leading foot, but overcorrected his mistake, which led to a disastrous consequence as the movement of the wire markedly increased. He knew he was about to fall.

He unclipped the short rope around his neck and dispensed with his balancing pole that arrowed towards the ground like a spear and after several seconds eventually embedded itself over half its length in the riverbank below. Time stood still as his heart raced. He knew he had one chance and one chance only to save his life and that was to grab the wire by both hands. He managed it and yet was aware this was only delaying the inevitable drop to the river below when his arms could no longer support the weight of his body.

He held on for dear life for what seemed like an inordinately long period, but was in fact only a matter of minutes. His arms ached and the pain from his muscles intensified. He was resigned to his fate, realising he was about to plummet to his death. The wind that had been his metaphorical downfall seemed to be getting stronger.

Suddenly, looking up he could see the underside of a helicopter dangling a rope ladder agonisingly close to his hands. Unfortunately the breeze had by now turned into a wind that had increased to ten kilometres an hour, fanned by the rotor blades, and was making the ladder sway at least two metres backwards and forwards. His muscles were now shouting at him in pain and he knew that in the next twenty seconds or so he would have to make a leap of faith and grab the ladder before his resistance gave way. He waited until it swayed away from him and then judged when it would sway back within his grasp.

Summoning the last ounce of strength from his

trembling arms he threw them towards a rung, any rung, on the ladder. His right hand managed to grab hold and he was now literally single-handedly dangling over the abyss. He then managed to grip with his other hand and the thought of his life being prolonged flooded his brain.

The helicopter did not descend, the pilot rightly choosing to try and get the stricken high wire walker back to the nearest terra firma as quickly as possible. That escape route meant flying sideways not down. Safety was agonisingly close as the chopper slowly, yet assuredly, was moving closer to the edge of the precipice from where Grant had set out. The pilot was desperately trying to keep a smooth flight as any sudden movement may have loosened the tenuous grip of his passenger.

His right hand was the first to surrender as it had been first to grab the rung; now he was back to a single hand-hold. Then his left, and weaker, hand began to tremble as the tendons tightened; the muscles had nearly had enough. The helicopter was now no more than thirty metres from the cliff edge. A gust of wind was the last thing Grant wanted at that point, but that's what he got, which accelerated his progressively weakening hold, gradually slackening until it eventually, reluctantly, capitulated.

He didn't want to die. There were so many things he wanted to do from his bucket list. Sadly, what he had partly achieved by this adventure would be his last. As he plummeted towards the Colorado River below he wasn't frightened. He just accepted his fate as a recreational hazard.

Falling, falling, falling; forever falling. Spiralling down, down, down; forever down.

As the ground rushed towards him, the impact of hitting it jerked Doug Grant awake from his nightmare.

"Bloody prostate," he mumbled to himself as he got up just after one in the morning and made his way to the bathroom. The little gland had interrupted his sleep every night for the last ten years. It helped if he drank less liquid before bedtime, although he knew it was better for him to stay hydrated. He switched on the bathroom light and started to relieve himself. As he gradually reduced the pressure on his bladder, his eyes moved from the urine flow and fixed on the window that was immediately over the toilet. Although the glass in it was frosted he could see what appeared to be a light flickering in his garden.

He abruptly finished urinating and rushed to the landing window to get a clearer view. To his horror he could now see his beautiful summerhouse ablaze. He rang the fire service and then, still in his pyjamas, he found his slippers, and rushed outside to turn on his garden hose and do what he could to douse the flames.

A fire appliance eventually arrived from the Devon Fire Brigade in Modbury, which was just over six miles away. The normal daytime journey time would have been over twenty minutes, but the firefighters arrived with commendable speed in a little over ten as no traffic was on the road at that time of the morning.

The big red appliance with blue lights flashing (but no sirens as there was no need to alert the whole neighbourhood) swept into the substantial drive and the firefighters went about their business as well-trained professionals. Soon after, another appliance arrived from Kingsbridge, about eight miles to the east of the village, and those firefighters promptly joined their counterparts. They were all undaunted in their task, although the prospect of salvaging anything of the summerhouse seemed remote. All of the firefighters were now clustered around the front and sides of the blaze.

"Gas bottles!" Doug Grant suddenly shouted remembering his free-standing gas barbeque was housed in the burning building. All of the figures clad in their traditional and distinctive yellow garb immediately retreated.

Moments later a gas cylinder exploded sending shrapnel flying across the garden. The blast was partially contained by a thick laurel hedge that bordered the lawn. Shredded leaves filled the night air like confetti. Two firefighters received superficial cuts from flying debris while the others escaped unscathed.

Soon after, the smoking ruins of the once beautiful summer retreat were just a smouldering pile of unrecognisable detritus punctuated by a blackened gas bottle that thankfully hadn't exploded. About half an hour after the last flames had been extinguished, one of the fire engines left, leaving the other to dampen down the gutted building.

The chief fire officer had alerted the police as he suspected arson and they soon arrived. There was little for them to do except make a record of the night's events and note what they had been told by the brigade commander.

Many of the surrounding houses came alive with lights and some people from them, clad in pyjamas and dressing gowns, were coming up the drive only to be ushered back by the police in case of further explosions. Most had a genuine desire to help; a few were just being nosey neighbours.

After an hour, all of the emergency services departed as well as the neighbours and Doug Grant was left sitting forlornly on his front door step surveying the remnants of his destroyed summerhouse. He was left asking himself why someone would want to do that. Why would they target him? Little did he know, that night he would not be the only one in Bolberry-on-Sea to suffer malicious damage to their property.

*

Abigail Croft, a retired headmistress and a long-standing member of the parish council, lived in a cottage called The Warren, which overlooked the sea. She was still just in her fifties thanks to the generous retirement package for teachers. Her bungalow, detached garage and garden were all pristine. She prided herself on her own appearance and the appearance of her property.

It was nearly 7am and, although it was still dark, she pulled back her curtains and casually glanced down over the front garden with its spotless lawn surrounded by well-trimmed evergreen shrubs. This ritual was performed every morning before she took her constitutional around her garden to breathe in the cool, fresh sea air.

The street light, which wasn't sited immediately outside her property, cast a weak yellow glow across her lawn, sufficient for her to notice something unusual. She couldn't make out exactly what it was, but imagined something must have blown into her garden during the night. She wasn't unduly concerned and stuck to her routine of going downstairs to make a cup of tea, which she would then bring upstairs and carry out her ablutions.

After she had changed and breakfasted she put on her outdoor boots and her Barbour coat and went outside. She first wanted to check what had blown onto her lawn in the night. The wind was not guilty. Nothing had been swept in overnight. She stood horrified when she saw the vandalism that had been caused to her immaculate grass. Scrawled across it in metre-high capitals and lower-case letters was 'VOTe Yes'. As she got closer, she could smell the stench of the bleach. This was no prank. Whoever had sprayed this unwelcome, and slightly sinister, message knew what the corrosive substance would do to grass. Because of the words, she rightly suspected that this was a serious attempt to intimidate her and to get her to change her mind on a planning matter being considered by the parish council; it was beginning to have the desired effect. This went beyond mere vandalism; this had threatening intent. The police were about to get their second early morning call of the day from Bolberry-on-Sea.

*

Mike Farthing, part-owner of Bolberry Garage, had been a parish councillor for over a decade. He lived in a cottage on the outskirts of the village and was an early riser. This particular morning he was feeling rather jaded as he hadn't got to bed until well after midnight. As usual he was out of bed before six o'clock.

He had his usual bacon sandwich for breakfast and three cups of tea; always three cups of tea. Dawn was awakening and true to his usual routine he put on his boots, grabbed his jacket and put it on top of his work overalls, making up his garage uniform, before walking the short distance to his detached double garage.

When he was a few paces from the door that housed his works truck (the other half of the garage accommodated his 1967 Aston Martin DB-6, valued at over six figures), he stopped dead in his tracks. In the early morning light he could clearly make out some graffiti on the door. In metre-high letters he read: 'VOTe YeS'.

Strangely, he was not unduly perturbed as he reached for his mobile and rang the police.

TEN

On the second morning after the body was washed up on the beach, the attempted murder at Bolberry Down and the interviews held by the senior detectives with the victim and his girlfriend, Inspector King had called a meeting at the police station to be attended by Sergeant Harris and Detective Constable Dyson. He started by reporting the crimes that had happened the previous night.

"We've had three separate reports about incidents last night, all in the village of Bolberry-on-Sea. The first reported incident is of the apparent arson of a summerhouse, the second a bleach attack on a lawn – where two words were written – and a third where graffiti was daubed on a garage door with the same two words: 'VOTe YeS'. The victims, all parish councillors, assume that it is linked to a planning application that is currently being considered by the council. The incidents have been recorded as arson for the summerhouse fire and malicious damage for the other two. The acting superintendent wants us to investigate these crimes as well as our current cases as the other detective teams are already stretched."

King wasn't at all sure that was the truth of the matter as he had spoken with his inspector colleagues. It was Roberts' way of directly adding pressure to the job and indirectly bullying his inspector into submissive behaviour as he sensed he hadn't got King's wholehearted support; he had his mind, but not his heart.

"We'll add them to our crime sheet and interview the victims," he said matter-of-factly.

Just then there was a knock on the door to the meeting room and it opened to reveal the giant frame of Alex Hammond filling the doorway. The detectives were surprised as he wasn't expected until later that month. After warm greetings and handshakes all round they were delighted to welcome him back. He had helped King's team on secondment recently and was now returning on a permanent basis. He addressed his new boss. "Sir, my court case finished early yesterday as the defendant pleaded guilty. I asked for my posting to be brought forward and here I am reporting for duty."

"That's a very timely entrance, Alex, and we are delighted you asked to rejoin us after the Cranson case and successfully prosecuting the villains who were stealing from farms around Dartmoor. We now have a set of new challenges, which I was about to outline; take a seat.

"Firstly, the body of a naked man was apparently washed up on the beach at Hope Cove the day before yesterday. I say 'apparently' as we haven't entirely dismissed that it could have been dumped there. We started an initial investigation by a search of the beach and also house-to-house enquiries to see if anyone had noticed anything suspicious. We await the pathologist's report before carrying out any further investigation.

"Secondly, two nights ago an investigative journalist was run off the road at Bolberry Down, close to Oceans Restaurant. Sergeant Harris and I have interviewed the restaurant manager and also the victim and his girlfriend who live in Plymouth. We believe this is drugs related as he has been researching the drug scene in London, Bristol and now Plymouth. It could be linked to the so-called County Lines gangs supplying drugs to small towns in the South West. The chief constable has been getting reports that drugs are flooding in all over Devon and the main entry points, anecdotally at least, would appear to be in South Devon.

"Thirdly, there are three reported incidents that happened last night in the village of Bolberry-on-Sea. One appears to be arson and the other two are recorded as malicious damage caused to a lawn by squirting bleach over it and the other graffiti on a garage door; both messages were the same, namely 'VOTe Yes'. We can't be sure, but due to the respective sizes of the letters it would appear that the 'e' is in lower case and the other letters are in capitals. We believe this is linked to a current planning application, which is being considered by the local parish council.

"We can't do anything about the body on the beach case until we get the pathologist's report, which is due tomorrow. In the meantime..."

King couldn't continue the briefing as the door to the interview room burst open and Acting Superintendent Roberts entered.

"Right, Inspector King, I'd like an update on what my team of detectives is involved in. What's happening with the body on the beach case and also the attempted murder at Bolberry Down?"

"Good morning, sir. Could I introduce you to Detective Constable Alexander Hammond, who has now joined us from Exeter Police. I'm pleased that it's happened sooner than planned due to a court case he was involved in finishing earlier than expected." Roberts ignored DC Hammond and continued to speak directly to his inspector.

"Why wasn't I informed that Hammond was joining us?"

"You were aware of his transfer, sir, and he took the personal initiative to ask for early release as his court case had finished early. We really could do with his help now. I assumed your counterpart in Exeter would have informed you."

"Well, she didn't."

The sheepish detective constable got to his feet and offered his apologies.

"I'm sorry, sir. It's probably my fault as the court case I was involved in finished rather abruptly only yesterday and I asked for my planned transfer to be brought forward. My inspector in Exeter was happy to release me once I had done all the paperwork relating to the case."

"I wasn't talking to you, Hammond," Roberts added indignantly. The acting superintendent neither accepted his apology nor welcomed him to the team, but moved on. "So, what's this meeting about?"

Not for the first time, and certainly not for the last, King bit his lip to prevent him saying something which he might later regret. Anyway, it would have been unprofessional and could have been classed as insubordination. He knew his detectives would make up their own minds about the attitude of the senior officer.

Irritated, but undaunted, King continued: "The team is discussing and actively pursuing three cases, sir. Firstly, we have the body on the beach at Hope Cove and we await the pathologist's report; secondly, there is the attempted murder of the investigative journalist at Bolberry Down possibly linked to County Lines that you asked us to investigate; thirdly, three incidents were reported last night at Bolberry-on-Sea, one we think was arson and the other two were criminal damage. I was about to brief the team and allocate them to these crimes when you came into the room."

"Well, let me give you your top priority. The chief constable is taking an active interest in the spread of illegal drugs. It seems they are coming into our patch initially and then being spread around the county. Why is it happening and why here?"

"The so-called drug barons are now targeting smaller provincial towns as their operations get squeezed in bigger cities."

Roberts was not amused as he meant to ask why Devon, not why was it happening. He turned away from the inspector to address the other detectives.

"Leave us now as I need to have a word with your inspector." It wasn't a request, it was an order. When Hammond, who was last out, closed the door behind him the acting boss once again addressed King: "Listen, Dickie, this has got to stop. You should have told me about the black guy joining us."

His description rankled King as he knew Roberts would never refer to Sam Dyson as 'the white girl' so why use that epithet to describe Alex Hammond?

"The black guy you refer to, sir, is DC Hammond and if you look at your emails, I informed you two weeks ago that he had been posted to us at his request." King's subtle attempt to rebuke him for his use of colour to describe a fellow officer missed its mark as Roberts ploughed on.

"Also I don't expect you to brief the detectives until you have discussed the cases with me. So in future I expect to be kept informed as to what's happening in the various cases so I can have my say on how you are proposing to deal with them. Do I make myself clear?"

The quietly seething inspector treated this as a rhetorical question and did not answer, and instead asked his own.

"I have outlined the three cases we need to investigate, sir. Please tell me how you would like us to proceed with them."

"I can't advise you on what to do. I haven't got enough information about these suspected crimes."

"Neither have we, sir. I was planning to find out more about each of them before having a meaningful briefing with you that I have already scheduled for tomorrow morning at eight thirty. I think you'll find an entry in your diary, sir."

"Okay, I'll go along with that approach for now. But I need to make it clear to you that I expect to be kept informed about each case and how the investigations are proceeding. Tell Detective Constable Dyson I want to see her now." With that he left the room before the inspector could ask him why he wanted to see the junior detective. Suppressing his anger, King sought out DC Dyson and asked her to immediately report to the acting superintendent. She asked her boss what it was about, but he was unable to tell her. He said that when she returned they would reconvene their meeting.

After five minutes, the nervous detective constable returned and appeared tearful. King asked to see her in the interview room and told Harris and Hammond to wait until he called them.

"What did he want to see you about, Sam? Do you want to talk about it?"

"The superintendent said he was a very busy senior officer and expected the most junior detective to bring him coffee in the morning and tea in the afternoon without him having to ask for it. So, he said that if he was in the station on any day, that's what he wanted me to do. He wasn't very pleased when I pointed out that on many days I am away from the station myself investigating crimes. He said if I was in, I was to get his refreshments. It wasn't a request, sir, it was more of an order."

King's by now subdued anger almost surfaced, but he was too professional to say exactly what he was thinking. He took out a sherbet lemon to soothe his annoyance. After a short while he said: "Leave it to me, Sam. I'll have a word with the acting superintendent." He placed great emphasis on the word 'acting'!

"I don't want to get into trouble, sir, for not carrying out an order."

Her boss reassured her that would not be the case. He called in Harris and Hammond, reconvening the meeting that had been so rudely interrupted by Roberts.

"Right, when we get the report from the pathologist on the body on the beach, I would like all of us to deal with that case, particularly if he thinks it should be a murder inquiry. Although Sergeant Harris and I have started the investigation on the attempted murder of the investigative journalist, I would now like you, Lucy, and Alex to make further enquiries. I will work with Sam on the incidents that happened last night at Bolberry-on-Sea. This will be part of her development. We'll leave in an hour to pursue those investigations.

"Lucy, if you could brief Alex and work out where we take that attempted murder case from here, we'll have another briefing session, possibly later today, and compare notes." Sergeant Harris was quietly dismayed that her working partnership with the inspector was temporarily at an end; at least she hoped it was temporary.

King decided to leave Roberts' order to Dyson about refreshment until later. He remembered the bullying case against his boss many years before, which eventually was not proven. He did not want a repetition and although he had originally planned to work with his sergeant, he decided to partner his somewhat emotionally fragile detective constable as his protective instincts were on full alert. He then corrected himself: she was not emotionally fragile at all, merely inexperienced and understandably lacking self-confidence. He wanted to monitor first-hand any harassment or bullying and if he witnessed it, this time he was determined that it would be proven.

ELEVEN

Before they left to pursue their respective cases after the meeting with their inspector, Dyson and Hammond met for a coffee in the station's canteen. Dyson told him of Roberts' refreshment order and of her concern.

"He's a bully, Alex, and he scares me. Did you notice the way he treated our inspector? Disgraceful!" There was no hiding her fear or her contempt. The burly detective colleague wanted to reassure her.

"Inspector King will deal with him, Sam, don't you worry about that. I have complete faith in him to make sure any harassment of junior officers, or other unacceptable behaviour, senior officer or not, will not be tolerated. My only concern is the inspector may not follow established protocols for dealing with people like Roberts. I could see him quietly seething and clenching his fists when we were kicked out of the meeting. So don't worry; he'll look after you and so will Lucy and I."

Dyson was somewhat reassured. "Thanks, Alex. I'm grateful to be working with our boss. As he said it'll be good for my development."

Hammond didn't think Richard King was being disingenuous when he chose to have Dyson working closely with him, but he knew the real reason why he'd made that decision and admired him for it.

*

Sergeant Harris was in the main office alone as her colleagues were grabbing a cup of coffee. She was rather crestfallen, not because she would be working with Alex Hammond as she liked him a lot, but because she wouldn't be working with her inspector. King sensed her disappointment.

"I owe you an apology, Lucy." King had quietly entered the room and pulled up the nearest chair so he was now sat very close to his sergeant.

"Apology, sir! What for?"

"For springing a change of partner on you without telling you first." She appreciated his apology, but that didn't change the decision.

"I was a bit surprised, sir. If I'm honest, I like working with you as we are a good team and I very much appreciate learning from what you do. Don't get me wrong, Alex is a great guy and I'm happy to have a partner like him. It's just we have a very good working relationship and I didn't want that to end so soon." She dejectedly looked down. King then did something unprofessional: he took her hand in his.

"Let me explain a few things, Lucy. In all honesty I made the decision on the spur of the moment that Sam would partner me on the current cases. Why? I think she is likely to be bullied by a certain senior officer and I need to be close to her should it happen so I can protect her. She will be an excellent officer in the future, probably a sergeant like you in a few years from now, but she needs to be given time to develop. I know she is naturally lacking confidence; that will come with experience. Right now she may not cope well with, what shall I say, unwanted attention and unwarranted criticism.

"That is the main reason I have paired her with me. But there is another reason why I want you working with Alex. He needs developing too and I think you are the right person to help him. It's a win-win for both of you as you will get satisfaction from bringing him on and he will benefit from your experience.

"One other thing I would add and that is we'll be working as a team of four on some cases and in the future no doubt we will work as a pair again."

Lucy Harris was reassured and they spontaneously hugged each other.

"Inspector! What the hell do you think you are doing? Embracing a junior female officer during working hours on police premises." His boss had walked in at the very moment of the embrace. King's suppressed frustration turned to anger.

"Listen, Roberts, I am dealing with a private matter with my sergeant so get out as we'd like to be left alone!" Roberts had received the message loud and clear and turned to leave the room, but stopped in the doorway and faced the one distressed and the other angry officer.

"You haven't heard the last of this, King!" and left the room slamming the door behind him.

"Sorry, sir. I hope I haven't got you into trouble."

The sergeant's tears of relief now turned to tears of sorrow and fear. Richard King hugged her for a second time for reassurance and as a show of defiance. After a fleeting moment, when she had stopped sobbing, he broke the embrace, leaned back and put a hand on each of her shoulders.

"Now you listen to me, Lucy Harris. Don't you worry about Roberts; I'll deal with him. You concentrate on the cases you're dealing with and developing Alex Hammond."

With that he left and made straight for his boss's office.

*

He didn't feel ashamed and had nothing to apologise for save telling a senior officer to 'get out!' He'd already worked on his insincere grovelling apology as he knocked on the door.

"Come!"

"Sir, I'd like to apologise for the manner in which I spoke to you just now. Sergeant Harris and I were having a private conversation and she became upset, that's why..." He was cut short.

"Save your breath, King. You've gone too far this time and I'm reporting you to the chief superintendent. I will recommend to her that you are suspended on full pay until the outcome of a disciplinary investigation. I will also recommend you are charged with intimacy with a junior female officer, whilst on duty and on police premises, and insubordination towards a senior officer. If proven I expect it will be classed as gross misconduct and you will be dismissed from the police service. Now get out!"

Strangely, King was not fazed by the verbal onslaught from his boss. He would keep doing his job until told otherwise. Also he was confident he had no case to answer and any inquiry would simply be an irritation he had to deal with alongside his crime fighting. Indeed, it would have to focus on why his sergeant was distressed and the underlying reason for his change of partner, namely to protect her from a potential bully.

He hoped that this would be about his behaviour and that his sergeant would be a witness not a co-defendant. He rationalised that in the meantime he must not let this impinge on his work as an inspector. There was no doubt he would prefer not to have the unwelcome scrutiny of a disciplinary investigation, but had faith that natural justice would prevail and expose the true unacceptable behaviour.

He sat in his office, alone and in reflective mood. Thoughts of his wife, tragically taken from him by her brain cancer, flooded his mind; his career in the police, now in jeopardy, with its exhilarating highs and devastating lows; the many successful arrests and prosecutions as well as the unsolved crimes, particularly where people, not property, had come to harm.

He had been lucky in his career as he had met, and worked with, some remarkable people. He would have liked to get on better with his present immediate boss, but he wasn't the cause of the breakdown in their relationship. He knew that his DCs, Hammond and Dyson, although 'work in progress', had great potential, which he wanted to develop. Then there was his sergeant. When they had hugged earlier, only in solace not passion, something stirred in him. Something he hadn't felt for a long time. What was it that had tweaked his psyche? Lust? No! Loyalty? Certainly. Love? Maybe.

TWELVE

Sergeant Harris and Detective Constable Hammond arrived at Bolberry Down, the scene of the attempted murder. Harris had regained her composure after the recent altercation between Richard King and Brian Roberts, reassured by her immediate boss to forget about it and concentrate on the investigation and the development of her new partner.

They were armed with the electronic transcript of the car-ramming event and the interview with the manager of Oceans Restaurant. Harris also told the DC about the interview she and their inspector had with the victim and his girlfriend.

Police tape was still in place, discouraging walkers from entering the scene of the crime. There were no obvious signs of the incident save for the flattened brambles where the car had plunged over the cliff. Both detectives strolled down the slope to the cliff edge and slowly walked back up, scanning the ground as they went, in the hope of seeing something others had missed. Harris knew that the one hard piece of evidence was part of a broken number plate that was assumed to have come from the ramming vehicle. The sergeant opened the boot of the police car and took out an evidence bag, which she passed to Hammond.

"Even if we had the whole plate, the chances are it was false and we'd be no further forward. However, I think we have to assume that this villain was so arrogant that he didn't bother to disguise the vehicle's true identity. After all, driving around with false plates risks falling foul of our Automatic Number Plate Recognition system. I don't mean for not being insured as I'm sure these crooks have all the money they want to pay for legality and respectability. But they don't like having their movements tracked or being seen in the wrong places.

"So let's work on the plate being legit as it's all we've got."

Hammond produced the broken middle part of the number plate from the bag and they both stared at it. He held it in his huge hands and made an observation.

"Just a thought, but I reckon the person driving the big vehicle this belonged to was playing for high stakes as he or she was prepared to kill the journalist. They might just be arrogant enough to have a personalised plate."

He took out his mobile and photographed the fractured part:

"It's like a giant jigsaw puzzle. The trouble is I've only got one piece! I'll work on a possible registration so we can identify the owner. It may be a long shot, but nothing ventured…"

Harris was happy to let him try to identify the rogue vehicle albeit she wasn't optimistic of him being successful. She wanted to explore other avenues.

"There is another piece of evidence we need to consider and that's Morris's car. When we get back to the station, check with Forensics, though I'm not hopeful we'll glean any more clues as to the make and model of the vehicle that did the ramming. It was obviously a heavy shunt as it broke the number plate and propelled his car over the cliff edge. I'd be disappointed if the team can't at least tell us its colour.

"There are two other lines of enquiry that I haven't completely given up on and the first is information from Morris about the people who know he's been poking around for his story on drug activity in the provinces and, more directly, in Plymouth. He is refusing to disclose any names, not from misplaced loyalty, more from protection of his income. If we blow his cover completely he feels that he won't get the story he's after and can't sell it to media outlets. He's playing a dangerous game. Richard, sorry I mean Inspector King, has warned him in no uncertain terms that he's playing fast and loose with his life. These drug gangs are ruthless and will go to any lengths to protect their livelihood.

"So I want us to see him again and put the frighteners on him before more harm comes his way.

His girlfriend, Karen White, could prove useful as I get the impression she too wants him to give us more information, so we need to see them together. Set up another interview with them at the station would you, Alex. Let's hope we're not too late."

Hammond asked: "You said there were two other lines to pursue?"

"Yes, and that's CCTV footage in nearby towns and certainly from any cameras on entry roads to Plymouth soon after the attack on Morris. Also from the A38 leading north to Exeter and west over the Tamar Bridge to Cornwall. If DI King is okay with what I am proposing I suggest we and DC Dyson split the footage three ways. It shouldn't be too arduous as it is time-specific. The crime took place at about eight o'clock that night so we need to view footage timed between then and, say, nine o'clock that evening. We are looking for a big, powerful car, probably a 4x4, and, according to Morris, with four spotlights on a bar over the cab. We'll have a chat with the inspector when we get back to the station."

*

"Well the car was pretty battered as you'd expect after plunging over the cliff onto rocks." A member of the forensic team was giving DC Hammond its initial findings after a cursory examination of Morris's car.

"The only thing I can say with any certainty is that the vehicle that hit the back of the car was black. We may be able to give you a more accurate description as to the type of black paint when we examine it under a microscope and break down the pigment. That'll take time, but should be done by this time tomorrow."

Hammond thanked the forensic officer and said he would return at the same time the next day. He also made a mental note to add 'black' to 'big, powerful car' on their CCTV viewing schedule.

*

Dan Morris and Karen White duly arrived at the police station in Plymouth via a back entrance. Hammond, with his sergeant's blessing, had convened a meeting there as requested to give it the gravitas it deserved. He had also arranged for it to be clandestine just in case Morris and his girlfriend had been followed. King was also supportive of the strategy.

Hammond had not been disingenuous when he told them the meeting was to provide an update on the investigation of the attempted murder. Morris and White were shown into an interview room and were soon joined by Harris and Hammond; the sergeant started the meeting.

"Thank you for coming in and apologies for the back door entrance, which was purely precautionary. This interview is not being recorded. Firstly, we'd like to update you on our investigations so far. Both DC Hammond and I visited the crime scene. We have also interviewed the manager of Oceans Restaurant and yourselves.

"We have had an initial report from our forensic team and they have ascertained that the vehicle that pushed you over the cliff was black in colour. Further tests are being carried out as we speak and we are hopeful that analysis of the paint's pigment will give us further help in identifying the make and model. I'll now hand over to DC Hammond."

"Thank you, sergeant. As you know, part of the number plate of the car that hit you was found at the scene. I have been tasked with trying to identify the full registration, which should lead us to the owner. I have a suspicion, no more than that, it may have been part of a personalised plate."

The sergeant continued: "Lastly, we will be examining CCTV footage from cameras at various routes out of the area looking for a big, black car with the spotlights you mentioned, Mr Morris. Have either of you any questions at this stage?"

Morris ventured: "I'm impressed by your thoroughness, sergeant, so thank you."

"We'll keep you updated if anything develops," Harris offered and then applied the pressure. "One last thing that my inspector discussed with you is your reluctance to name any of your informants or people linked to your journalistic work that may give us a fasttrack to apprehending the offender. This is a serious business, Mr Morris. Your life could be in danger."

Karen White implored: "Come on, Dan. You could have been killed. We can't lead our lives forever looking over our shoulders. We've had the hit-and-run and your car being vandalised. What next?" She clearly understood the seriousness of the situation and was pleading with her partner to give names to the detectives. Morris was, surprisingly, unmoved. Possibly driven by a mixture of journalistic etiquette, a determination to uncover drug-related criminality, carefree stupidity and sheer bloody-mindedness. His stubbornness was not appreciated by Harris and Hammond, but they didn't show their irritation. His mind was made up.

As the reluctant journalist and his concerned partner left the station by using the back entry as an exit, the sergeant shrugged.

"If he'd given us names, the inspector may have offered police protection, but no doubt our Mr Morris would have declined it. We'll just have to go with what we've got. The scary thing is as we get closer to the bad men the likelihood of retribution increases on him. Oh well, it's his funeral."

She hoped that those words would not prove to be prophetic.

THIRTEEN

King and Dyson arrived at Bolberry-on-Sea to interview the parish councillors who had been targeted the previous night. Before seeing the three people, the inspector had asked to be taken to the field, part of Ringmore Farm, where the building of the twenty-five executive homes was planned. The two detectives stood just inside the entrance to the ten-hectare field and gazed down at the nearby beach and the sea beyond. After sucking a sherbet lemon in silence for a few seconds, King spoke.

"Stunning view. You can see why the developers want to build here."

They both stood and stared in wonderment as the field gave way to sand, then sand to sea – that was Ayrmer Cove – and the English Channel in the far distance. After a quick mental calculation and conversion by him he offered: "Ten hectares means each plot will have roughly an acre of ground. Depending on the build quality and obligatory sea view, we are talking about really big money to be made from this site." They stood for a few more minutes until the sherbet lemon had finally dissolved. The silence was broken by Dyson.

"Thank you, sir," she said sheepishly to her inspector without any apparent link to anything in particular. She had eventually realised that he paired them to protect her from Acting Superintendent Roberts who had unsettled the junior detective constable by his overly aggressive manner towards her. By using her as a working colleague in the 'field', her inspector could vouch for her effectiveness and also witness any inappropriate behaviour by the senior officer towards her, if it happened when they were together.

"You don't need to thank me, Sam, you are quite capable of looking after yourself. I wanted you working with me to help your development, as with more experience I think you've got a bright future as a detective. You've already shown that in the last case we successfully handled when that criminal gang were stealing from farms on Dartmoor. One thing's for sure and that is your development isn't going to be improved by fetching cups of coffee for lazy senior officers." King spoke the truth – as well as having his other motive – and gave her a knowing grin that made the diminutive detective feel ten feet tall.

They admired the view for a few more minutes before the peace was shattered. Two scrambler motorbikes, ridden by young men, suddenly appeared over the brow of the hill from the direction of the farmhouse. They appeared to be on a mischievous mission as they criss-crossed very close to the detectives, swerving at the last second, without any real intent of stopping. Dyson retreated behind her inspector who was unmoved. It appeared they were the advance party as a man on a quad bike soon joined them, skidding to a halt barely a metre from the indomitable inspector.

"This is private property. Who the hell are you and what do you want?"

King had had enough of belligerent farmers in his last case and wasn't about to humour him. He responded rather tersely, but without overt antagonism: "We are detectives investigating incidents that happened in Bolberry-on-Sea overnight. I am Inspector King and this is Detective Constable Dyson. Perhaps you'd like to tell us your name." It was delivered as a command rather than a question and no 'sir' was added.

"Oh, sorry, but with all the debate about my field, I'm a bit wary of people coming to view it. I'm Joe Garner and those are my boys; they didn't mean no harm. This is my land that's up for sale. I'm hoping the developers will buy it off me if they can get permission from the bloody planners. After all, they have promised to build a brand new community centre if they are allowed to build the houses. God knows the village needs one as the listed ramshackle village hall is on its last legs."

King was proved right, he was a farmer.

"Well, Mr Garner, in future I suggest you address people with a little less hostility. Also, your sons were trying to intimidate us!"

"Oh, don't mind Wayne and Buzz, they were just having a bit of fun."

"Perhaps they'd like to continue their bit of fun at the police station in Plymouth?"

Garner turned away from the detectives: "Okay, boys. Fun over." With that they did one more defiant pass and disappeared over the brow from where they had come. Suitably rebuked, Garner also left without another word. The detectives didn't know it, but the 'boys' were local tearaways who often rode through the village on their scramblers, too fast and too noisy. They were very friendly with Lucas Peverell, the curate at the local church who was also a biker.

Sherbet lemon time again for the inspector – Dyson thought back-to-back sweets were unusual – but it had the desired calming influence.

"Right, let's find out what's been going on here in this lovely village. Who have you lined up for us to see first, Sam?"

"Mr Doug Grant, his summerhouse was burned down, then Miss Abigail Croft, bleach message on her lawn, and finally Mike Farthing who had graffiti daubed on the garage door at his home. We can leave the car in the village hall car park, sir. All three properties are within walking distance of there." When they arrived she referred to Google Earth on her mobile and set off for their first interview.

They opened the five-bar gate and noticed a chain, with a combination lock, dangling from the catch on the gatepost. As they walked up the drive that led to Doug Grant's front door, King was scanning the ground as he ambled over the gravel. He was always on the lookout at a crime scene for any small piece of evidence that may have been missed by others. He drew a blank, so approached the front door and rang the bell. It was answered by a man in his mid-to-late fifties, slightly overweight and dressed in jeans and a T-shirt with 'I HAVE SEX DAILY DYSLEXIA' emblazoned on its front. The inspector suppressed a smile.

"Mr Grant? Mr Doug Grant?" Although the inspector knew he was at the right house as evidenced by the charred remains in the corner of the garden, nevertheless he needed to establish to whom he was talking.

"Yes, that's me. Thanks for coming. I've taken the morning off work so I could see you." Grant had assumed they were police and after introductions the inspector wanted to find out more.

"So, sir, please tell us what happened last night."

"Well, I woke up from a nightmare at about one o'clock and wanted a pee. I saw through the frosted glass in the bathroom window a flickering glow. When I checked it out from the landing window I could see my lovely summerhouse was ablaze. I called the fire brigade and used my garden hose to try and put out the fire. The guys arrived quite quickly considering how far they had to come, but they were too late to salvage anything. What's more they could have been seriously injured as a gas bottle exploded."

"You had barbeque equipment in your summerhouse? Had you used it that day?" King was subtly checking out if the fire could have been caused by the owner's neglect.

"Hardly, inspector, it wasn't exactly a balmy summer evening last night."

"So what do you think happened?"

"Well, it's obvious to me, someone set fire to it."

"If it was arson, why do you think you were targeted?"

"I had no idea until I spoke with Abby and Mike this morning, sorry, I mean Ms Croft and Mr Farthing. Now it's pretty obvious the attacks are down to this confounded planning application that the council's considering. They had messages left that clearly referred to it. I don't think it's any coincidence as we three have spoken out against it; someone is trying to get us to change our minds. If I were you I'd interview those bloody developers. They've got the most to gain from all this."

King ignored the allegation. Grant continued what was fast becoming a rant.

"I'm not Mr Popular as I speak my mind, but this is heavy stuff. I can't think of anyone I've upset enough for them to torch my summerhouse apart from the developers. We had a site meeting with them recently about the proposed development, which most of the councillors attended; two district councillors were also there. A whole gang of us walked up to the field at Joe Garner's place at Ringmore Farm to look at the site. He'll get a pretty penny if he sells the field to the builders. Reckon it'll cost them a million. Of course, that's if they get planning permission."

"What was the outcome of the site meeting?"

"That was just so we could hear more about the plans. We had an extraordinary meeting in the village hall and the same people attended, with over fifty of the villagers there. Some see this as a good thing, while most see it as the thin end of the wedge. They feel if they don't object to this then more and more houses will be built in the village or surrounding countryside."

"What was decided at these meetings?"

"You don't know how these planning things work, inspector. Nothing's been decided yet. The actual decision will be made at our next monthly parish council meeting towards the end of the month."

The inspector was partially persuaded at what might have triggered the offences, but at the same time was keeping an open mind.

"So I assume at the second meeting in the village hall, councillors indicated their voting intentions and that is when you and others said you were against it?"

"There are no flies on you, inspector. That's exactly what happened and I wasn't alone."

King ignored the slightly patronising response. "Who else is opposed to the development?"

"Abigail and Mike obviously and Kirsten Massey is against it too I think, but she couldn't make the second meeting, while some of the others are hedging their bets, or should I say are being indecisive."

"Kirsten Massey? Is she another councillor?"

"She is and although she wasn't at the village hall meeting, I think she made her intentions clear at the site meeting. If you ask me the vote's going to be very close and I for one won't be changing my view just because some bastard torched my summerhouse." As an afterthought he added more venom: "Oh, and the developers have promised to build a new community hall if the application is approved. I ask you, have you ever seen a more obvious sweetener than that?"

King didn't comment on the not-so-veiled bribe accusation, but, as ever, did not simply accept the obvious.

"You said earlier that you couldn't think of anyone you have upset enough for them to torch your summerhouse. Have you had any altercations or disagreements with anyone recently?" The wily inspector had assessed Grant's personality as someone whose outspoken manner could easily offend.

"Not really unless you count the spat I had with my local garage over some work they did on my car that I wasn't happy about. I know about motors as I am in the trade. I could have got it sorted at my place in Exeter, but wanted to put a little bit of business their way. I'd asked them to sort out a problem on my Merc as it kept cutting out. I told them it was probably some dirt in the carb. Well, they said they fixed it, but the damn thing cut out again on my way back from the garage. I had a real go at Mike Farthing and he apologised. He was a bit vague as to what had been done, so I reckon it was probably his partner who did the work. Anyway, Mike apologised and fixed it; we're still good friends."

King thought the incident was hardly worthy of arson retribution.

"One last thing, Mr Grant. Do you chain and lock your five-bar gate at night?"

"I do, inspector. Every night just before it gets dark I lock it with the chain and combination lock. It wouldn't stop a person, but no cars can come into my property. I feel safer that way. It deters any passing person or animal from wandering in."

"Thank you, sir. You have been very helpful. Before we leave we would just like to have a look around your garden, just in case the culprit left any incriminating evidence. There's no need to take any more of your time. If you think of anything else that may help, please let us know." He gave him a card with his police station contact details, not his mobile phone number.

The two detectives split up and searched opposite sides of the garden hoping to find an empty petrol container – unlikely, but worth a look. Close to the entrance gate, King bent down on his haunches and began studying the gravel. He'd missed something on his first casual inspection. He took out one of those neatly folded unused tissues and picked up an object.

King ambled to the five-bar gate and his detective joined him. She sensed a personal development opportunity and she was right.

"When I enter a crime scene, Sam, my senses go into overdrive. I'm always looking for anything that might help us solve the crime. Most often I find nothing of note and even if I find something, it doesn't necessarily mean it's in any way connected to the crime. Just now I found this object on the drive." He, once again, took the tissue handkerchief from his pocket and carefully unfolded it to reveal a button about the size of a pound coin and about as thick. On closer inspection it had on it some lettering: HONI SOIT QUI MAL Y PENSE. Dyson peered at it without touching and then her boss continued with the detection lesson.

"As I recall the phrase translates as 'Evil be to him that evil thinks' or something like that. It looks to me like it came from a military uniform and, although the motto is in French, I think it comes from a British Army regiment. Could be unconnected, but I might get Forensics to have a closer look at it. One possible explanation is that the perpetrator climbed over the five-bar gate as it was locked using the chain and combination lock Mr Grant mentioned. If the person is fairly short and, say, was wearing a big coat, in trying to slide over the top bar of the gate this button could have been pulled off his coat. If they are going to climb over a gate, country folk tend to do it as close to the hinged end as possible, as it puts less strain on the gate. It is more stable or rigid close to the hinge rather than the latch end."

With that King closely examined the top of the gate closest to the hinge with Dyson also moving closer.

"See here, Sam. There is a mark across the top bar from one side to the other, fairly close to the hinge. I reckon the person tried to slide over the gate and that's when the button snagged on the wood and eventually came off. So, from that you can begin to build a picture of the person who may be responsible for the offence. Possibly ex-military and probably fairly stocky in stature. But a word of caution: don't become fixated on that particular piece of evidence as I could be completely wrong! Always keep an open mind, Sam. Pursue the probable and pursue the plausible. Let's move on.

"We need to find out more about this planning application and the two meetings that have been held so far. Knowing how parish councils work, as I was a councillor myself as a young man, I would think a record was kept of the second meeting at least. See if you can get hold of a copy as it would give us background on what's going on and probably put into context what Grant has told us and what we're going to hear from the other two.

"I'd like you to conduct the next two interviews, Sam. Who's next?"

Slightly taken aback by this surprising elevation, the detective quickly regained her composure.

"Miss Abigail Croft who lives just around the corner at The Warren. She is expecting us about now."

FOURTEEN

King and Dyson moved on to the second victim's property, a cottage in its own grounds. Following the summerhouse fire, this time it was the resident's lawn that had been defaced by a corrosive liquid. The detectives stopped to inspect the vandalism on the front lawn. 'VOTe YeS' had been scrawled in metre-high lettering on the otherwise pristine grass. The stench of bleach hung in the air. Dyson was taking the lead as main questioner, so she used the ornate brass door knocker to signal their arrival. A middle-aged woman answered wearing an elegant floral dress and full make-up. It wasn't what the detectives were expecting of a retired headmistress.

"Good morning. Miss Abigail Croft? I am Detective Constable Dyson and this is Inspector King." She nodded to acknowledge who she was and who they were.

"If you don't mind I'd prefer to be addressed as Ms," the spinster said without hostility.

"Apologies. We can see the vandalism on your lawn, Ms Croft. When did you first notice it?"

"It was early this morning when I looked out of the window. At first I thought it was some debris blown in overnight, but then on closer inspection I saw it was a message."

"And what do you make of the message?" Dyson probed.

"'VOTE YES' can only refer to the planning application I am totally opposed to and someone is trying to frighten me into changing my mind."

"Do you think the applicants could be responsible?"

"Who else? The developers have the most to gain, don't they?"

Dyson nodded several times as she made an entry in her notebook.

"I understand from your near neighbour, Mr Grant, the victim of an arson attack, he too is opposed to the application and thinks the developers have questions to answer."

"He is, and so is Mike Farthing who I spoke to on the phone earlier. He has had his garage door defaced with the same message."

With that the three moved from the entrance of the cottage to her lawn and all gazed at the letters written in bleach. The pungent smell seemed to fill the whole garden. They all stared at the menacing message: 'VOTE YES'. King looked at the lady and thought he detected apprehension bordering on fear.

"They've done this and the other things – what might they do next?"

Dyson tried to be reassuring. "These attacks have

put everyone on their guard and they'd be foolish to try anything else. Also it is now a police investigation."

She tried to sound convincing, but Abigail Croft was far from being convinced. The troubled homeowner told the detectives about the site meeting and the subsequent meeting in the village hall, echoing Doug Grant's summary, but perhaps with a little less vitriol.

Dyson didn't bother asking her if she could think of any other motive for the vandalism as she knew she wasn't looking beyond the obvious. She reiterated that she thought the developers were responsible; the discussion with Doug Grant had made a lasting impression on the retired school teacher.

"Thank you, Ms Croft. We are now going to have a word with Mr Farthing. If you think of anything else that you believe will help us, please call me on this number." She handed her a card with her extension at the police station. With that they left.

Dyson started walking down the drive. "Mr Farthing lives a little bit further on, sir."

Just by the gate that marked the entrance to the cottage, the inspector stopped again.

"Before we see him, Sam, I wanted to cover a couple of things. Firstly, do you think we should carry out a search of the garden just to see if we can find a discarded bleach bottle or anything else that the person who did this was careless enough to leave behind?" Dyson knew where he was coming from and they split up and started their search.

After several more minutes the inspector abandoned the search as they hadn't found anything. Once again by the entrance gate the inspector wanted to ask his detective another question.

"So, Sam, how did you think you did with Ms Croft's interview?"

"I thought it went pretty well, sir. It's clear who she thinks defaced her lawn and the reason why they did it."

King took out a sherbet lemon – by now well above his daily quota – and Dyson waited patiently; she was slightly anxious at what he was about to say.

"I mentioned earlier, Sam, that I wanted you with me as part of your development." Dyson bit her bottom lip as she rightly feared some feedback coming her way.

"The picture is becoming clearer on these attacks that, on the face of it, do seem to be linked. Who do you see as the likely perpetrators?"

"Well, obviously the developers, sir. They stand to make millions of pounds if the planning application is approved."

"Anyone else?"

Dyson looked pensive and a little flummoxed. The wily senior detective sucked and then spoke when the detective didn't offer any other possible suspects.

"It seems that the common denominator to these attacks is the planning application, but let's not be too quick to condemn the developers for now, whilst acknowledging they have a lot to gain. There are a number of other people with vested interests in the outcome of the planning application, not just them.

"As detectives we need to keep an open mind. If we don't, we could be in danger of making the facts or evidence fit our prejudices or preconceived view. We need always to be looking beyond the obvious, whilst not ignoring it. Who do I think is responsible for the vandalism and the arson? True, the developers have a highly profitable vested interest, but so does Mr Garner, the farmer we met earlier on, who is selling them the land. Also the business people in the village could see their livelihoods given a boost, so it is very much in their interest that the development goes ahead. Neither can we rule out some perverted vendetta against these councillors by someone using the planning furore as a cover for their retribution. Granted the last one is very unlikely, but nonetheless possible.

"So, Sam, you not only asked Ms Croft a leading question by asking her if she thought the developers were responsible, but when she said she thought they were, you nodded several times as if in agreement. We have to remain impartial and not be seen as biased.

"You also told her of the conversation we had with Mr Grant and that we were going to speak with Mr Farthing. As a general rule in any investigation, I don't divulge what other witnesses have said or tell a witness who else we plan to interview. I learned my lesson many years ago when dealing with a case. I divulged to a witness the name of another person I was planning to interview and it resulted in one attacking the other and causing serious injuries, all because of what I had said.

"We could have asked her if she'd noticed anyone snooping around her place lately and had she upset someone recently that could make this a retribution crime. Those questions may not have given us anything, but unless we ask we may never know." King knew he was in danger of being labelled a smart alec, but had faith that Dyson didn't think that, but feedback overload was a distinct possibility. High risk, but he had started so he was going to finish.

"Any thoughts on the 'VOTe YeS' graffiti?" he asked, but Dyson was too dejected to speak. King answered his own question.

"It looks like a mix of upper and lower case with the 'e' the only lower case letter. However, the 'v', 'o' and possibly the 's' could also be lower case just enlarged to make the letters uniform height. Is this important? Will it help lead us to the writer? It may or it may not. As detectives we mustn't take things at face value. We must always think laterally. Unlikely, but from now on we must be watching for anyone who mixes upper and lower case when writing. It could suggest involvement in these crimes." The young detective was looking increasingly crestfallen.

"Now don't take this the wrong way, Sam. I'm giving you feedback and telling you about how I operate and also about the mistakes I made as a junior detective, when I was inexperienced, so you won't make them too. I'm also pointing out to you the things I do and look for when on an investigation.

"Okay. Let's see what Mr Farthing has to say about his garage door."

King knew Dyson was hurt by what he had said, which wasn't his intention. He was, however, confident she would analyse it, learn from it and move on.

"As arranged, Sam, you lead again."

The junior detective gave him a rueful smile that he didn't see and thought to herself: *No pressure then!*

FIFTEEN

The third, and last, victim they planned to interview lived a short distance from their second interview. As they walked neither detective spoke as Dyson was reflecting on the feedback her boss had given her. She was determined to quickly learn from it and demonstrate to him that she had.

"Do you still want me to conduct this interview, sir?"

"Of course." King, showing mock surprise, knew this was an ideal early opportunity for her to prove his faith in her.

On arrival at Farthing's place, the detectives ambled up the gravelled drive towards the house taking them past the double garage. Dyson began studiously scanning the ground, particularly in front of the defaced door, and also walked along one side of the building. A blue Nissan pick-up truck was parked in the drive. Farthing lived in a rather dilapidated three-bedroom bungalow by himself, having been widowed several years before. His garden was unkempt just like the owner. Before Dyson could use the doorbell, he opened the door.

He had been to work at the garage he owned and returned after being contacted by the detective. Several days' growth of beard was clearly evident. He had a newspaper in one hand and a pipe in the other. He was obviously having his mid-morning break at home. Introductions followed and Dyson started her second interview that day.

"Thank you for returning from work, Mr Farthing. You rang the police earlier to report some vandalism at your property. When did you notice the graffiti on your garage door?"

"Soon after I got up. I'm a fairly early riser and after breakfast I was about to get my van out of my garage to go to work and that's when I saw it. I rang the police and still went off to work as I couldn't do anything about the damage until you'd seen it."

"You didn't hear anything or see anything suspicious before you went to bed or during the night?"

"No. I didn't notice anything out of the ordinary. I sleep pretty soundly and it was a complete surprise when I saw what they'd done. When you rang I was at my garage in the village and I came back here. I left Jim Preston, my partner, to look after the place, but I could do with getting back shortly."

"Have you any idea what the vandalism is about, sir, or who would want to deface your garage?"

"Well, because of the two scrawled words, I assume it's linked to the planning application the council's considering. I've made it clear I'm not in favour of it, the same as Abby; that's Ms Croft. I doubt that any newcomers would bring their fancy cars to my garage for service or repairs. Besides that I like the village as it is and if this application is successful others may soon follow."

"Have you had a disagreement with anyone recently? Someone who might have wanted to spite you?"

"Not that I can remember."

"I understand the parish council has held two meetings recently. What was discussed?"

"The first was a site meeting and the developers were telling us what the houses would look like. They also showed us where the approach road would be so the new owners' cars wouldn't have to come through the village. The second meeting was in the village hall and all the councillors were asked their view of the planning application. The public also came along and I would say the mood was generally not in favour, although there were some very good reasons put forward for approving the application.

"Minutes of the second meeting were prepared so you can read what happened for yourselves."

"Have you a copy by any chance, sir?"

"No. I binned them soon after they were delivered by the clerk to the council. I know a copy was pinned to the notice board outside the village hall; you can also read them on the council's website." Dyson had already made a mental note to print a copy when back at the station as her boss still liked paper.

"Thank you, I'll go online when we get back to the station. Could we have a closer look at the graffiti?"

All three went to inspect the garage door with 'VOTe YeS' scrawled across it.

"I spoke to Abby and Doug and they suspect the developers. Is that who you'll be pursuing?" Farthing's mind was made up, possibly persuaded by his two council colleagues.

Dyson wasn't about to make the same mistake again.

"We are keeping an open mind as to who might be responsible. We need to complete our initial investigation and assess everything we've seen and been told. We'll have a look around your garden and your garage if we may and see if the perpetrator left any incriminating evidence."

Farthing became a little agitated.

"Why do you need to look in my garage? I keep it locked as I have a valuable motor in there so they couldn't possibly have got in and left anything in it."

"We need to be thorough, sir. I notice the side door to your garage has a Yale lock and the visitor last night could have easily picked the lock and been in and out without you knowing." Dyson knew that scenario was unlikely, but getting the owner to confirm nothing had been disturbed in the garage would rule that out of their investigation.

"The key to the lock is on my other set of keys, which are at work. I really need to be back at my garage as I left Jim on his own. So if you don't mind I've helped you all I can and I'd like to get back now."

Dyson was suspicious as to why Farthing was reluctant to unlock the side door, but didn't feel she could insist if he didn't have the key. She also mused that if he used the battered pick-up truck to go to and from his workplace, why wouldn't he keep his house key and home garage key on the same keyring as the truck?

"Okay, sir. Thank you for your time. Please let us know if anything else comes to mind about the incident." She gave him her card, he took it and got into his Nissan and, with spinning wheels on the gravel, he was gone.

King started looking more closely at the drive and surrounding area, but no buttons had been inadvertently left behind at this crime scene. Dyson reached for her mobile and started taking pictures of the graffiti. She then walked around the side of the double garage again. A wall prevented her walking all the way around, but towards the back she once again saw the side door with the Yale lock. It also had an old-fashioned Bakelite handle, used simply for pulling the door open once the lock had been disengaged.

She tried the handle, hoping it had been left open, and was not surprised to find it locked. What did surprise her was when she took her hand off the handle she found black paint on her hand. King was looking around the other side of the garage and when they met back at the front, she showed him her hand.

"What do you make of this, sir?"

"Perhaps the graffiti artist tried the side door after painting the front?"

"I'm not sure, sir. Did you notice Farthing seemed very reluctant to let us see inside his garage? I'm thinking he has something to hide. Anyway, if our graffiti artist did try the door, could we get Forensics to get a fingerprint from the handle? It may be the only slip-up he or she made. If we could get a print, link it to this crime, we potentially solve three crimes at once, providing we could get a match."

King reached for a sherbet lemon and Dyson knew to wait patiently for a response.

"It may be a little unorthodox, but ring Mr Farthing and tell him what we've discovered and that it could lead to a positive identification of the person who defaced his garage. As he's busy, he doesn't need to come back. There's a screwdriver in the boot of our car and looking at the handle it's only held on by three screws so I could take it off. Tell him we'll pop a receipt for it through his letterbox and return it as soon as it's been forensically examined."

Dyson took out her mobile and rang the garage owner. After a brief conversation she hung up.

"He wasn't too happy, sir, but he said to go ahead as he's too busy to come back. He also said that he doesn't often use the side door so it shouldn't be a problem. However, he wanted the handle back as soon as we've finished with it."

King went to fetch the screwdriver and it only took him a few minutes to take out the screws that secured the handle, all the time wearing blue latex gloves. They were partly not to smudge any existing fingerprints and partly not to get his hand covered in black paint like Dyson. He carefully placed the handle in an evidence bag, held open by his detective, and let her have it for safe keeping and reference to Forensics when they returned to the station. Still sucking his sweet he wasn't sure if this would prove to be a breakthrough.

"Just to be sure that the paint on the door handle matches the paint used as graffiti you'd better take a sample of it. Ideally, we need Farthing's prints as well to eliminate him, but let's see what Forensics comes up with first. They'll need yours too, Sam, as you touched the handle as well."

It was now late morning and they had done all they could in Bolberry-on-Sea. As they were about to get in the car, King paused and they faced each other over the car roof.

"I'm not going to ask you how the interview with Farthing went, Sam, I'm going to tell you. I couldn't have done a better job myself."

That morning, in the space of a few hours, Dyson had experienced the highs and lows of being a junior detective; she was quietly proud of how she had taken her inspector's feedback and put it into practice.

SIXTEEN

Early morning and the various cases being investigated by the team of detectives were keeping them busy. King had regular meetings with his team to ensure they were all aware of what was going on. Sometimes necessity might mean a crossover was needed or all of them working on the same case due to escalation. The inspector arrived early and was immediately summoned to see Chief Superintendent Harper in his office; he knew what he wanted to see him about.

"Come in, Inspector King, and sit down. Acting Superintendent Roberts has spoken to me about something that happened yesterday between you and him and also involving Sergeant Harris. He has asked that disciplinary action is taken against you and you be suspended until it has been concluded. Before I institute those procedures, I'd like to have a word with you as I only have his account of the incident. So what happened?"

"Well, sir, I was speaking about a private matter with my sergeant in the main office. I had just told her that although we usually partner each other, I would be partnering Detective Constable Dyson in the current case we have under investigation. I made the change mainly so I can develop Dyson while I'd like Harris to develop DC Hammond who has recently joined us from Exeter Police.

"She was very disappointed as we've worked together for some time. She became emotional and I was comforting her when Acting Superintendent Roberts entered the room. He saw us hugging and put his own, but wrong, interpretation on it. I was annoyed at his interruption and told him to get out. I now regret speaking to a senior officer in that manner." Harper leaned back in his chair and didn't speak for a few seconds, which seemed a lot longer to King.

"I see. Are you prepared to apologise to him?"

"I already have, sir, but my apology wasn't accepted."

"Okay, Inspector King, here's what I'd like to do to deal with this matter. I cannot condone you speaking to a senior officer in the way you did. However, if we start disciplinary action against you it will be a long drawn-out procedure, possibly involving another force, and consume many, many hours of valuable police time. I do think Acting Superintendent Roberts understandably misinterpreted the embrace between you and Sergeant Harris. That leaves your insubordination.

"I will speak with him and ask if, in the light of your explanation over the embrace, he will accept an apology from you for what you said to him. If you will accept a verbal warning as to your future conduct, I am confident I can get him to agree with my proposal and we will regard the matter as closed. If either of you don't agree, disciplinary action will follow. Do you accept my proposal?"

The wily inspector thought for moment and realised his acceptance would completely exonerate Roberts and the verbal warning would be like 'the Sword of Damocles' hanging over him. His consent would also mean that natural justice would be denied and Roberts would continue to act unfettered. Balanced against those compelling reasons not to accept what had been offered by the chief superintendent was no disciplinary hassle for him and, crucially, his sergeant's reputation would not be unfairly tarnished over Roberts' spurious complaint.

"I accept, sir, and thank you."

"Excellent, Richard. I'm sure Acting Superintendent Roberts will also be persuaded to accept it." With that the inspector left by one door and Roberts, who had been asked to remain on standby to be recalled, entered by another.

Fifteen minutes later, King was summoned again to the chief's room. Roberts and Harper sat on one side of a large desk and the inspector was invited to sit on the other. King thought, judges and defendant. Harper was quietly pleased with his unconventional mediation.

"I have explained my proposal to Acting Superintendent Roberts and he has graciously agreed to accept an apology from you as an end to this matter. I think a formal apology is in order, inspector."

"Fuck you two. I'll take my chances, so let the disciplinary procedure start, which I am confident will expose Roberts for the bully he is and hopefully scupper any chance he has of promotion." That's what King wanted to say, but, firstly, he never swears and secondly, for the sake of others, particularly Sergeant Harris, he was prepared to eat a slice of very bitter 'humble pie'. He duly apologised and the acceptance was not as gracious as he would have liked as it took the form of a simple nod of the head. Matter closed… or was it?

He was about to leave, but Harper didn't want to miss another opportunity to remind senior officers of their responsibilities.

"Before you go, Inspector King, the chief constable has been getting reports from all over the county of an alarming rise in drugs coming into our area. From Tavistock in the west, Barnstable in the north, Exeter in the east, across Torbay and, of course, as both of you are very aware, here in Plymouth.

"The chief has anecdotal evidence that most of the drugs are coming into the area through the south of Devon as we have many miles of unprotected coastline. Information from surveillance and arrests elsewhere suggest that somewhere down our way is a major store of cocaine and cannabis that is then distributed around the cities, towns and villages in the county. You know it's not just about the drugs. Increasing drug use leads to other crime, which is rising exponentially all over our beautiful county. So there's a lot resting on your shoulders to catch the people behind this evil trade. I know progress is being made and I want that accelerated."

*

It was the day after King and Dyson had visited Bolberry-on-Sea and Harris and Hammond had made further investigations about the attempted murder case. All the detectives, save for the inspector, had spent some time viewing CCTV images of roads to and from the ramming crime scene, as yet to no avail.

After his meeting with the chief superintendent earlier that morning and his second apology to Roberts, King invited his immediate boss to a briefing meeting with his detective team for an update on the progress being made on several cases. Roberts had declined attending and told the inspector to see him after that meeting and briefly outline progress. King masked his relief at his non-attendance.

At 8.30am he and his three detectives met in the interviewing room. At his request Dyson reported on the interviews they had held at Bolberry-on-Sea the previous day.

After her fairly detailed verbal report, the inspector asked Harris and Hammond if they had any questions. They didn't so he asked for an update on the attempted murder case.

Sergeant Harris then gave an update on that case mentioning Morris's continuing reluctance to divulge his sources. She then handed over to DC Hammond who held up an evidence bag containing the fragment of the registration plate left at the crime scene that he was proposing to analyse further, with a view to identifying the full registration of the vehicle. King wished Hammond good luck with that particular part of the investigation, with more than a hint that he thought it was an impossible task.

The inspector's own report, of the body on the beach case, related to the pathologist's autopsy. John Gleeson had confirmed his earlier assessment as being fairly accurate when he had first seen the body at Hope Cove. King read out a synopsis of the detailed report: the dead man was a male between thirty-five and forty years old; 177 centimetres (about five foot ten inches tall); ninety kilograms in weight (approximately fourteen stone); ten kilos overweight (one and a half stone) according to Body Mass Index; a smoker; regular dentistry and his front left incisor was made of pure gold; suffered a blow to the back of his head with a round object that was slightly bigger than a baseball bat. The blow was of sufficient weight or delivered with sufficient force to fracture the base of his skull; due to the effect of the seawater, time of death was estimated at approximately 3am on the morning the body was found; he was not dead before he entered the water. Conclusion: death by drowning while concussed from the contusion of the skull. After King finished his synopsis he handed out copies to each detective.

King remembered what Dr Gleeson had said about the expensive watch the corpse had been wearing. He produced an evidence bag containing the Rolex Submariner gold watch and passed it to DC Hammond. He asked him if he could use it to try and identify the man, acknowledging it was probably yet another difficult task to add to the identification of the number plate fragment. He was playing to his strengths.

The inspector had also received a report on the black leather rectangular box with a green strip of leather sewn on it from end to end. This had been found by his sergeant on Hope Cove beach, quite close to the body. Forensics reported that it was a cigar box that was from Naples in Italy. They didn't offer any more than that, intimating it was up to the detectives to pursue that lead. Once again the inspector delegated that task to DC Hammond as solving puzzles was fast becoming his forte.

Before King summarised the meeting and decided how the investigations should proceed, he asked his detectives if they had anything to add and Dyson spoke.

"Yes, sir. As you know, I mentioned to you a couple of weeks ago about a suspicious house I pass on my way to work from where I live in the Millbay Docks area of the city. For the benefit of the others, this takes me past the back of Union Street and over the last month I've frequently noticed that an end-terraced house always has the blinds down. As I pass the place on my way to work and way home, I have seen different people entering and leaving the property; it looked rather suspicious and I wondered if drugs were being traded. I thought it may be a 'cuckooing' house. Have there been any developments, sir?"

King duly provided an update: "When Sam mentioned the house to me, I spoke with a colleague of mine, Inspector Best from the Drugs Squad. As we all know, when the so-called County Lines drug gangs invade a smaller town or city they sometimes befriend a drug user and gradually take over their place and use it to trade drugs – hence the term cuckooing. That said, they may not actually kick out the occupier who is most likely a tenant. Keeping him in the house and under their total control suits their purposes.

"Inspector Best had ordered the house be kept under surveillance for a week and that ended last Friday. He thinks this is a key drugs trading place. He's waiting for a full report before deciding what to do. Early reports do suggest that an unscrupulous gang have taken over the house. I'm meeting with him later today and we will be involved in any bust. So, well done, Sam."

With that the briefing ended and the inspector made his way to his acting superintendent's office to brief him on the points raised at the meeting.

"Come," Roberts replied to the knock on his door.

He listened as King briefly outlined the progress on the different investigations. The inspector knew he wasn't really listening to the detail of his report as he didn't ask any questions. He even let pass the term 'cuckooing', and the inspector doubted he knew what it meant, such was his disinterest. When he finished, as promised, he wanted to address another matter.

"There's one other thing I'd like to raise if I may, sir?"

"Yes, what is it?"

"I believe you've asked Detective Constable Dyson to get you refreshment in the morning and the afternoon if she's in the station?"

"Yes, what of it?"

"She hasn't complained, sir, but is worried as she spends quite a lot of her time out on investigations and won't always be available to get you drinks. I have approached one of the admin staff, Betty James, and she is very willing to make sure you get your refreshment throughout the day."

"Okay, I'll let Dyson off, but I'm not happy she didn't just get on with it as I'd told her to."

"Thank you, sir, I'll tell her."

With that King left the irascible senior officer and went straight to an interview room and shut the door. He took out a sherbet lemon and did something he seldom did. Rather than sucking the contents out of the boiled sweet casing, he bit hard on the shell so the powder exploded in his mouth.

He muttered under his breath: "One day, Roberts, one day!"

SEVENTEEN

DC Hammond was busy during the day involved as he was with ongoing investigations, so it was in the evening he spent some of his free time working on his giant one-piece jigsaw puzzle. The fragment of number plate retrieved from the scene of the attempted murder on Bolberry Down posed a very difficult, if not virtually impossible, challenge to identify the vehicle to which it belonged.

His sergeant had just received the report from Forensics so he knew the ramming car was black in colour.

He didn't have the fragment, but that didn't matter as a picture of it was all he needed. After he'd eaten his dinner, he reached for his mobile and selected Gallery from his home screen. He quickly found the photograph he'd taken of the evidence:

After a few false starts he decided on his methodology. Much was based on conjecture, but after two hours he had worked out some possible names, if indeed it was, as he suspected, a personalised plate. If it wasn't, he'd wasted those hours of his leisure time. He would need to check them out against the database at the Driver Vehicle Licensing Agency and see if he got a match. By a match he was hoping that one of the names searched drove a black 4x4 and lived close to Plymouth or at least in the South West.

*

The diligent detective was at his desk earlier than the official eight o'clock start time, despite having worked until nearly midnight on the 'jigsaw' piece.

After running some checks he was waiting for his sergeant as she arrived for work. He waited until she had taken off her coat and asked her to listen to his hypothesis.

"Great work, Alex. I'd like you to tell the rest of the team what you have deduced at our briefing meeting that starts shortly."

The inspector had convened an update meeting for 8.30 postponed from the previous afternoon. He knew people were at their sharpest first thing and had also invited his acting boss after his hostile reaction at not being kept up to date with investigations; Roberts didn't actually reply to the invitation with "if I must", but that was how King had interpreted his non-verbal response.

At 8.35 the acting superintendent entered the

main room where all four of the detective team were patiently waiting. A chair was left empty at the head of the table and he duly sat down.

King spoke: "Sergeant Harris has told me that DC Hammond saw her first thing this morning and he has made a potential breakthrough on the attempted murder case; so let's call it breaking news. I thought you might like to hear his account first hand."

"Thank you, sir. I was asked by Sergeant Harris to do some investigation into the one concrete piece of evidence, namely the fragment of the registration plate left by the vehicle that rammed Mr Morris's car over the cliff at Bolberry Down. I started with the presumption that someone playing for such high stakes, being prepared to murder the investigative journalist, was wealthy and would do anything to protect their ill-gotten gains."

"Highly speculative, detective," Roberts interjected, but Hammond was not fazed by his interruption.

"I made an assumption that we are looking to identify a person that, in all probability, has an egotistical, narcissistic attitude to life, so much so that they would have to own a personalised number plate." Before Roberts could once again question his approach Hammond quickly continued.

"Before I left work yesterday, Sergeant Harris told me that Forensics had verbally informed her that the vehicle that hit Morris's car was black. I realised I was making a lot of assumptions and fully expected some to lead up blind alleys, but ever hopeful that my hunch may eventually pay off."

The acting superintendent let this quantum leap statement pass without an acerbic comment as even he realised he was tracking too many negatives.

Hammond then held up an A4 print, taken from his mobile, so all those present could see the image of the plate fragment. He used Blu Tack to stick it to a whiteboard behind him.

"From 2001, registrations were in a sequence: letter, letter, number, number, letter, letter, letter. As you all know, the number, number indicates the year of manufacture. So yet another assumption was that the fragment followed that sequence.

"My first thought was that when people are trying to devise a registration plate that spells their name or nickname they see if any numbers in the modern sequence could be read as a letter."

Roberts couldn't resist making an exaggerated gesture of looking at his watch in a non-verbal 'Get to tho point' gesture. Hammond continued pointing at the image attached to the whiteboard.

"From the piece of plate we have you can see a '1' and a '3'. When shown close together those numbers can be read as a 'B'. The next letter could be a 'P' or a 'B' or maybe even an 'E'. I discounted the 'P' as that letter would not normally follow a 'B'. I decided to pursue the 'B' and would come back to the 'E' if I drew a blank with 'B'."

Roberts yawned.

"So I was working with 'BB' as part of some sort of name, whether a Christian name, a nickname or a surname, though I thought surname the most likely. I reasoned a vowel must precede 'BB' so came up with permutations. I produced a list of likely names with the middle three letters." By way of illustration, and to aid understanding, he picked up a marker pen and began writing down one side of the board as he spoke.

"I came in this morning and began to run the names through our link to the DVLA database in Swansea starting with 'ABB' followed by 'EBB' and so on. I couldn't think of many credible surnames that would fit the sequence: letter, A, B, B, letter, letter.

"Anyway I came up with names and Googled them just to make sure they are actually used as surnames. For example I excluded CABBOT as it isn't used as a surname. My list of about twenty names included GIBBON, ROBBIE, COBBLY and RIBBON. I drew a blank with the first few I tried as none of the owners were registered to drive a black 4x4. Then I came up with a name that I believe could be the owner." He then sketched on the board the missing ends of the plate:

The owner of this registration plate is a Mr Simon Webber, insured to drive a Ford Ranger and its colour..." – Hammond paused for effect – "... is black! Furthermore Mr Webber lives in the village of Moorhaven not far to the east of Plymouth."

Dyson was the first to react: "Brilliant work, Alex."

Roberts was less impressed: "Seems to me there was a lot of guesswork, detective, and luck. Also we cannot be certain this isn't a coincidence."

King couldn't let his boss get away with that less than positive synopsis, but knew he mustn't become insubordinate.

"As you know, sir, our job can at times require guesswork and also a slice of luck, but if you have very little evidence when investigating a crime, guesswork becomes a legitimate method of detection. Of course, this should not be the sole determining factor when prosecuting any individual. It has to lead to other incriminating evidence and be corroborated.

"What DC Hammond has achieved is a remarkable piece of detection and given us sufficient circumstantial evidence that this vehicle, not necessarily Mr Webber himself, was used in an attempted murder crime. However, we won't be racing around to where he lives with several squad cars that slide to a halt on the gravel drive illuminating his house with flashing blue lights. No, he will be invited to attend the station with his solicitor, if he so chooses, and will be interviewed under caution. That could lead to his arrest if we are not satisfied with his explanation as to why his vehicle, albeit on circumstantial evidence, appears to have been used in a crime."

The acting superintendent wasn't happy.

"Thank you, inspector, but I don't need a lesson in correct police procedures. All very interesting, but I have some urgent matters to attend to, so if you'll excuse me." He was clearly irritated and wasn't seeking permission to leave.

King could have offered more advice to his belligerent boss following his rebuke, but thought he'd gone as far as he felt appropriate in front of the other detectives. As Roberts left the room, nobody spoke; it was as if someone had hit a meeting pause button. As the overall boss closed the door behind him, the inspector slowly reached into his pocket and took out a sherbet lemon and popped it into his mouth. His team knew to adopt a dignified silence as they let his evident anger dissipate.

Soothed by his effervescent sweet he continued: "I was hoping that the acting superintendent would have stayed for the rest of the briefing as I know he is keen to keep abreast of our work."

The detectives reviewed the other cases they were dealing with and King thanked them for their updates before setting out the next steps.

"Right. Sam and I will continue working on the Bolberry-on-Sea crimes and talk further with Inspector Best about a possible drugs bust. Lucy and Alex, I'd like you to pay a visit to Mr Webber's home this afternoon and, despite what I said earlier, you'd better have a squad car with you in case it turns nasty. Depending on how your interview with him pans out, either bring him back with you, if you think he's involved in the ramming of Morris's car, or invite him for interview tomorrow morning here at nine o'clock. Mention he will be interviewed under caution so he might like to bring his legal representative with him."

King's approach was cautious when dealing with people he assumed were rich and powerful based on fairly flimsy evidence; he was mindful of how the police had treated Sir Cliff Richard and the subsequent defamation case.

"While you're there, if the black 4x4 is on the drive, check that Alex was right about the plate, see if it's got four spotlights and have a look at the front of it for any sign of a collision. Don't arouse suspicion about the vehicle as we may end up bringing it in for Forensics to give it a going over.

"Right, I'll now brief the acting superintendent about the progess we've made on the other cases." He wanted to add, "if he's interested", but he knew that would have been inappropriate.

EIGHTEEN

D C Dyson had printed out a copy of the extraordinary meeting minutes from the Bolberry-on-Sea Parish Council website following the interviews with councillors the day before. She and her inspector had been told of a meeting regarding an outline planning application to build luxury homes on the edge of the village. They were directed to the website and Dyson knew that her boss would prefer a paper copy rather than reading it on screen. King found the copy on his desk and, after putting a sherbet lemon in his mouth, he began reading:

BOLBERRY-ON-SEA PARISH COUNCIL

**MINUTES OF AN
EXTRAORDINARY PLANNING MEETING**

Held at Bolberry-on-Sea Village Hall on Wednesday
13th March 2019 at 7pm

ATTENDING

PARISH COUNCILLORS: Colonel M Davenport (Chairman); Ms D Proud; Mr D Smith; Reverend Robert Brown; Mr G Harkness; Mr T Bayliss; Ms J Ferris; Mr M Farthing; Mr D Grant; Ms A Croft; Mr S Osbourne. Apologies for absence: Ms K Massey.

DEVELOPERS: Mr S Webber and Mr L Simpson (Directors of Build Great Homes Ltd)

DISTRICT COUNCIL PLANNING OFFICERS: Mrs D Norris and Mr P Armitage

MEMBERS OF THE PUBLIC: Fifty-five members of the public attended the meeting.

1. CHAIRMAN'S OPENING ADDRESS
The chairman opened the extraordinary meeting and welcomed those present. He said it was a single-issue meeting to discuss whether to accept or reject an outline planning application that had been made to the district council on behalf of Build Great Homes Ltd. He informed those present that the application related to land to the west of the caravan park at Warren Point above the small secluded bay called Ayrmer Cove. Permission was sought for the building of twenty-five two-storey detached houses on a ten-hectare field, which was currently part of Ringmore Farm. The houses would form Burgh Island View and would not impinge on the South West Coast Path. Access would be by a new single-track road, with passing places, from the existing farm entrance. All the parish councillors attended a site meeting held the previous week and also representatives from the developers and two district councillors.

Notices relating to the application had been displayed for the statutory period at the site. Plans of the proposed development had also been displayed in the village hall. The chairman reminded the councillors that the developers had pledged, if their application was successful, they would build a new community hall, to replace the dilapidated village hall, that would contain a library, café and a function room.

The meeting was open to the public, but the chairman made it clear that they were observers and were only allowed to speak when the meeting was opened to the public, when questions would be invited.

2. PURPOSE OF MEETING

The chairman informed the meeting of its purpose. The plans for the proposed development had been on display in the village hall for two weeks and they were also available on the district council's website. A site visit had been held the week before this meeting, attended by the parish and district councillors and two directors from Build Great Homes Ltd. This meeting was arranged to allow the local councillors and the public to express their views.

He stressed that parish councillors would vote on the outline planning application at its next monthly meeting.

3. POINTS RAISED BY COUNCILLORS

3.1 Mr G Harkness spoke in favour of the application as he felt the houses would not be seen from existing dwellings and the new residents would bring prosperity to the local businesses. He acknowledged that as the local butcher he would welcome increased trade and did not see the dwellings having an adverse effect on the village as it was over half a mile away. He also said that the primary school in the village was short of pupils and could close. The new families were sure to have need of the school.

3.2 Ms A Croft was totally opposed to the new development as it would further deface the coastline she had walked for many years. She had opposed the caravan park when it was originally formed and she saw the proposed buildings to be a further blot on the landscape.

(Note: Her comments drew applause from some members of the public and the chairman said they should remain silent or they would be asked to leave.)

3.3 Mr M Farthing supported Ms Croft as he thought the village didn't need more dwellings, particularly as they were unlikely to be in the price range of local people.

3.4 Ms D Proud disagreed with the view expressed by the previous speakers and welcomed twenty-five more families to the area and the new community hall.

3.5 Mr D Grant was against the development purely for, as he called it, NIMBY reasons. He wasn't against progress, but 'not in my back yard'. Furthermore he thought the offer by the developers to build a new community hall was an obvious bribe to get their application approved.

(Note: The chairman rebuked Mr Grant for his use of the word 'bribe', saying it was out of order.)

3.6 Mr D Smith supported the application as the local area would benefit from an influx of more people who would use the facilities, including his pub, provided by local businesses who were finding it increasingly difficult to make ends meet as Gavin, the local butcher, will testify.

(Note: His comments drew laughter from the public.)

3.7 The Reverend Brown did not object to the planning application, but was concerned that the new dwellings would become holiday homes and only be occupied for some of the summer months. He suggested that the parish council approve the application, and advise the district council it should be subject to a binding covenant that the prospective buyers must use the dwelling as their principal place of residence, as opposed to using it as their second home. The reverend commented that his proposal was a measure designed to decrease the proportion of holiday homes in the village and not to prevent progress.

3.8 Mr T Bayliss thought there was plenty of scope for further development. As for the earlier comment that the development would be a blot on the landscape he said there was no bigger blot than the existing caravan park.

3.9 Ms J Ferris said she could see both sides of the discussion, but was generally in favour of the development.

3.10 Mr S Osbourne said when the village was first formed, historical records showed it had a church and a few cottages. If further development hadn't been allowed we wouldn't have the lovely village we have today. He said he was not a Luddite and thought further development should be allowed. However, he did have some concerns about the impact on the environment.

3.11 The chairman said, like Councillor Ferris, he too could appreciate the differing views expressed. He was undecided on the matter and acknowledged that he would have the casting vote if the other councillors were equally divided when the proposal was put to a vote at the next meeting.

4. QUESTIONS FROM THE PUBLIC

The chairman invited questions from the public and said they should be addressed through him.

Q. I'd like the builders to answer a question. How much profit will your company make if the houses are built?

BGH Ltd replied: I'm afraid that information is classed as commercial in confidence. We are a developer with a good reputation for building quality homes and, as you will have seen from the plans, we have designed them so they are aesthetically pleasing and will be built in traditional style as we are aware of the prestigious location.

Q. Not a question as such, but an observation. The councillors who are in favour of the development mostly stand to profit from more homes. I would urge them to set aside their personal gain and to think of the impact on our coastline and the environment.

Planning Officer replied: Mr P Armitage informed the meeting that an Environmental Impact Assessment had been carried out and a copy could be obtained from the council offices. There was no objection to the application from an environmental perspective, but the developers would have to meet certain requirements to reduce the impact on the habitat of some wild animals that currently use the field and surrounding hedges.

(Mr D Smith suggested the developers should build some executive rabbit hutches.)

Q. Why can't the developers build on brownfield sites rather than using a field still used for grazing?

BGH Ltd replied: We do build a high proportion of our developments on land that had previously been developed and was no longer in use. However, we also like to offer our customers the choice of more exclusive houses in prime locations.

Q. If the parish council approve the application will the district council planners also approve it?

Planning Officer replied: Mr P Armitage said that district councils are under pressure from central government to allow building to take place whenever possible to boost the number of homes as a shortfall is predicted in the not too distant future. We increasingly take note of the views of local councils' advice so it is likely the district council will be guided by the parish council decision.

Q. I'd like to ask the developers what their motive is for building a new community hall if it isn't to curry favour?

BGH Ltd replied: The offer to build a new hall for the village is a gesture from the company for allowing us to build quality homes in your village. It is not a bribe as someone said earlier, more an act of appreciation.

Q. Do the developers aim to comply with Section 106 of the Town and Country Planning Act 1990 and make some of the new houses suitable as social housing?

BGH Ltd replied: A very good point. Can I just correct you with the term social housing, which allows individuals with very little or no income to live in a stable and secure home provided by the local authority. In the case of this development, we considered affordable housing, where a house is offered for sale or rent at a price below market value, as part of a government or local council scheme. We believe, because of the nature of the proposed development, neither social or affordable housing schemes apply. However, I go back to my previous answer referring to the gesture the company has made to build a new community hall.

5. CONCLUSION OF MEETING
The chairman asked all the parish councillors to reflect on the points raised at the meeting and said they will be asked to vote on the outline planning application at the monthly council to be held later that month.

MEETING ENDED AT 7.52pm

(MINUTES PREPARED BY MR G BARTON, CLERK TO THE PARISH COUNCIL)

*

The inspector had made his sherbet lemon last until he had finished reading the minutes of the meeting. He now felt better informed and they put into context the interviews held with the councillors who had been subject to the attack on their property. His job was not to influence the outcome of the parish council's decision on the planning application, but to combat the evident intimidation of those councillors who were against the development and also to arrest whoever was responsible for the criminal behaviour.

Although the directors of Build Great Homes wouldn't answer the question about build cost and profit, King knew that this was a multi-million pound investment; that didn't mean to say they were behind the threats as there were others who would benefit from more homes in the village. Just then Dyson passed his desk.

"What did you think of the minutes, sir?"

"Very interesting, Sam, and gives me a clear insight into the background of what we are dealing with in Bolberry-on-Sea. One thing troubles me though and I am surprised it wasn't picked up at the meeting by a councillor or a member of the public."

"What's that then, sir?"

"The so-called 'bribe' of the developers offering to build a new community centre to replace the village hall that is in desperate need of repair."

"What about it, sir?"

"Do you recall the conversation we had with Farmer Garner on our very own site visit?"

She referred to her notebook: "Do you mean the bit about the proposed new community hall? He said 'God knows the village needs one as the listed ramshackle village hall is on its last legs.' That bit, sir?"

"That's the very bit, Sam. And what is the key word in that passage?"

Dyson looked nonplussed.

"The word 'listed'. If it is Grade II listed it can't be knocked down and rebuilt. Therefore, the promise to provide a new community hall means they will have to find a new site. Now I wonder where that site would be? Wherever it is, and if it isn't already land owned by the council, it would attract a very good price from the developers."

NINETEEN

DC Hammond's examination of the number plate fragment left at the scene of the attempted murder of Dan Morris had led him and his sergeant to the village of Moorhaven to the east of Plymouth. As they drove up the ungated drive to the home of Simon Webber in their unmarked car, a liveried police 4x4 containing two uniformed officers was waiting just outside the entrance to the property. The detectives walked to the front door of the substantial house with stables attached.

The black 4x4 they were interested in was not on the drive. Instead, parked in front of a double garage was a top-of-the-range Volvo displaying its own personalised number plate WEBB5 1, yet another example Hammond thought of a number being used as a letter.

Before their visit, DC Hammond had made discreet enquiries about Webber. "He is not a licensed gun holder, sergeant." If he had been they would have been more cautious in their approach.

"He's a self-made millionaire who in his early career owned a glass-making factory and for the last twenty years has been one of three directors of the building company called Build Great Homes Limited."

Simon Webber could have added that he was a very keen cyclist and a lead singer in an acapella quartet. He was proud to be a ten-handicap golfer, but was never quite able to make the magic single-figure golfing milestone that only one per cent of the amateur golf players in the world achieve. In view of his advancing years he had resigned himself to the fact that he wasn't going to improve his golf game and, anyway, he preferred to be on his bike. He and his fellow directors, Len Simpson and George Lawson, had been founder members of their building company having met when they were all members of Thurlestone Golf Club. Webber and Simpson were already in partnership as builders and Lawson had his own building company. What started as casual conversation during a round of golf developed into the amalgamation of their building expertise and the formation of Build Great Homes Limited. The four-year-old company had flourished and its annual profit was now measured in millions rather than tens of thousands.

With the uniformed officers waiting a short distance away in case they were needed, Sergeant Harris rang the doorbell. It was answered by a lean, middle-aged man of above average height.

"Can I help you?"

"Good morning, sir. Are you Mr Simon Webber?" He nodded his confirmation.

"I am Detective Sergeant Harris from Plymouth Police and this is Detective Constable Hammond. We are making enquiries about a case and we believe you own a black 4x4 Ford Ranger motorcar with the registration WE13BER, is that correct, sir?"

"I don't personally own it. It's owned by our building company and it's used as a general-purpose vehicle by the directors and the site manager in charge of any of our construction sites. Why do you ask?"

"We have reason to believe that it was recently used to commit a crime. Where is the vehicle now, sir?"

"A crime! What crime and when?"

"The night before last a car was forced over a cliff at Bolberry Down. Fortunately the driver managed to jump clear. We have reason to believe it was your company's 4x4 that rammed the other vehicle. Judging by the registration you would appear to be the owner and driver." Not quite an accusation, but not far short. Webber looked slightly shocked and at the same time perplexed, but recovered his composure.

"Looks can be deceptive, sergeant. As I've said already, a number of people use it. All three directors of the company have their own cars – me, Len Simpson and George Lawson – and as an affectation we all have personalised plates as well as the 4x4. George has the plate LAW50N, while Len has LEN 1. As you can see I have WEBB5 1 on my Volvo as my friends call me Webbs.

"I'm the registered keeper, but a number of people are insured to drive it as it's used as a sort of utility vehicle. It's useful for carrying people because it can seat five or we use it to transport small building supplies because of the cargo bay at the back. Currently we have a site over in Dartmouth. Sometimes authorised people use it overnight, but more often than not it's locked up in the garage of our show home on site."

Undaunted, Harris wanted a more accurate location for the vehicle.

"As we have reason to believe the vehicle has been used in a crime we will need to inspect it and also interview all those who had access to driving it, particularly on the night before last. Do you know who was using the vehicle then?"

"I know it wasn't me, but offhand, I don't know who had access to it that evening. I would have to ask my director colleagues or the site manager."

"Could you do that, sir, and while we wait could you also identify where the vehicle is now?"

"I'll have to make some phone calls; my mobile is indoors."

"We'll come in if you don't mind, sir?" The sergeant wanted to eavesdrop on the telephone calls to check he was not warning someone of their interest in the 4x4.

"Of course you can come in; I've nothing to hide." Webber had regained his self-assured manner.

From what the detectives could hear it appeared that he wasn't warning anyone of the police enquiry, merely trying to establish the whereabouts of the vehicle as requested. After three phone calls, with the detectives only hearing one end of the conversations, Webber put down his mobile phone and gave them the information they were after.

"The 4x4 is at our current construction site over Dartmouth way where we are currently building executive homes overlooking the River Dart estuary."

He gave them the address of the site and continued: "It's used during the day, particularly by our site manager, Greg Carter, and, as far as I am aware, it was locked in one of the show home garages on site on the last two nights. So I'm sorry I can't confirm who was driving it the night before last as I thought it was garaged. Are you sure you've got the right vehicle?"

Harris, without wishing to appear rude, ignored his question.

"Where are the keys to the vehicle kept when it is housed in the show home garage overnight?"

"Because the site is nearing completion, the study in the show home doubles as an office and in there is a locked wall cabinet with the keys to all of the completed properties. Any of our sales people can get the keys from there and take prospective buyers to show them around houses. The road around the site can get very muddy with lorry deliveries, so it's better if we take them to the houses. Also, the keys for a number of vehicles used on site are kept in the cabinet, including the keys of the 4x4."

Harris wasn't entirely satisfied with the explanation, but accepted it on face value.

"And where were you the night before last, sir?"

"I was rehearsing with three other guys. I am part of a barbershop quartet and we use a hall over in Kingsbridge to rehearse. I guess we started about 7.30 and finished around ten o'clock. We then went for a beer in the Creeks End Inn in Kingsbridge and left about half past ten."

"Please give the detective constable the names and contact details of the other members of your singing group who can corroborate your whereabouts that night."

The sergeant was satisfied he could account for his whereabouts on the evening in question, subject to verification.

"Okay, sir, I'll tell you what we'd like to do. DC Hammond and I, plus the two officers who are waiting outside, would like to visit the site in Dartmouth now. It is likely we will need to take the vehicle back to the station for inspection, so please contact your Mr Carter and tell him that it mustn't leave the site. We should be with him in about three quarters of an hour."

"You're impounding our vehicle?"

"As I mentioned already, we suspect it was used in a serious incident I referred to earlier and I would like our forensic people to have a look at it, if you have no objection?" Harris was being polite, but Webber knew any objection would have been futile.

"Depending on the outcome of our site visit and discussion with your Mr Carter, it may be necessary for you and others, who had access to the vehicle, to attend Charles Cross Police Station in Plymouth where all of you may be interviewed separately under caution. Of course, if that happens you are quite at liberty to have a legal representative with you. I will contact you again if I need to formally interview you and the others."

Webber was again a little nonplussed, but reached for his phone and contacted the Dartmouth site as the detectives left.

The two-car police convoy headed for Dartmouth and because of some traffic congestion due to roadworks, they arrived at the site closer to an hour after they had left Moorhaven village.

They were greeted by a person in a contradiction of clothing; he was wearing a suit and wellington boots. He introduced himself as Greg Carter the site manager. There, on the drive of the show home, was the 4x4 with the distinctive personalised number plate of WE13BER, displaying four spotlights over its cab. He knew what they had come to see, being forewarned over the phone. He duly handed over a set of keys for the vehicle. One of the police officers, who had followed the two detectives to the site, took possession of the keys, but did not drive the vehicle away; he waited until the detectives had finished their enquiries in the show home.

Carter showed them the substantial steel cabinet that housed several rows of keys on hooks, each with a number directly above it. Hammond wanted to ask a question.

"So, Mr Carter, who has access to this cabinet?"

"Well, I do and, of course, all three directors. Our sales people may drive it during the day if they need to run an errand or meet potential buyers. They'll help themselves to the keys if the cabinet is unlocked, which it is for most of the day as they also need access to house keys."

Hammond pressed: "So there is no record of who uses the vehicle or at what time?"

"No, I'm afraid not."

"Who was the last person to use it two days ago?"

"One of the plumbers, Lewis Slinger, popped to Kingsbridge that afternoon to collect some special part to finish a job in a house. When he got back, George, sorry, Mr Lawson, wasn't best pleased as he wanted to use it. I don't know what for and he wasn't back by the time I locked up. His Jaguar was on the show home drive when I left to go home. I locked the cabinet in the knowledge that Mr Lawson had his key. I assume he would have garaged the 4x4 on his return and locked the key in the cabinet."

"Why did he use the 4x4 if his own car was here?"

"You'd have to ask him that, detective."

"Am I right the site is not secured overnight?"

"Yes you are, as some of the new builds are now occupied, so they need access. The show home is locked together with the compound where we keep all our materials and other vehicles."

Harris noticed what looked like a small cashbox in the corner of the cabinet.

"You lock up the cash with the keys?" She pointed at the cashbox.

"No. That contains all the duplicate keys for the vehicles."

"Please can I have a look?"

With that Carter retrieved the box and handed it to the detective.

"So you don't lock the box?"

"No point if the cabinet is locked."

"Which key is for the Ranger?"

Carter put his fingers in the box and moved the keys on fobs about.

"The spare key for the Ranger isn't here," he said looking nonplussed at the detectives. "Someone must have used it and not returned it." He then looked shocked, realising the significance of what he'd just said.

After a few more general questions the detectives felt they had all the information they were going to get and decided to have a conversation in private. The uniformed officers left with one driving the 4x4 after giving Carter a receipt for the vehicle. Advised by DC Hammond, the police driver donned blue latex gloves before driving away.

Harris and Hammond walked to their own car, not to leave, but to privately discuss what they had been told; Harris asked Hammond for his views.

"Well, sergeant, I gave the front of the vehicle a cursory inspection and I couldn't see any marks on it at all. In fact the plate was so clean it looked as good as new! What appeared to be proof that Webber was our man is now in doubt, as from what he's told us, and the site manager's replies, it is purely circumstantial evidence that Webber was responsible due to the fact the vehicle is used by others. Although it would appear there is restricted access to the cabinet, and therefore the keys to the 4x4. I think we need to speak with all of the people who use it. They'll all have to provide an alibi of their whereabouts for the night of the attempted murder.

I would suggest we wait for the forensic report to see if we can get confirmation that the 4x4 was actually the vehicle involved in the attempted murder bid before we hold interviews, starting with the other two directors. By the way, I think we should ask them to fingerprint the key fob. I'm not optimistic it'll tell us anything, but it's worth a try. Hopefully the report will be available tomorrow depending on what else they've got on."

"I agree, Alex, but for now we'll assume it was that vehicle. Please tell Mr Carter we'll be back in the morning at nine o'clock and we'd like to see him and the people who had access to the key cabinet. Importantly, those interviews should include Simpson and Lawson. Following those discussions we'll decide whether to speak to them again under caution back at the police station. Ask Carter if he can provide a room for us to hold the interviews. Seems to me he's got plenty to choose from." After speaking once again with the site manager, Sergeant Harris had the final word before they returned to Plymouth.

"My gut feeling is that one of these people connected to Build Great Homes Limited is either responsible for what happened to the investigative journalist or knows who attempted to murder him. What I don't understand is if Morris, as we suspect, has upset the drug dealers and they want him dead, what's that got to do with this building company?"

TWENTY

On Thursday afternoon, King and Dyson were still at Charles Cross Police Station in Plymouth awaiting the report from Forensics on the door handle of Farthing's garage at his home. The other information that Dyson eagerly awaited in particular was the result of the surveillance of the suspected drugs den, which she had drawn to the attention of the appropriate team within the National Crime Agency the previous week.

The two detectives waited in their main office and were first joined by Richard King's colleague, Inspector Jim Best, and one of his team, DC Ken Baxter, who had carried out the surveillance prompted by Dyson. Baxter gave a verbal report and reassured his colleagues that he would leave the written version for them, but by telling them what it contained, it would allow them to ask questions.

"The property was kept under surveillance by me for five days. It is an end terrace, rented from Plymouth Community Homes, and the tenant's name is John Gilmour, who is known as 'Gilly'. He does have a criminal record for petty theft on more than one occasion, but was recently charged with dealing cocaine; he was eventually acquitted by order of the presiding judge due to lack of evidence.

"The rent for the property is a hundred a week, paid monthly in advance, out of an account in the name of a Mr Ron Bathe, not by Gilmour. I've checked this out and Bathe's address is fictitious. Money is paid into the account every month sufficient to cover two months' rent. The council doesn't query the fact that the tenancy agreement is in Gilmour's name and yet the rent is paid monthly by direct debit by another person; all they are interested in is non-payment.

"Over the five days that I watched the place, the property was visited daily by six or seven people, a mixture of men and women, and a different one came on the hour every hour from ten o'clock until four o'clock in the afternoon, staying for no more than five minutes each visit. However, on Monday, Wednesday and Friday, Gilmour left the property at approximately fifteen minutes before midday and took the fairly short walk to the Plymouth Pilgrim pub, arriving just before noon. On every occasion he wore a backpack back to front; in other words with the pack on his chest rather than his back.

"He usually spent an hour at the pub on those days, there being a steady stream of customers during the time he was there. I assumed they were meeting with him, but wasn't sure. So, last Wednesday I entered the pub soon after Gilmour, ordered a drink and sat in the bar pretending to look at my mobile whilst observing the comings and goings. He was not in the bar area when I arrived and later emerged from the back of the pub then left. On the pretext of using the toilet I went to the back of the pub and observed a poolroom behind the bar; I assume that's where he trades.

"Meanwhile back at his property, further covert surveillance over the week revealed it appears to be a classic 'cuckooing' set-up. It all points to a gang of criminals, possibly from Manchester, Birmingham or London, who have taken over Gilmour's place to sell drugs. So his property is being used as a drug trading post and he is either a willing accomplice, particularly as his rent is being paid by someone else, or he is being forced to allow it to be used as a drugs den.

"Some of the people that I observed going into the house appeared to be regulars as I recognised them as return callers. I estimate that during the five days I observed both his property and the pub, he would have seen over fifty people; if he's dealing, as I suspect he is, that's an awful lot of drugs. Plus any dealing he does at weekends, which I didn't observe.

"I have got photographs of the callers to his terrace house, not the pub as I didn't want to arouse suspicion. A regular at the house has a semi-circular scar on his right cheek. He is not known to the police in Devon and I'm checking with other Forces."

King wanted to ask a question: "Wouldn't wearing his backpack back to front arouse suspicion?"

"You're right, inspector, but I can only assume that the contents are very important to him. He mixes with some pretty desperate people and this is his way of guarding his livelihood. Interestingly he wears it the orthodox way when leaving the pub, because, I assume, by then it's empty."

King wanted to know more.

"Has the pub landlord got form?"

"Strangely, no. He would probably plead ignorance of what was going on if he was raided. When I was in the pub, Gilmour arrived and ordered his pint and I saw him give the landlord a £20 note and didn't get any change. If that happens every time that's £60 a week he's getting for turning a blind eye. That doesn't include any weekend trading."

"What about the visitors to the house; any identified?"

"Two have been done for petty theft and another two are convicted drug users; as far as we know they're not pushers. That's to say they haven't been convicted of dealing drugs."

DC Baxter then turned to speak directly to the inspectors.

"My advice is to carry out a simultaneous raid on the pub and Gilmour's house. That way you'll net the biggest number of druggies and their drugs."

King agreed: "I think you're right, detective. We could arrest Gilmour at his place, but I'd sooner catch him dealing his drugs in the pub. Also, if he's been 'cuckooed' we need to catch the criminals who have made him do their bidding and they are likely to be at his house." He consulted with his inspector colleague.

"What do you think, Jim, a joint operation on both places?"

Inspector Best concurred: "Yeah, I think that would deliver the best result."

King then asked: "So, DC Baxter, if we're going to bust both simultaneously, what's the best time, do you think?"

It was recognised that he was probably in the best position to answer that question, due to his week-long surveillance, and both inspectors looked in his direction; he took the hint.

"I'd say about fifteen minutes after Gilmour has entered the pub on a Wednesday or a Friday would maximise arrests. One other thing for our colleagues who don't routinely deal with drug busts: when we strike, strike quick. These villains are past masters at quickly disposing of evidence by whatever means they can if we give them time."

His boss, Best, supported his point: "Ken's right about speed of action, which will mean, probably, a dozen officers at each place when we go in."

A few minutes earlier, King had surreptitiously popped a sherbet lemon into his mouth and had listened intently while the other detectives were outlining the joint operation.

"I agree about speed being of the essence at both places and particularly the raid on the pub. However, I think that rather than predetermining the time to strike, it would be helpful if we had someone in the pub, with a direct link to waiting officers, who could advise when best to start the operation." He paused and after Jim Best had nodded his approval to this suggestion continued: "I have just the person in mind to do that job."

A further meeting was arranged to be attended by all the detectives when detailed planning would take place. This was provisionally arranged for the following Monday morning with the two-pronged drugs bust for the Wednesday, two days later. King agreed with Best that he would invite the acting superintendent to the meeting, as the raids would require his blessing and authorisation of the substantial resource. With that Baxter passed a copy of his report to King and he and Best left the room.

"Okay, Sam. Let's grab a coffee and ask Forensics to meet us here in fifteen minutes so we can get an update on Farthing's door handle."

*

An enthusiastic laboratory technician, who had recently joined the Forensic Screening Unit direct from university, announced her arrival with a knock on the door just as King and Dyson were finishing their coffee. She handed her two-page report to DC Dyson and verbally summarised its content. The confident lab technician briefly outlined what she had been asked to do and quickly concluded that there were only two sets of fingerprints on the door handle that was smeared in black paint. She discounted Dyson's, who had supplied a copy of hers to the lab, but the others did not show on the criminal database. The paint was urethane, which she stated is used on cars as it provides a good finish, doesn't run, dries off quickly and is durable.

King was impressed and when she had finished, he thanked her and wished her well in her chosen career as she left the room.

"Well, Sam, what do you make of that?"

"I think, sir, that Mr Farthing has a lot of explaining to do. We can assume the prints on the handle are his as he is a regular user, which begs the question why didn't he mention the paint on the handle when we interviewed him? Unless, of course, he put it there, presumably by accident. Also I assume as a garage owner he would have easy access to the type of paint that was used as graffiti on his own garage door!"

"I agree, Sam. Let's look at what else we've got on and then we'll pay him another visit and this time unannounced at his place of work."

TWENTY-ONE

Before Sergeant Harris and DC Hammond left the police station to interview the Build Great Homes directors and others who had access to the 4x4 at the company's Dartmouth site, Forensics had informed them of the initial findings following its inspection.

The verbal report was delivered actually right next to the black Ford Ranger in a huge garage with the detectives attentively listening. Its front number plate had been removed. The forensic officer pointed out a sizeable dent in the bodywork that would not have been evident if the plate had been in place. He then took a tape measure out of his pocket and measured from the centre of the indentation to the floor and applied the button on the tape case, which held it in the measured position. Carrying the tape, he then walked to the corner of the vast workshop and pulled back a tarpaulin to reveal the back of Morris's battered Land Rover. This exposed the tow ball that was fixed quite high up onto the chassis of the car and he offered the tape case to the ball and the tape end to the floor. The message was clear: in all probability the tow ball had caused the dent and the Ranger was the ramming vehicle. Any doubt was further reduced as it was revealed that the paint on the tow ball matched that of the 4x4.

The forensic officer also observed that the removed plate looked brand new, but manufacturer information had been erased. Armed with this initial report the detectives had what they wanted to pursue their investigation.

As promised they were back at the Dartmouth building site at precisely nine o'clock. They parked their unmarked car on the roughly tarmacked site road, which would get its smoother topcoat when building was complete.

As the driveway to the show home, where they planned to interview several people, was fully occupied by other vehicles, they parked on the road. As they walked up the path to the front door both detectives noticed that the parked cars respectively carried the number plates LEN 1, WEBB51 and LAW5ON. As they entered the immaculately presented house they were greeted by an avuncular figure. He was a dapper man, over 190 centimetres tall with a full head of hair and carried an air of confidence that didn't seem out of place. His tanned face evidenced a stay in hotter climes. He was dressed rather like you would imagine a country landowner to dress: tweed jacket, cavalry twill trousers and brown brogues. All that was missing was the gentleman farmer's flat cap. In his lapel he wore an enamel pin badge showing two lions rampant either side of a shield with the capital letters PARFC shown underneath.

In view of the nature of the investigation, Harris did not think handshakes were appropriate, but neither was no salutation.

"Good morning, gentlemen. I have already met Mr Webber. I am Sergeant Harris from Plymouth Police and this is Detective Constable Hammond."

"Good morning, detectives, my name is George Lawson and I am a director of Build Great Homes. I understand you wanted to interview all the people with access to the Ford Ranger? Could I introduce Len Simpson and, as you said, you've already met Simon."

"Could we speak privately as we have a development we need to report to you before we begin our interviews?"

"Certainly, please follow me." With that Lawson ushered them into a room off the hallway of the show home, which in future would be the dining room of the house, as evidenced by eight chairs around a central table. The directors sat at one side of the huge table and the detectives on the other. As he looked across at the three men, Hammond privately thought to himself, *See no evil, hear no evil, speak no evil*, but quickly admonished himself for being too judgemental. Harris brought him back to the real world.

"Gentlemen, thank you for meeting us here this morning. I have to tell you that before coming here we were informed by our forensic team that, from a preliminary examination of your company's Ford Ranger, it was indeed the vehicle used in the ramming incident."

All three looked visibly horrified, partly because of the seriousness of what had just been said and also because that meant all three were suspects. Webber's reaction was less exaggerated than the other two because he knew he would be exonerated after the detectives had contacted his alibi witnesses.

Simpson was the first to regain his composure.

"Come on, sergeant, why would any of us, or the others who use the 4x4, want to do harm to this journalist?"

"I didn't say he was a journalist," Harris responded and left the statement hanging in the air. Simpson quickly realised the implied accusation.

"It may not have been reported in the papers yet, sergeant, but it's all over social media that this chap was an investigative journalist. I simply can't see the connection you're trying to make between him and BGH."

"I'm not trying to make a connection, as you put it, sir. The forensic examination of your company vehicle has made the link."

Lawson wanted to calm matters.

"I think what Len's trying to say, Sergeant Harris, is we are all flabbergasted that our company vehicle could be implicated in such a heinous crime. I'm sure we all accept what your forensic people have discovered, but can't think why it was used or by whom; it simply beggars belief."

"Well, that's what we are trying to find out, Mr Lawson. Why it was used and by whom. We have spoken with Mr Webber already, so could I suggest we start by informally interviewing you, Mr Simpson, and then we'll speak to you, Mr Lawson, followed by Mr Carter. Perhaps Mr Webber could arrange for them to wait in your reception area?"

Lawson and Webber left the room and Simpson remained. He was older than his fellow directors, mid-sixties, with no hair, not overweight and with a penchant for wine. A thought flashed through his mind about not cooperating with the interview until the company solicitor was present, but reasoned that might imply guilt and he wanted to avoid any unnecessary attention on himself.

"So, Mr Simpson, where were you during the early evening three nights ago?"

"That was Monday night? I was out walking my two dogs. Let me see. I left my house in Frogmore with Layla and Oakleigh at about six thirty and drove to a lovely place called Slapton Sands; they love to run along the beach and dodge the waves as they come on shore. I suppose I was there for about an hour so got back around eight o'clock or maybe just before."

Hammond spoke: "I know Slapton Sands; that's not far from Dartmouth?"

"I know what you're getting at, detective, and no I didn't go to our site and pick up the Ranger. From Dartmouth to Bolberry Down, where this incident occurred I understand – according to social media – must be about twenty miles, which would have taken me, what, forty-five minutes. So that's over an hour and a half there and back and then home to Frogmore from Dartmouth another half an hour. I don't drive that fast, detective." His regained confidence was short-lived as Hammond persisted.

"Did you see anyone while you were walking your dogs, Mr Simpson?"

"No, it was a bit wintery that night so there wasn't anyone else around."

"What about your wife? Could she vouch for what time you got home?"

"No, she was out at a meeting of the local library in Kingsbridge and didn't get back until about nine thirty. She can certainly confirm I was home then and that our dogs were worn out. I'll leave you to work out timings, but I can assure you I was walking our dogs and not ramming a car over a cliff!" Confidence again restored, he was verging on becoming indignant.

Harris changed tack as she wanted to understand how the business was run as it might give a clue as to who was the most regular user of the Ranger.

"The three directors of Build Great Homes, do you all get involved in all aspects of the business or do each of you concentrate on certain aspects?"

"I don't quite see why you're asking me that, but George, that's Mr Lawson, acquires building plots for the company and seeks planning permission, while Simon, Mr Webber, deals with sales. For my part I am the one mainly responsible for getting the houses built. Obviously, there is some overlap in duties, but that's broadly how we operate."

"So, do I gather that you would be the biggest user of the Ranger utility vehicle as you are on site most?"

"I suppose I am, but I didn't use it last Monday evening."

"Remind me. Who actually uses it?"

"The three directors, Greg Carter, the site foreman, and occasionally sales staff to take prospective buyers to a new house on site. The roads can get very muddy so we don't want them walking."

Harris didn't think there was much more to be gained from speaking with him, so terminated the interview.

"Thank you, Mr Simpson. Could you ask Mr Lawson to come in, please?"

While they were waiting the sergeant spoke to Hammond. "Well, our Mr Simpson couldn't provide a satisfactory alibi; let's see if Lawson can."

"Come in, Mr Lawson, and have a seat." He had barely sat down before Harris continued: "Why were you using the Ranger on the day of the incident and yet you left your Jaguar parked outside the show home most of that day?" Harris had observed Inspector King use this shock questioning tactic, but Lawson was unfazed.

"I had some business to attend to in Plymouth and Exeter. I needed to see the company's solicitor about some land we are looking to buy. I also had to visit the Planning Department for South Hams District Council in Totnes. I deal a lot with the planners as, obviously, we don't buy land without planning permission."

"That didn't answer my question, Mr Lawson."

"Oh, why the Ranger and not my Jag? That was because I needed to drop off four bags of cement to another site in Salcombe where we're finishing off a garden wall. Better to use the Ranger as those bags are heavy."

"But why were you not back before this site was closed at the end of the working day?"

"After my meeting with Paul Armitage, a member of the planning committee, we went for a drink. So I got back here soon after six o'clock, locked up the Ranger and later stopped in the Ferry Inn in the middle of Salcombe, which is not far from where I live. Bob, the landlord, will confirm I arrived about half six and left just before eight o'clock."

Hammond made a note to check out his story. He was fairly confident it would be confirmed by the landlord as the director's confidence was bordering on smugness.

Harris thanked him for his time and she and Hammond then spoke to the sales people who occasionally used the Ford Ranger. Their movements on the night in question were recorded and would be checked. In her mind, Harris quickly dismissed them as not being involved in any criminality. After all they didn't have the key to the secure cupboard so could not have gained access after hours.

Lastly, they spoke once again with the site manager, Greg Carter. Hammond opened the questioning: "So, Mr Carter, it has been confirmed by our forensic people that the company's 4x4 was used in an attempted murder. The three directors and you are the only people with access to the cupboard containing the keys. Where were you last Monday evening when the offence was committed?"

"I can assure you I had nothing to do with this and the Ranger wasn't even on site when I left after work. So why is it necessary to tell you where I was?"

The detectives could spot an evasive answer a mile off and Hammond wasn't about to let it pass.

"Where were you, sir, between leaving work and, say, eight o'clock that evening?" The reluctant site manager didn't answer straightaway. He then sighed as he knew there were two ways of answering this question and he chose to be truthful.

"If you must know I was seeing one of the sales girls. I locked the show home having taken a key to a completed house on the estate, that is unoccupied, and we met there for about an hour or so before going home."

"And I assume you weren't discussing sales figures?" Hammond rather facetiously added.

"Look, I don't want my wife to find out. She thinks I was working late."

"Who were you with?"

Carter was hesitant, but quickly realised it was better to be honest.

"June, who you interviewed earlier. She'll confirm what I've told you. By the time I left the site, Mr Lawson's Jaguar had gone and I assumed the Ranger was in the garage. I didn't bother returning the key of the unoccupied house we'd used until I arrived for work the next day as I knew it wouldn't be missed."

Hammond had a few alibis to check out and assured Carter of discretion when speaking with his co-worker following their assignation.

It was now approaching lunchtime and Harris and Hammond returned to their car. It was left to the sergeant to summarise their morning's work.

"Well, Alex, the mystery deepens. Despite our early thoughts, Webber doesn't appear to be our man. Simpson's movements on the evening in question cannot be corroborated. Lawson's alibi will probably check out, but I'd like someone else to have seen him during the early evening as the landlord of the Ferry Inn could be 'tame' and, given a sum of money, he would have been only too eager to back up Lawson's story. There again, the director could be perfectly innocent of any involvement in the crime.

"Carter's account of his movements, assuming June of Sales confirms their hanky-panky, was interesting and does seem to confirm Lawson had left the site, by the time of the ramming, as his Jag was gone when the two lovers emerged from their clandestine tryst. Of course, we can't completely rule out Carter, as after kissing his mistress goodnight, there was nothing stopping him jumping in the 4x4 and carrying out the evil deed.

"There is one thing we haven't explored and one thing I don't quite understand." Hammond wanted to test his growing experience as a detective.

"Let me guess, sergeant. Although there were only four people that had access to the secure key cupboard, and thus access to the Ford Ranger, we can't rule out a duplicate key has been made or the missing spare Ranger key was given to a third party.

"The thing that doesn't make sense, sergeant – assuming the Ranger had been returned to the show home garage by Lawson last Monday night – is how it could then be used and damaged in a hit and run that same evening and yet appear perfectly undamaged the following morning when people turned up for work?"

"Got it in one, Alex. Let's go and talk to Inspector King."

TWENTY-TWO

It was the evening of the monthly Bolberry-on-Sea Parish Council meeting held in the Grade II listed village hall. All the councillors were present and over fifty members of the public, including Mr Armitage from the district council, as the village came under his jurisdiction for planning. Also in attendance was Farmer Garner who had a particular interest in one of the items on the agenda: the right decision from his particular perspective would mean the value of one of his fields would rise at least ten-fold.

Although the meeting was scheduled to start at 7.30pm, it was delayed by ten minutes while additional seating was set out at the back of the hall in the form of foldaway chairs from the storeroom. Usually meetings attract about ten members of the public, but this was not a routine meeting.

The chairman, Colonel Davenport, was delighted to see that all the parish council members were in attendance. He opened proceedings and welcomed the members of the public before informing them of their status. Using his most authoritative army tone

166

he told them that it was a closed meeting, meaning they could not participate unless invited to do so. He thought to himself that emotions would be running high and he was right.

He knew that the vast majority of the public attending were only interested in one particular item on the agenda and, generally, were not in favour of more houses being built in the village. He could have brought the item forward, but he was a stickler for correct procedure and unilaterally decided that the captive audience should listen to other village matters before their sole item of interest as they might learn something. The standard items, as determined by protocol, were duly set out in the agenda:

1. APOLOGIES FOR ABSENCE
2. APPROVAL OF MINUTES OF LAST MEETING
3. MATTERS ARISING
   3.1 Dog fouling
   3.2 Repairs to the village hall roof
4. CORRESPONDENCE
5. FINANCE
6. PLANNING APPLICATIONS
   6.1 Executive properties development
   at Ringmore Farm
7. ANY OTHER BUSINESS
8. DATE OF NEXT MEETING

While item 3.2 was being discussed, people present cast their eyes to the ceiling and saw various brown patches suggesting urgent repairs were required.

Having dealt with CORRESPONDENCE and FINANCE the chairman eventually moved on to the most contentious item on the agenda: PLANNING APPLICATIONS.

In between CORRESPONDENCE and FINANCE items, Jim Preston slid into the back of the village hall. Like the others he was only interested in one agenda item; unlike the others he wasn't prepared to sit through the 'twaddle' of the other items as he disparagingly called them.

"The next item is Planning Applications and the council has one application to consider. I would draw councillors' attention to the application that was attached to the agenda for the meeting of which I am sure you are all well aware. This relates to land to the west of the caravan park at Warren Point above the small secluded bay called Ayrmer Cove. Permission is being sought for the building of twenty-five two-storey detached houses on a ten-hectare field, which is currently part of Ringmore Farm. The houses would form Burgh Island View and would not impinge on the South West Coast Path. Access would be by a new single-track road, with passing places, from the existing farm entrance.

"For the benefit of the record for this meeting, I have been informed by the police that there have been two acts of vandalism in the village and one of arson directed at councillors that are apparently linked to the planning application. I have spoken to the councillors affected and they are happy for the vote to proceed at this meeting.

"The outline plans were displayed here in the

village hall for two weeks. Councillors then recently attended a site meeting and also a subsequent meeting in this hall, which was attended by the public, the landowner, two district councillors and representatives from the developers, namely Build Great Homes.

"Both of those meetings were to help the parish council to decide whether they are in favour of the application or against it. I do not propose to have further discussion about the proposal at this meeting. All councillors have had a copy of the application for over a month and plenty of opportunity to discuss it, both formally at the meetings and informally with parishioners and amongst themselves.

"It is now the parish council's duty to vote on the application and I propose to do this by a show of hands."

"Point of order, chairman." Farthing raised his hand to attract Davenport's attention. "This planning application is very contentious and has set councillor against councillor. In order to maintain a harmonious relationship within council, I propose the vote should be done by secret ballot."

Before the chairman could answer the Reverend Brown was quick to respond.

"If I may, chairman, I would like to comment on that proposal. I understand why Mike has made his suggestion as I too have heard completely opposing points of view, sometimes very forcibly expressed. However, all I would ask, chairman, is it best for the view of each councillor to be known on this matter or live with mistrust that can, sadly, be the outcome of undisclosed voting? It is up to councillors to accept whatever is the consensus decision and then move on."

"Thank you, reverend. First of all could I ask the parish clerk for his view on the proposal for a secret ballot as a constitutional procedural point?"

The clerk to the council, George Barton, evidently wasn't too impressed at being drawn into the debate on such an emotive subject, partly because he was busy scribbling away making a record of the meeting, but mainly because he didn't want to be embroiled in what was a highly contentious issue. However, it was right and proper for him to advise the council on a procedural point. He did his best to sidestep responsibility.

"Well, chairman, I do not think the Code of Conduct, under which all local councils operate, covers this specific point. I would say that a secret ballot is at the discretion of the chairman. All I would add is the public have elected the councillors and should be aware of the voting intention of each councillor."

The 'ball' was firmly back with Colonel Davenport. Not only did he not mind having to make the decision, due to his army training as an officer, he revelled in it.

"Of course, I am aware of the criminal act that three of our councillors have been subjected to, apparently in order to intimidate them into supporting this application. Equally, I think the reverend makes a good point. Secret voting can breed suspicion. Councillors need to vote with the greater parish community in mind rather than their own personal view, though I respect their right to follow their own conviction on the matter. In this particular application there are compelling reasons for granting it and compelling reasons for rejecting it.

"The voting will be by show of hands. No more delay. There are twelve councillors eligible to vote. All those in favour of granting outline planning permission for the application, please raise your hands now."

The arm of Dave Smith, the local publican, was the first to shoot up, quickly followed by Gavin Harkness, the local butcher, and Dawn Proud, Making Waves hairdresser.

Postmaster Ted Bayliss confidently thrust his arm in the air and as he did so glanced at his partner, Jane Ferris, expecting her to follow suit. When she didn't he continued to stare at her with a quizzical look and, eventually, in a disbelieving way.

The chairman waited patiently as he suspected others were still wrestling with their consciences. The young PE teacher, Scott Osbourne, was expected to vote in favour, but simply stared ahead without moving a muscle. The chairman didn't move either, but not because he was dithering.

There were several sharp intakes of breath from the public and a few councillors when Mike Farthing was the last to vote with an almost apologetic wave of his hand.

"Are you voting, councillor?" came the abrupt question from the chairman. Farthing's arm then extended to confirm his voting intentions. It at last became clear why he wanted a secret ballot: he desperately wanted to keep in favour with the woman he craved, but the proposed development offered an even bigger prize. If looks could kill the one he got from Abigail Croft would have struck him dead in an instant.

The clerk was diligently noting who had voted. After another agonising pause, the chairman considered all those who wanted to had cast their vote.

"Will those against the outline planning application please raise their arm now."

Almost as if they had rehearsed it, the arms of Doug Grant, Abigail Croft and Kirsten Massey were raised in unison. Rather hesitantly Jane Ferris sheepishly raised her hand. The eyebrows of her long-term partner, Ted Bayliss, were also raised as his eyes were now wide with shock. Another pause by the chairman unwittingly increased the tension in the room.

All those in the hall weren't sure if the young teacher, Scott Osbourne, was even aware of what was going on – perhaps planning tomorrow's lessons – as he continued to stare straight ahead. It was his way of dealing with his conscience. The Green Party got his vote at General Election time, but he wanted the local school to survive and more families moving into the area would secure it: environment versus education. He was concerned about yet another drain on the planet's resources, but wasn't a Luddite: carbon footprint versus progress. Environment won and he slowly raised his arm. His vote was duly recorded by the clerk.

"Abstentions?" Davenport asked and the Reverend Brown unsurprisingly for, as he was generally an even-handed man of the cloth, raised his arm. The chairman then raised his arm almost like a salute.

Realising he was the last to vote, Davenport turned to the clerk: "George, please would you inform the meeting of the votes cast."

"The votes in favour of the application total five; the votes against the application total five; abstentions total two votes. As chairman you have the casting vote, colonel." Colonel Davenport, once again due to his army training, was used to pressure and was not fazed by what he had to do, yet paused for a few seconds and stared, once again, at the ceiling, but this time oblivious to the brown stains. Despite his initial abstention he was generally a decisive man; he didn't usually do dithering.

"This puts me in an invidious position as I abstained because I was in two minds and still am. I can see the potential benefits to the wider community, but I can also see the potential damage to the environment as well as the development defacing our coastline." He paused not for effect rather because he was on the horns of a dilemma.

"After very careful thought, on balance I object to the proposed development. The planning application is refused. Any other business?"

This sudden, almost abrupt, and certainly dramatic announcement drew gasps from the public and an equal number of smiles and frowns from the councillors. Some members of the public clapped while others cried, "Shame!" Davenport called for order and, not really wanting any other business, confirmed the date of the next meeting and declared the meeting closed.

Much discussion followed among the public. The planning application had divided the community as well as the parish council. Such an emotive decision would obviously have repercussions.

Abigail Croft walked out of the village hall without acknowledging Mike Farthing.

Ted Bayliss was speaking to his partner, Jane Ferris, trying to understand why she had voted against the application, but, in fairness to him, without rancour.

Dave Smith was philosophical and likened it to 'Bloody Brexit' as that issue had divided a country. He left with Doug Grant who was pleased without gloating; they both retired to the Duke of Cornwall to have a 'life goes on' drink.

Farmer Joe Garner stormed out and every person there knew why. He wasn't the only disgruntled attendee; there were at least two others. Jim Preston left shaking his head in disbelief. District Councillor Paul Armitage was quietly seething and left the meeting muttering to himself: "What a bunch of bloody tossers. Couldn't organise a piss-up in a brewery!"

TWENTY-THREE

John 'Gilly' Gilmour was twenty-eight, unemployed and unemployable. He'd been a drug addict since he became a teenager and had spent half his adult life in institutions or prison. As ever he was in debt to his supplier for over £500 and because of his addiction, the debt would never be paid off as interest was added month-on-month. He had unwittingly created the perfect vicious circle. He had to have drugs, which cost him money, and couldn't afford to reduce his debt; he didn't do 'cold turkey'.

After paying for his meagre living, any cash he had left over from his Universal Credit payment, which wasn't much, was soon swallowed or sniffed up to feed his habit. He lived in fear and ecstasy: fear of what might happen to him if his supplier decided arbitrarily that enough was enough and the debt had to be repaid and ecstasy from his latest sniff. Then one day he was given a chance to discharge what he owed; however, it wasn't without risk.

When his supplier fuelled his habit at his end-of-terrace house in exchange for what little money he had, the pusher gave him a message from a nameless person who he knew existed, but had never met. He was being given the opportunity to wipe out what he owed if he was prepared to carry out a task set for him by the boss of his supplier: to Gilmour this was Hobson's choice.

A meeting was arranged for him and he knew this was one date he could not afford to miss. On a dark and cold evening he caught a bus into Plymouth and arrived in the city centre at 7.45. The short walk to the Crowne Plaza Hotel, close to Plymouth Hoe, took him less than ten minutes and he waited a discreet distance from the entrance foyer until it was two minutes before his eight o'clock appointment.

He had been instructed to report to Room 162 at the Crowne Plaza at precisely that time. He had been specifically told to knock on the door of the room and wait until he was invited in. He nonchalantly entered the hotel, and, bypassing reception, walked towards the bar area. Before reaching it, he diverted to the stairs that led to the rooms at first-floor level and above. It was now 7.59 and he followed the sign on the corridor wall that indicated the way to rooms 101 to 162. The passage with rooms off both sides was deserted and he soon found his meeting place, which was the last room at the end of the corridor. A 'DO NOT DISTURB' sign hung on the door handle.

He gave the door a gentle knock and waited. After a few seconds, a voice from inside the room commanded: "Enter." Tentatively he opened the door and was surprised that there were no lights on in the room, it being solely and dimly lit from the corridor lights.

"Shut the door," a voice ordered and Gilmour was then left in complete darkness. Suddenly a very bright light was being shone directly at his face.

"Sit down." From the peripheral glare of the spotlight, the addict could just make out a chair immediately in front of him. As he sat down the angle of the spotlight was altered to keep the main beam on his face. He could barely make out the silhouette of the person giving him orders from behind a desk. Not only could he not see him, he was being spoken to through some sort of voice synthesiser. Even a simpleton like Gilmour reasoned the distorted voice and dark room was to keep the person's identity a secret. There was no greeting offered.

"You owe me big money, Gilmour, and if I don't get the debt settled within a month I will not be a happy man. However, I'd like to give you the opportunity to cancel the debt, but in return, I need you to carry out a task. You have a choice: you can either leave this room now and I want my money within thirty days or you can carry out the task. However, you have to decide now before I tell you what the task is; once I have explained it you must carry it out. Do you understand?"

He hesitantly nodded his understanding. His second Hobson's choice in as many days. He thought that if he walked away now, in a month from now he might never walk again. Dithering, he knew the likely consequences of not accepting the task, but he didn't know what it was and, once told, he was compelled to carry it out. Damned if he didn't take the task on and, probably, damned if he did.

"Make your mind up, Gilmour!" the voice demanded from the darkness.

"Task!" was his terse reply.

"You are going to a rugby match. Under the chair you are sitting on is a holdall; don't touch it. I will tell you what it contains: a black hoodie, a pair of black trousers, a pencil torch, a pair of black gloves, a magazine, size eight black boots and £30 in cash. That money will pay for your admission to the ground and your drinks for the evening. You will also find a Plymouth Albion rugby shirt and cap."

Gilmour thought to himself that although he had no interest in the stupid game of rugby, he would happily watch it if it meant his debt was cancelled. What's more his drinks were being paid for. There had to be a catch.

"Tomorrow you will attend match day at Brickfields Recreation Ground at Damerel Close wearing the rugby shirt and cap. It's an evening match, kicking off at half past seven. When the game is over, you will go into the main bar and order a drink. You are only allowed a maximum of three pints throughout the evening and you must not, repeat not, get drunk. Also no fix that evening; do I make myself clear?" The last question was delivered in a raised voice. Gilmour squinted and nodded briskly.

"You can buy your drinks using the cash in the holdall. Then you can watch TV or read the magazine. Do not attract attention to yourself. Sit in a corner and don't engage in conversation. During the evening when you go to the toilet you will locate the changing rooms, which are on the right-hand side down a corridor off the bar area. When you return to the bar, go via the entrance hall to the club and look for the alarm system, which is in a small cream-coloured plastic box with a flip-down front. It's about halfway up the wall to the left of the main entrance. The alarm is activated by the last person to leave the club and is set using a four-digit code; that code is 1876. Memorise it, Gilmour, as you will use it later as the same code deactivates the alarm."

The person conducting the interview marvelled at the information people were prepared to part with for as little as fifty quid. There again, he probably could have saved himself the cash payment and guessed the number: Plymouth Albion Rugby Football Club was founded in 1876.

"Following that, return to the main bar and after half an hour go to the toilet again. This time when you come out, enter the home dressing room provided it is empty. If it isn't you will return to the main bar, order another drink and then repeat what you did previously half an hour later, until the changing rooms are no longer occupied. Don't leave an unfinished drink when you are not returning as that may arouse suspicion.

"Once inside the changing room, if no lights are on just use the pencil torch and you will see in one corner a pair of double doors with EQUIPMENT STORE shown on them. The room contains corner flags, a large sack of rugby balls and several tackle bags. You will hide in the equipment cupboard until the club closes, which I anticipate will be shortly after midnight. You will remove the rugby shirt and cap and put them in the holdall; put on the gloves I have provided and you will then be completely dressed in black.

"Having carefully checked the club is empty and closed, move to the alarm box and, still using the pencil torch, deactivate the alarm. This must be done at precisely twelve thirty; not a minute before and not a minute later."

By this point Gilmour was suffering from information overload, but knew he had to concentrate and remain attentive as any hint of disinterest would be quickly spotted in the glare of the spotlight still trained on his face.

"After deactivating the alarm, move away from the entrance doors as a 4x4 will enter. Two men, also dressed in black and wearing balaclavas, will locate the free-standing safe, which is in a room behind the bar and bolted to the floor. They will use wire ropes attached to the vehicle to wrench the safe from its floor fixing. When that is done, you will help them lift the safe into the car, if necessary with the aid of the on-board winch. You will then leave with the men and they will drop you close to your home. Any questions?"

That signalled the end of his instructions, but not the end of the meeting.

"Right, Gilmour, briefly outline your task to me."

"When I leave this room I take the holdall with me and tomorrow evening I dress in the black clothing and wear the Plymouth Albion rugby gear on top of the other clothes so I look like a team supporter. After the match I use the bar and watch TV or read the magazine. At some point in the evening I go to the toilet and check where the changing rooms are and the alarm system. I return to the bar and get another drink. When the changing rooms are no longer being used, I use the pencil torch and hide in the equipment store. After midnight, I carefully check that the club is empty and if it is I deactivate the alarm, using the code 1786 at precisely half past midnight."

"No, you cretin, it's 1876."

"Oh yes, 1876. Then I stand clear of the doors as the 4x4 enters. I then help the men get the safe into the back of the vehicle. I leave with them and they drop me close to my house."

By this time Gilmour was sweating profusely and shielding his eyes from the blinding light. Even with his limited brainpower, he mused it would have been easier, and more comfortable, to have simply blindfolded him.

"That is your task to discharge your debt to me. Do not talk to anyone about it and, Gilmour, there will be repercussions if you fail. Leave now."

TWENTY-FOUR

As advised by Inspector King, investigative journalist, Dan Morris, had changed his routine following the attempt on his life, but some routines were sacrosanct. Most Friday nights he met up with his friend from Ivybridge who caught the six o'clock bus into Plymouth and met Morris at his apartment overlooking Sutton Harbour. The ritual of discussing topical sporting issues and life events was a glorified pub crawl and one they really enjoyed. The friends visited a number of hostelries in the Barbican area of the city. They would pick three each from the range of pubs they regularly visited on any Friday night. They would choose in turn, always mindful of proximity to the one they were currently in. They would have a pint in each unless the conversation and the beer were particularly good.

They always started in the Kings Head near the old bus station and had their usual tipple (a pint of Timothy Taylor brewed in West Yorkshire). This particular night, after the Kings Head they moved on to the Minerva Inn, the oldest pub in Plymouth, which was established in the sixteenth century (HSB was the chosen bevvy at that pub). Next was the Three Crowns (Legacy), then the Queen's Arms (Salcombe Gold) and on to the Navy Inn (Atlantic). Next was the Dolphin Hotel (Betty Stogs), made famous by the artist Beryl Cook. The two friends loved that pub as, although it was rough and ready, it had something other pubs found difficult to generate: atmosphere. Whether it was because its ambience reflected a truly anachronistic ale house, or possibly because by then they'd had six pints each, was open to question.

After eating an excellent fish and chip supper from the Harbourside restaurant at a table street-side, their evening was nearly complete.

The two friends would then walk unsteadily through the Barbican heading for Royal Parade where Morris would see his friend safely on the bus back to Ivybridge. The problem with this was they had to pass Kitty O'Hanlon's and with twenty minutes to spare before the bus left, a nightcap was required. A whiskey each (Jamesons) followed by a quick dash for the Totnes bus via Ivybridge.

After seeing his friend safely aboard, he started to walk back, albeit not in a straight line, to his apartment. His path home took him back near Kitty's place. When they had left the bar in a hurry to catch the bus, a band had just started playing. Dan Morris liked them so much he decided to call in again. He had another whiskey and listened contentedly to the music.

It was gone midnight and light rain was falling when he finally left, taking a few back alley shortcuts as he knew his girlfriend would start to worry if he wasn't home soon. By now the harbour and residential area surrounding it was deserted.

He was less than a hundred metres from his front door, gingerly walking on the wet cobbled street, which led to his apartment block. As he staggered closer to home he thought he glimpsed some movement in a recessed shop doorway that was in the shadow cast by a feeble street light. He wasn't unduly perturbed as a number of rough sleepers inhabited the Barbican as there are usually rich pickings to be had from the revellers whose generosity for some increased exponentially as they consumed more alcohol.

The journalist veered towards the doorway and put his hand in his pocket to bring out some loose change. He was happy to give to someone less fortunate than himself. As he approached the doorway he slurred: "Here you are, mate, have a drink on me."

He could now see that the man in the doorway was dressed in dark clothing and had a scarf around his face that he initially thought was to keep out the chill of the night, before realising it was to hide his identity. The man lunged towards Morris who, in surprise and his alcoholic haze, was completely defenceless.

"This'll teach you to meddle in our affairs, you bastard!"

In his inebriated state, Morris saw the arm of the man thrust towards him and only at the very last moment did he fleetingly see the long thin, stiletto-like blade. He made a grab for his assailant in a rather pathetic attempt at defence. The loose change he was holding fell onto the cobbles and the coins rolled away in an ungrateful manner.

The attacker and his victim were now only a few metres from the edge of the harbour wall. Morris clutched his stomach and fell to his knees. The man ferociously kicked him in the head and he was sent sprawling backwards. The beer, the fatal stab wound and the vicious kick to his head made everything a blur. Was this really happening to him or was it a nightmare?

The last thing he ever remembered was being dragged by his ankles, his head bumping over the cobbles and being thrown into the water. The sudden chill of the black liquid in other circumstances may have shaken him to life; sadly, for Dan Morris it was to usher him to his death. He was never a good swimmer and fully dressed, suffering from an excess of alcohol, a stab wound and a severe blow to the head, the chances of surviving the now icy harbour water were zero.

*

Karen White, Morris's live-in girlfriend, looked at her watch; it was half past midnight and she started to worry. She tried his mobile several times and got no answer. A call to his friend who he had spent the evening with confirmed he had left Dan at precisely 10.30 as that was when his bus left. She decided she would wait for another ten minutes and if he hadn't come home or contacted her by then, she would call the police.

Following her call, four police cars were outside the apartment in a matter of minutes. While two officers asked her some questions, the other six, armed with torches, walked along the harbour side on the route she thought that Dan would have taken to get back to their apartment. Up ahead, they saw something glistening on the cobbled road and discovered it was a mobile phone. One officer noticed a slightly deeper puddle in one of the many valleys created by the cobblestones and, on closer inspection, she realised it was blood.

Within the next five minutes four more police cars arrived and an ambulance. Fifteen minutes later a police boat could be seen moving slowly and eerily around the boats moored in the harbour with a spotlight trained on the water.

A ghostly quiet settled over the scene punctuated only by the gentle, almost apologetic, chug of the police boat engine. Police all around the harbour wall shone their torches on the water.

Suddenly a shout of "Over here!" filled the night air and all the officers rushed to where the call had come from. The body was close to some steps down into the water, which made recovery easier. Within a matter of minutes the body of Dan Morris was lying back on the cobbles, about thirty metres from where he had been thrown. Two paramedics were kneeling over the lifeless body. They knew that CPR was futile. One looked up at the circle of gazing helpers and shook his head.

The police knew they had to do two things. The area would have to be secured and Karen White would have to be given the dreadful news. A female police constable self-nominated to carry out the latter task, while her colleagues taped off the whole length of one side of the harbour.

In tragic circumstances like this, the volunteer woman officer knew she might not have to say anything to the recently bereaved partner or, at most, say, "I'm so sorry…" It was never easy; nor would be the questions that would have to be asked in an attempt to apprehend the culprit. King and his team of detectives would have to investigate the murder as they were dealing with the previous attempt on Dan Morris's life. Their investigation of this murder would start at first light. The illegal drug trade had cost the life of yet another person; or had it?

TWENTY-FIVE

Modern policing is different from twenty years ago or, indeed, even ten years ago. The change was primarily due to the cutbacks in budgets, due to the financial crash of 2008 and the consequent reduction in the number of police officers and administrators. Therefore, crimes now had to be categorised and graded. Reported petty vandalism and even burglaries, where there was no threat to the occupants, would receive an incident number and precious little else. If these crimes and other minor misdemeanours are at one end of the criminal spectra, murder is at the other.

King and his small team of detectives arrived at Sutton Harbour early on the morning after the murder just as dawn was breaking. There was still considerable activity at the murder scene. The inspector's philosophy on criminal investigations was simple: the more serious the criminal act, the greater the demand for the involvement of all his team; that would ensure the best chance of identifying the culprit, leading to the prosecution of the person or people responsible.

The whole of one side of the harbour had been taped off and the actual spot where the journalist had been killed was now shrouded in a square blue tent. There were several forensic people clad from head to toe in their white plastic one-piece overalls, white slip-on bags over their feet and blue latex gloves. They were carrying out a painstaking search of the ground around the harbour; two were working exclusively in the tent.

Several police vehicles were parked just outside the exclusion zone. Morris's body had been removed and now lay motionless and lifeless on the pathologist's white marble table. Examining Morris's body would be John Gleeson's first task of the morning. The body of a murder victim would queue jump other bodies linked to other less serious circumstances. The clinical investigation of the body could give crucial evidence of the likely perpetrator; the postmortem would be carried out in a shorter timescale than normal and a detailed report would follow the thorough autopsy.

Even though the area immediately around the murder scene had been thoroughly searched, the detectives formed a line as they approached the protective tent hoping to discover something, anything, that might give a clue to the murderer. King pulled back the tent flap and nodded to the two forensic officers who were taking samples from the cobblestones where the body had lain. The blood had dried black. Every spot would have to be collected and analysed in the hope that some was not from Morris on the offchance that he had drawn blood from his assailant.

Sadly, the murder weapon had not been left at the scene, unless it had been discarded in the harbour. King reasoned that the murderer carrying out a premeditated attack, which this appeared to be, was very unlikely to dispose of his knife by simply throwing it into the water where it could be retrieved. Nevertheless, police drivers were busy searching the bed of the harbour just in case he had been careless.

One of the forensic officers showed King the best evidence they had, which was the imprint of the heel of a shoe, or more likely judging by the size, a boot. This partial footprint had been painstakingly photographed and if it didn't match Morris's footwear, it had to belong to the person who took his life.

The inspector knew that there were three sources of help in an investigation of this nature: firstly, the scene of the murder; secondly, any witnesses, who may not have actually witnessed the murder, but may have seen someone or something that night; finally, the most fertile source for clues as to the murderer's identity might not necessarily be found at the scene. Although he conceded that the partial footprint was a positive lead, he also suspected that because of Morris's profession as an investigative journalist, there were people who would be pleased to see him dead. It was the detectives' job, using all three sources, to find a link to the killer, if such a link existed.

There was very little else the detectives could glean from visiting the murder site itself, but the inspector wanted them to get a true sense of what had happened and, at the same time, show due reverence to the victim.

After a few more questions to the forensic team from King, all four detectives moved on to the unenviable task of speaking with Morris's girlfriend, Karen White. A police constable stood guard outside the door to the apartment she shared with Morris. This served a dual purpose: to keep away any unwanted attention from the press; and also to deter any attack from the murderer, or accomplices, determined to destroy any incriminating evidence that Morris may have gathered on them.

In answer to one ring of the doorbell, the door to the apartment was opened by Mrs White, Karen's mother, who was staying there in support of her distraught daughter. King and Harris sat on a sofa opposite the Whites; the inspector wanted to make the interview as painless as possible, but knew that was not going to be easy. DCs Dyson and Hammond stood discreetly at the back of the room.

"I want to begin by apologising for intruding on your grief. The tragedy last night must have been devastating for you, his family and everyone who knew him." He could have paused while Karen White sobbed into her handkerchief, but knew the whole interview punctuated by such pauses would only prolong what was clearly an ordeal for the distressed girlfriend.

"I just need to ask you a few questions. Can you think of anyone who could have done this and why?"

"He didn't tell me much as he thought it best I didn't know what he was doing. I do know he was getting close to some sort of outcome. I could always tell as he got edgy and went quiet. Also his timekeeping would become erratic. We would arrange to meet and then he'd be late or cry off. I assume it was because he needed to be totally flexible to respond to what he was investigating. That's what happened the night he was nearly forced over a cliff on Bolberry Down; he was late for our dinner date.

"I do know he had continued to pursue the so-called County Lines gangs, so I assume it's those bastards that did this." This was the first sign of anger that Karen White had shown as she was gradually coming to terms with the full impact of her loss.

"I wish I could be more helpful, but I now know why he didn't tell me anything: he was protecting me."

"There is something you could do to help us catch the person who did this."

"Anything, anything at all, Inspector King."

He nodded in the direction of an antique bureau in the corner of the room.

"Just as a matter of interest, is that where Mr Morris did most of his work?"

"Oh, that old thing. Yes, he spent many hours sat at it with the drop-leaf front down and his laptop plugged into the socket next to it. A sort of ancient and modern approach. It belonged to his parents and he was very fond of it. He did most of his work on his laptop, but did use the bureau for filing papers and other things he used. He liked all the little compartments."

"I'd like my detective team to have full access to

any files that Mr Morris had and particularly his home PC, if he used one, his laptop and mobile phone. In fact any records he kept relating to the investigation he was involved in. Also, I assume he had a contact at a national newspaper that he had organised to publish his exposé? We'd like his or her name please. Did he keep a diary or just use the calendar on his mobile?"

"He mainly worked on his laptop, which is encrypted and I think you already have his mobile as that was found at the…" She stopped herself from saying 'murder scene', suppressed a sob and quickly regained her composure.

"Actually, he did keep a pocket diary as he preferred paper to electronic means for recording his appointments; wait there, inspector."

She then rapidly got to her feet and left the room. In her absence nobody spoke. When she returned, gone was any hint of self-pity. Her red, tearful eyes were suddenly replaced by a fierce determination to do all she could to help catch the killer. She came back carrying a laptop, diary and a small cardboard box, which later was revealed to contain some paper files.

"There you are, inspector. It's all yours and if I can think of anything else I'll get in touch straightaway."

"Could one of my detectives look in the bureau drawers, please?"

She nodded her approval and Dyson began opening the drawers. Strangely, there was very little in any of them or, when she dropped down the leaf, in the cubbyholes.

"Thank you, Ms White, please do let me know if you think of anything else."

He handed her a card with his mobile and landline numbers on it. He didn't usually hand out his card to anyone as he would rather them ring the main police station in Plymouth; he made an exception in her case.

"Rest assured that I and my team will do everything we can to catch the person who killed Mr Morris." With that, Hammond, who had relieved her of what she was carrying, walked out of the room and all the detectives left.

Once outside the apartment, as there was no one else around, King addressed his team in the lobby area of the block. He first primed Hammond to get the laptop to the Cyber Crime Unit to decrypt it; Dyson to see what information was on his mobile phone; and Harris to do a day-by-day analysis of his diary and other files. For his part, he would set up door-to-door enquiries and would liaise with the pathologist.

"I know we weren't supposed to be working on the weekend, but we need to crack on with our investigation. However, before you can make a start on the jobs I've allocated, some will require others to do their bit before we can get rolling. In the meantime it would be useful if we did a bit of old-fashioned knocking on doors while things are still fresh in the mind of residents. I don't propose visiting all the apartments in the high-rise blocks, so, Sam, if you could arrange some incident boards and put one in the main entrances to the blocks and also at the entrance to the harbour. Usual thing 'Incident here around midnight on Friday...' and so on. I'll arrange for an Incident Support Unit to be parked near the scene later this morning, so if a resident saw anything last night they can simply approach the van. While you're arranging the signs, we can do some cold-calling on other low-level properties in the vicinity, after doing whatever you need to prepare your tasks. As it's the weekend there's a good chance we will find people at home.

"For the rest of today and tomorrow we can all continue with our work on this case. If you come across what you think is a good lead, please let me know. Also I'd like a team meeting first thing on Monday morning, which the acting 'super' will be invited to attend, as we need to review where we are with the various investigations, including this one.

"You've all seen how devastated Karen White is and how she is determined to help us catch the scumbag that killed her man; we must not fail her."

TWENTY-SIX

On the day of the match, 'Gilly' Gilmour arrived at the Brickfields stadium, home of Plymouth Albion Rugby Football Club in time for the Saturday evening kick off. He carried out his task to the letter as he knew any mistakes would be punished. He watched the game, wearing home team kit, with mock interest and made his way to the bar after the final whistle. If asked the score he wouldn't have known.

All was going to plan, although when he first went to the changing rooms, someone was sweeping out mud, various discarded medical tape and plenty of chewed orange peel, so he returned to the bar. He ordered his third pint and read the *Rugby World* magazine once more until he had nearly memorised the articles, without understanding anything about the sport.

Again he finished his drink and took the empty glass to the bar signalling his imminent departure. He relieved himself in the toilet as he knew he was in for a long night. He was also relieved at last to find the changing room empty and in darkness. He closed the changing room door behind him, took out his pencil torch and located the walk-in cupboard marked 'EQUIPMENT STORE'. It contained a set of ten so-called corner poles, six rugby tackle bags and a large string sack full of rugby balls. He hid behind the bags, lying on one in relative comfort, with the others stacked upright around him. Then he waited. He was content to lie there until all others had left; his contentment didn't last long.

After half an hour he could hear the door to the changing room being opened and some loud voices, which sounded like several men entering. He moved from his prone position to a crouch in case he needed to make a run for it. Although he still felt relatively safely hidden, he was still on edge.

He was suddenly shaken out of his safety zone when someone opened the door to the store and reached in for the bag containing the rugby balls; he took one out. The man was so close that Gilmour could smell the beer on his breath. As the store door was closed he was once again plunged into darkness and it sounded to him like the men were having an impromptu training session. There were many expletives uttered and much raucous laughing and cheering. Fortunately, it ended after ten minutes and the equipment store door was once more opened and the rugby ball unceremoniously thrown inside clattering against the wall and hitting Gilmour on the head. They eventually left, slamming the changing room door behind them, leaving the drug addict to his nocturnal vigil.

Time passed slowly and he began to feel drowsy.

He was drifting in and out of sleep because of the beer, the lateness of the hour and he was once again lying fairly comfortably on a foam-filled tackle bag. He reached into his pocket and took out a stick of Wrigley's Spearmint chewing gum in the hope that mouth activity would be an antidote to drowsiness and stimulate his saliva glands as his mouth was starting to get dry. In the darkness of the cupboard he carelessly discarded the white sleeve and silver wrapping paper of the gum; after ten minutes' chewing, the gum had lost its flavour. All it did was intensify his thirst and he had to get rid of it. In the darkness, he reached out and stuck it on the inside of the door frame. Time passed slowly and the effect of the beer began to tell as he drifted into a longer doze.

He awoke with a start and, realising he had fallen asleep, was terrified that he had slept through his deadline. Fortunately, his body clock must have reminded him of his task as a quick look at his watch using the torch showed it was now twenty past midnight.

He crept from his hideaway, switched on his torch and gingerly opened the changing room door to be met with total silence and total darkness. There was no sound coming from the main bar area or any other area of the club. The capacity of the stadium was officially recorded as accommodating over 8,000 people; the attendance now was one.

Using his torch, he made his way to the front entrance and stood close to the alarm as he counted down to the crucial time. Looking at his watch he punched in the four-digit code at precisely half past midnight.

Meanwhile, two men clad in black, wearing balaclavas, drove up to the main entrance to the rugby ground. The padlocked entrance gates provided little resistance as one of the men, using bolt cutters, made short work of the chain. With the gates wide open the other man drove the black Nissan Navara into the ground. The gateman then shut the gates so no passers-by would be alerted to their presence.

Gilmour stood back from the doors to the club. At 12.32 just using sidelights, the 4x4 almost silently reversed close to the double doors and stopped. A quick check from his mate that he was lined up correctly and, with a swift rev of the engine, the driver engaged reverse gear and accelerated backwards at speed. The doors were no match for such power and sprung open, showering the bar area with glass. The car continued reversing more slowly now across the room, crunching over the broken glass and stopping just before the bar. None of the men spoke. The gateman jumped over the bar and into the back room taking one end of a rope wire with him; the other was firmly attached to the Nissan.

After a minute he came out and put a thumb up to the driver who eased forward as the wire became taut. He then applied more power and after a matter of seconds the rope man held up his hand to indicate he wanted the driver to stop. The bolts that had anchored the safe to the floor had succumbed. The two men then beckoned Gilmour over to them and the three men dragged the safe unceremoniously through the bar access gap and across the floor to the 4x4. With some difficulty they managed to get it into the back of the vehicle without having to use the on-board winch.

The gateman clapped his gloved hands together to get Gilmour's attention. He then pointed at the till and did a yanking movement, indicating he wanted him to bring it from behind the bar and not to worry about unplugging it! The driver and the gateman were busy making the safe secure with a twine rope to any anchor points they could find in their car and then covering it with a rug. They were also checking nothing incriminating had been left behind.

In the few minutes it took the men to carry out these tasks, Gilmour did as he was instructed. But his mouth was by now parched, partly because he hadn't had a drink for several hours and also because of nervous tension. He saw his chance due to the slight delay. Grabbing a glass from the shelf under the bar, he helped himself to less than half a pint of lager, which he immediately downed in one or two gulps to quench his raging thirst.

He then yanked the till from its central position along the back of the bar and it came away surprisingly easily. The driver pointed at the till and then the front footwell, indicating where he should put it. The hand signals continued: thumbs up then one thumb jerked backwards in a 'get in the back' gesture to Gilmour. There was just enough room for him to squeeze in.

The driver then carefully retraced the way he had come in, passing the wrecked entrance doors on the way out. The gateman had gone back to the entrance gates in readiness for their departure. The car exited the ground and stopped. The gates were pulled closed and the useless chain was wrapped around where they came together to appear security had not been breached.

Gilmour was dropped off close to his home without a word being spoken. When in his end terrace, he sat in his armchair comforted by the fact he had successfully completed his task and thankful he was now debt free. He reached for some white powder and rewarded himself.

The drug baron estimated the contents of the safe to be in excess of £15,000 as he knew the week's takings were not banked until Monday and several functions had been held at the club that week, including the recent home match. He knew his man, armed with a disc cutter, would make short work of the safe.

At that moment, he was blissfully unaware of the consequences of Gilmour's illicit late-night drink in the rugby club or the discarded gum. If he had been, the debt would not have been cancelled and the punishment would have been swift and severe.

TWENTY-SEVEN

It was now Sunday morning and there was still activity at the scene of the murder in Sutton Harbour. DC Hammond was back at Charles Cross Police Station in Plymouth busily scrolling through the documents on Morris's laptop after it had been decrypted by the Cyber Crime Unit. DC Dyson was with him getting data from his mobile.

King and Harris were helping with house-to-house enquiries and keeping in touch with the mobile on-site Incident Support Unit.

The blue tent used by Forensics was gone as was the police tape from around part of the harbour. The incident boards, arranged by DC Dyson, remained and King had decreed they would be in place until the following Sunday in case some visitors were creatures of habit and only visited on a Friday night; did he but know it, but that decision was to yield an unexpected bonus of information the following week.

Taking a well-earned break from doorstepping local residents, King, Harris and uniformed officers were drinking coffee and munching a late breakfast of burgers or bacon rolls from the famous Cap'n Jasper's quayside fast food kiosk. No new information was forthcoming, which didn't surprise the inspector as most residents would have been tucked up in bed after midnight at the time of the murder.

Harris's mobile rang, which usually signalled trouble. She listened and thanked the caller.

"Sir, a report of a break-in at Plymouth Albion Rugby Club has just been received. Apparently it happened last night and has only just been phoned in when a keyholder arrived to restock the bar."

"Okay. We'll leave off from here as we're nearly finished anyway and take a look at the rugby club. That won't take all morning so hopefully we'll be back here before lunchtime to wrap things up. I'll let the uniformed sergeant and the support unit know what we're doing. When we get back, lunch will be on me from that little café around the corner. Let's go, sergeant."

Sergeant Harris was absolutely delighted to be back working with Richard King and he was pleased they were a pair again.

"Sir, sir!" a voice called out from the Incident Support Unit trying to attract his attention before he left on yet another mission.

"In response to one of the incident boards, a dog walker, who was out quite late on Friday night, reported that he had seen a person acting suspiciously around midnight. The person, he thinks it was a man, was lurking in the shadows cast by the harbourside lights. He didn't get a good look at him, but remembered what he was wearing. He had on a long greatcoat like they used to wear in the war – a sort of military overcoat. He also had a scarf around his face." The inspector thanked the officer on duty in the support unit and told her they were briefly leaving to investigate a break-in and would be back around lunchtime should any other information be received.

As Harris drove to Plymouth Albion Rugby Club on the west side of the city, King asked how she was getting on with DC Hammond. She told her boss that he was one for the future. He was developing into a very good detective. She stopped herself saying that he was a good partner to work with, which she believed, as she was ever hopeful of resuming her partnership with King on a more permanent basis. Harris then chastised herself for her rather selfish approach and to ease her conscience added: "I think in a couple of years he will be sergeant material."

She drove into the Brickfields ground, home of the city's foremost rugby side, and parked next to two liveried police cars. Police tape was strung across the battered entrance doors to the club.

A police constable introduced the detectives to the keyholder who was the only person to have entered the clubhouse that morning. When the police arrived he was politely asked to wait outside as the building was now a crime scene. He told the detectives that he saw the damage when he arrived shortly after half past eight that morning. He confirmed the safe had been taken as well as the till. From a cursory look around all the rooms, he said those two items appeared to be the only things missing.

King walked into the bar area closely followed by Harris. He crunched over broken glass and stopped in the middle of the big room. He took out a sherbet lemon and put it into his mouth. His sergeant smiled to herself and thought it was just like old times. She knew not to interrupt.

"So, it looks like a classic ram-raid," and having noticed the alarm keypad when he entered continued, "but why didn't the alarm sound?" He sucked on.

"In a moment, sergeant," King was planning, "I'd like you to interview the keyholder and find out how many other people hold keys. But first let's have a look around the place and then when we come back here we'll give the bar room closer attention. I'm thinking of possibilities as to why the alarm apparently wasn't set by the last person to leave the club last night – either in error or by design – so find out who locked up. If it was the man waiting outside, check how certain he was that he actually set the alarm.

"If it was him who locked up and he's certain he activated the alarm, it was either deactivated by him, another keyholder later that evening or someone who was aware of the combination to switch it off. He could have hidden somewhere in the club and killed it before his friends arrived. Ask the chap if the last person out checks the building to make sure it's empty. The question is where would the accomplice hide?"

Both detectives headed for the toilets thinking a cubicle would make a good hiding place if the villain crouched on the pan so no feet could be seen by anyone casually checking under the raised partition. They could see no evidence of footprints on the closed lids of the pans in either the gents' or ladies' toilets. That didn't completely rule them out, but made them unlikely hiding places.

The away team dressing room was spartan. Just a square room with long wooden slat benches around the four walls and access to a bank of showers. The home dressing room was similar only bigger and in the middle it had a medical couch for treating players. Harris walked across the room to open double doors marked 'EQUIPMENT STORE'. She peered in and reported it contained corner flags, rugby balls and several rectangular plastic-covered large foam wedges with straps. King enlightened his sergeant and called them tackle bags. She was about to close the double doors when the inspector asked her to wait.

"Seems like an ideal hiding place to me. You can't be seen and the changing rooms aren't used after everyone has showered; they're all in the bar area or the toilet. Let's have a closer look."

Both detectives then began emptying the store, more in hope than expectation of finding any incriminating evidence.

"Well, well. I wonder if our little sneak thief left this behind?" King said as he gingerly picked up the small rectangular white sleeve of a chewing gum wrapper. Harris took out an evidence bag from her coat pocket and the inspector, holding it between thumb and forefinger, gently dropped it into the bag; the silver foil quickly followed.

"I reckon he or she must have been hiding for some time and after a while chewing flavourless gum can get tiresome." With that he began to inspect the cupboard, which was only lit by the light from the changing room. His sergeant passed him her mobile with the 'torch' symbol on. Using the bright light from the phone he inspected the tackle bags, but ignored the rugby balls as he thought they were unlikely to be used for gum disposal. Although he had a torch, he ran his index finger around the inside of the door frame. "Bingo!" he cried as his fingers hit the small ball of gum.

"Maybe nothing to do with the break-in, but worth fingerprinting the wrapper and DNAing the gum."

They then returned to the bar area and once more crunched over thousands of glass shards as they made their way to where the safe had once stood. The back counter showed a slightly darker patch where the till had sat. King stopped to survey the scene, glancing this way and that.

"How would you describe the actual bar and surrounding surfaces, sergeant?"

Harris thought it a strange question, but replied: "Clean and tidy; no clutter."

Then he held out his hand towards Harris: "Exactly. Evidence bag, please, Lucy."

He then walked behind the bar and turned the bag inside out and placed his hand in it. He then picked up a solitary half pint glass from the counter, withdrew his hand so the glass was now inside the bag, but was untouched by King's fingers.

"I think the counter had been cleared of glasses and wiped down before the bar people left the club. It's just a hunch, but I think thieving is thirsty work." His sergeant understood what he was intimating; this is what she so missed about not working with him. On her training course to become a detective they didn't really cover how to follow a hunch; it was strange, she thought, and rather compelling just how often her boss's hunches paid off.

"If you have a word with the keyholder as we'll need to track down all the other people who have access to the club, particularly those that know the alarm code. Also ask him to estimate how much money was taken. Forensics will be here soon and you can give them the gum and the glass then. Then you can tell the keyholder he can clear up and got a glazier in when they've left. I'll speak with the uniformed guys just to see if they can add anything. When you're ready we'll get back to the harbour and I'll treat you to that lunch I promised to buy you."

Rather churlishly and yet with desire in her heart, Harris whispered to herself: "I wish it was dinner!"

TWENTY-EIGHT

Early on Monday morning at Charles Cross Police Station in Plymouth, Inspector King had convened a meeting to be attended by his team of detectives and his boss, Acting Superintendent Roberts. About half an hour before the meeting was due to start, DC Dyson passed her inspector an envelope she had received that morning from clerk George Barton containing a copy of the minutes of the Bolberry-on-Sea Parish Council meeting when the councillors had voted on the controversial planning application. This was a draft as he still needed to check his work before publication.

"It makes interesting reading, sir, and voting intentions were not all they seemed."

King was intrigued and as he was fully prepared for his own meeting and with his interest sufficiently piqued, he took out the minutes from the envelope and quickly found the agenda item of interest.

His own meeting time arrived. At a convenient point, Inspector Jim Best would be asked to join it when the drug raids on Gilmour's house and the Plymouth Pilgrim pub would be planned in outline and approval sought from Roberts. Best is an inspector in what used to be called the Drug Squad; in modern police parlance he was now part of SOCA (Serious Organised Crime Agency).

"Good morning, everyone. A lot of criminal activity has taken place over the last week in our area and I have called this meeting so we are all on the same page and to decide what action to take and by whom. Obviously, catching the murderer of the investigative journalist Dan Morris must be our top priority, but not to the exclusion of the other crimes."

He then directly addressed his boss. There was residual deep-seated animosity between the senior officers, but King was too professional to let it show… for now.

"The meeting will bring you up to speed, sir, as to what the team has been investigating recently. DC Dyson and I have worked together, while Sergeant Harris and DC Hammond have investigated other crimes. However, in view of the seriousness of the murder, I have involved the whole team on that case; that will give us the best chance of identifying the culprit. We think the murder could be drugs related and our investigations to date suggest that some of the other crimes also involve drug dealing. To that end, as you know, sir, I have been working closely with Inspector Best and he will join us later in the meeting when we decide, with your approval, what action to take against a suspected main dealer."

Roberts nodded his understanding and King thought, for a change, he looked engaged and attentive. Due deference by his subordinate officers usually won his approval.

"Let's start with the body on the beach at Hope Cove, which was discovered over a week ago. DC Hammond was tasked with discovering the identity of the dead man who is thought to be a foreign national or an illegal immigrant." King nodded in his direction.

"Thank you, sir. The starting point was the expensive Rolex watch the corpse was wearing when he was found. I contacted the manufacturer at its headquarters in Geneva, Switzerland. The company keeps meticulous purchase and service records and when I gave them the serial number they identified the original owner as a Mr Marco Coppola who lives in Naples. He bought the watch there in June last year and paid over 30,000 euros for it. The 'MC' etched on the jade ring he was wearing seemed to confirm the owner.

"I informed the Italian police about the body on the beach and the expensive Rolex. They have made enquiries and have been to the address I gave them from the factory records. A few days later, an officer rang me from Naples as he thought I might be interested that Mr Coppola owned a boat called *Marcass*. The police are searching the marinas in Naples for the boat.

"As it is a murder case, and in all likelihood the vessel has been used to transport drugs, when they find it they will compare DNA samples of Mr Coppola from our database with what they discover on the boat. I've asked them when they locate it, if the yacht's Global Positioning System could be investigated by the manufacturer. I understand that from the computer memory in the device, they can plot the co-ordinates of any voyage recently taken and historically track the boat's passage. I gave them the date when the body was found on the beach and asked for the yacht's movements a week either side of that date.

"The cigar box, found on the beach at the same time as the body, was manufactured by Toscano in Tuscany and each cigar that would fit into the two-finger case retails at about fifty euros. So, it would appear that Mr Coppola has some very expensive tastes; with the help of our Italian colleagues I hope to establish how he funds such a lifestyle."

King congratulated the detective: "Good work, Alex. Any questions for DC Hammond?"

Roberts asked: "Will the Italian police charge us for their investigations?"

"I asked them that, sir, and they said as Mr Coppola is an Italian citizen and as it appears he has been involved in a crime, they will bear the cost."

King wanted to move on: "Last Tuesday evening three crimes were reported in Bolberry-on-Sea: one of arson and two of criminal damage. I'll now ask DC Dyson to update us on the progress of our investigations."

"The inspector and I interviewed the three victims and we are not satisfied with the testimony given by a Mr Farthing, who owns the local garage and petrol station. Although he appears to be a victim, some evidence we found at his home would suggest he could be responsible for defacing his own property.

We have reason to believe he has not told us the truth so we intend to pay an unannounced visit to him when that can be arranged."

"Thank you, detective. Sergeant Harris will update us on the attempted murder inquiry."

"DC Hammond had identified the vehicle used in the ramming of Mr Morris's car on Bolberry Down from a fragment of the front number plate and Forensics has confirmed it was the vehicle we suspected. However, it isn't as straightforward as it appears as many people have access to it. We have interviewed the directors of the company that own the vehicle, Build Great Homes, and also the people who work for the company. We are still trying to determine who was driving on the night Mr Morris was forced off the road."

"Thanks, sergeant." King continued: "That leads us on to the murder of Mr Morris, which I will cover. I have spoken with the pathologist, John Gleeson, and he has confirmed the weapon used was a narrow-bladed implement, rather like a stiletto, not a flat-bladed knife; he could deduce this from the puncture wound. It had penetrated the victim's ribcage just below his right nipple up to a depth of approximately fifteen centimetres or six inches, possibly suggesting the attacker was left-handed. As a result the victim had lost a significant amount of blood. However, the cause of death is the same as Mr Coppola's, namely drowning due to the amount of water in his lungs. In his report the pathologist concluded that if Mr Morris hadn't drowned in all probability he would have bled to death.

"Our inquiry will be guided by the information held on Mr Morris's mobile and, particularly, his laptop, which has been decrypted by the Cyber Crime Team. As he was investigating the drugs trade in the South West, particularly towns and cities in Devon, it would appear likely that his murder is in some way connected with the County Lines gangs.

"John Gleeson did recover one interesting piece of evidence when he carried out the autopsy. Morris's right hand was clenched tight and due to rigor mortis it had to be cut open. When he did, he found the fist had been clutching a button, presumably ripped from his assailant's coat. On closer inspection it had on it some lettering: HONI SOIT QUI MAL Y PENSE. In his report, for the sake of completeness, the pathologist had added the translation from the French: 'Evil be to him that evil thinks.' DC Dyson and I know where the button came from! It's from a military uniform of the Royal Engineers regiment. How do we know? Because we found the self-same type of button on the drive of one of the houses that had been vandalised at Bolberry-on-Sea. What I can't understand is the link between that and the murder in Sutton Harbour.

"Later this morning we hope to have information from Morris's laptop and mobile phone, together with whatever was in the folders we have taken from his flat. I'm hopeful this will provide some leads that will help catch the person responsible for his death."

Turning once more to his boss, King summed up: "So you see, sir, we have made significant progress on some of our investigations and will make the murder inquiry top priority when we access Morris's laptop and mobile.

"Sergeant Harris will cover the latest crime we are involved in, sir, which happened late on Saturday evening."

"We attended Plymouth Albion Rugby Club because it had been ram-raided on Saturday evening, stealing the safe and the till. They were taken and the amount of money stolen is estimated as over £15,000. The theft wasn't discovered until the morning. We do have two leads, namely a glass we think one of the robbers may have used and also some discarded chewing gum; they are currently with Forensics for analysis."

Roberts had listened intently and, apart from his questionable manner and interpersonal skills, he was a shrewd detective.

"I am slightly concerned, inspector, that your team may be overstretched. You rightly identified the murder investigation as your top priority with the attempted murder not far behind. In other words, because they appear to be linked, solving one might help solve the other. I am tempted to get another team of detectives to deal with the robbery at the rugby club, but will leave it with you for the time being as you have already begun the investigation.

"I think the shenanigans at Bolberry-on-Sea will have to wait, as will the death of Mr Coppola. Depending on how the murder inquiry proceeds, and what resources it requires, I will have to keep a watching brief on your ability to cope with your team's overall workload."

King wasn't entirely sure how his boss could differentiate between two dead bodies whilst accepting Coppola's death was unexplained. He didn't want to admit it, but took Roberts' point, particularly as he wanted the meeting to move on to the drug raids.

"I understand the point you are making, sir. If you're happy to move on I'd now like to ask DC Dyson to contact Inspector Best so he can join the meeting?" Roberts nodded his approval and a few minutes later, the inspector entered the room and took a seat.

King continued: "Two weeks ago, DC Dyson personally identified a house that appeared to be a drugs den. We informed Inspector Best who authorised a week-long surveillance and I'll now invite him to update the meeting on what his detective observed."

Inspector Best outlined what the surveillance had found and it appeared that the main resident, John Gilmour, was allowing his house to be used to trade drugs. He said he was either complicit or he had been cuckooed, knowingly allowing other drug dealers to use his place, possibly under threat of violence if he refused. Either way the inspector had little sympathy for him and referred to him as a crook with some venom. (Privately, talking to Richard King, he would have called him scum.) He went on to report Gilmour selling drugs himself some lunchtimes at his local pub.

Best then mentioned the earlier discussion he'd had with Inspector King when a simultaneous raid on the house and the pub had been suggested with which he agreed. He was now seeking Roberts' approval for the outline plan for the raids.

"What resources will you need to carry out these simultaneous raids?" Roberts reasonably asked; Best had a ready answer.

"I think it would be advisable to have a dozen officers at each of the properties to deal with arrests as we're not sure how many users we'll catch. The officers may only be required for less than an hour at the pub and the house and then half a dozen of my team can search Gilmour's house after any occupants have been arrested. So, as this is our area of expertise, I would suggest my detectives, initially supported by uniformed officers, concentrate on the house, and Inspector King's detectives, also supported by uniformed officers, deal with the pub. When we last met he suggested that one of his detectives could go undercover before the raid at the Plymouth Pilgrim pub, suitably wired, and could tell the other officers the best time to strike; that would also trigger the raid on the house.

"If you are in agreement with that strategy, sir, I will work on more detailed planning of the raids with Inspector King."

"Before I answer that, inspector, what risk assessment have you done? What I'm alluding to is the possible need for armed officers on either or both raids."

"I have assessed the need with my superintendent, sir, and as we anticipate the criminals will be low level as many will just be users, we do not expect them to be armed. We think uniformed officers wearing protective clothing will be sufficient."

Inspector Best's decision not to use armed officers was soundly based and probably saved the life of one of the criminals.

"You require a significant number of officers to carry out this operation and I would be loathe to authorise such a number if they were required for a longer period. However, as you have explained, most would only be involved for a relatively short period, so I am prepared to authorise the operation." With that Roberts quickly rose to his feet and left the room.

Having gained approval for their outline plan, Best and King would do the detailed planning together before meeting with the teams to co-ordinate the raids. Neither expected to catch 'the big fish', but over-confident dealers can make mistakes.

As the meeting ended and the detectives went back to the tasks in hand, King asked DC Dyson to stay behind.

"As you know, Sam, we've a lot going on at present and despite what the acting superintendent said about priorities, I think it's time to wrap up one case. You and I, together with two uniformed PCs, will pay that unannounced visit to Farthing at his garage this afternoon. If you could arrange for a squad car to be ready and briefed by two o'clock we'll see what he's got to say for himself."

TWENTY-NINE

The two-car convoy arrived at Farthing's garage close to the centre of Bolberry-on-Sea unannounced as planned. The forecourt was big and would have parked nearly twenty cars, but only four spaces were occupied, one by a motorbike on a stand with a black helmet on the seat. The workshop was substantial, its footprint being about the size of a tennis court. Its outward appearance was tired and, naturally enough, maintenance of vehicles appeared to be the priority for Farthing and his work partner, Preston, rather than maintenance of the building. It had a brick façade and, on one part of the front, a wide aperture for vehicle access, with an up-and-over roller shutter door. On the other side a standard door – its frame blackened by greasy hands – marked 'ENTRANCE'. The paint on the door and adjacent window was badly flaking and the roof was rusty corrugated iron. King muttered to DC Dyson that this was one building that definitely was not listed. Both detectives were thinking the same thing: this was a business that was run down and struggling to make a profit.

Their arrival didn't spark any activity and the two uniformed officers stood by their liveried car while the detectives walked towards the entrance. They noticed that the workshop wasn't equipped with a hydraulic lift, so underside mechanical work was done below floor level from a pit about a metre wide, two metres deep and six metres long. In order to inspect the underside of a car, a mechanic had to slide into the pit and work with his arms above his head. The detectives had seen Preston before and now they knew one possible reason why he always looked miserable: his working conditions.

They walked into a small office area, which housed a counter and, behind it, a desk and chair. The desk was littered with car manuals, small engine parts and dirty coffee cups. The counter had on it a page-a-day diary, well thumbed by oily hands, a calculator, a card machine for taking payment and a receipt book.

Judging by the entries in the diary, which the detectives rightly assumed was for logging jobs, business was not brisk. The receipt book was open with its carbon paper slightly protruding and the paper receipt on top was blank in readiness for the next payment. King gently lifted the blank form on top, the carbon sheet and the blank copy underneath to look at copies of the last receipts. Still holding the book open he gestured with his head for Dyson to look at the copy of the last receipt. They both looked at each other and nodded in unison at the significance of what they had just read.

While they waited for someone to appear, the

detectives continued to look around them, taking in every aspect of the room. Dyson then noticed a button on the wall by the counter, like a front door bell, and a sign that read: 'PLEASE RING FOR ATTENTION'; she duly pressed it.

Farthing appeared through a door at the back of the office rubbing his hands on a rag. When he saw them he recoiled slightly before regaining his composure.

"Can I help you, detectives?"

"Good afternoon, Mr Farthing. We've come to return your door handle and we need to ask you a few further questions." King was polite, but firm. "If you could accompany us to your house, we would like to have a look inside your garage. You can travel in the police car that's outside."

Farthing went ashen white and didn't say another word: he wasn't hostile, rather adopted an air of resignation. He grabbed his jacket off the back of the chair in the office, went back out of the door into the workshop and called out to Jim Preston he would be back soon.

Dyson thought to herself that was likely to be a longer time than soon.

King and Dyson led the way, closely followed by the marked police car, and after a few minutes pulled into Farthing's drive. All five people were now standing on the gravel as the inspector began to ask a series of uncomfortable questions.

"When we visited your property last Wednesday, after you reported that graffiti had been daubed on your garage door, you left to return to your work.

My detective constable tried the door handle of the side entrance to your garage as we wanted to look inside; she got black paint on her hand. Our forensic people have since confirmed two things: firstly that the paint on the door handle is the same paint that was used for the graffiti. Secondly, there were only two sets of fingerprints on the door handle, one was Detective Constable Dyson's and, we assume, the other set is yours; that can easily be checked. So we have asked ourselves how did the black paint get on the handle?"

"I remember now, when I saw the graffiti on the garage door I was going to clean it off and wanted a rag from inside the garage. When I realised I had paint on my hand I assumed the culprit must have tried the door to see if they could take something or do more damage to my property."

"Why didn't you mention this before as we told you we were taking the door handle for possible fingerprinting? If Forensics confirm your prints are the only others on the handle that doesn't explain your story of the culprit leaving paint on it. One possible explanation, Mr Farthing, is that you painted the graffiti on your own garage door."

"Why the hell would I deface my own garage door?"

"That's what we were hoping you'd tell us. Leave that there for the moment as I'd like to mention two other things. I've read the minutes of the last parish council meeting when a vote was taken on the planning application at Ayrmer Cove. From what I gather from the minutes of the previous meeting, held in the village hall, to discuss the application, and also from interviewing you over the graffiti attack, you were against the development and yet you voted in favour of it at the meeting. What changed your mind or was your apparent objection just a sham?" King wasn't in the mood to wait for an answer and he might not have got one anyway.

"But let me tell you of the most damning evidence against you, Mr Farthing. When we were waiting in the office at your garage earlier there was a receipt book on the counter and I decided to see how business was doing."

"You had no right to look at that without a warrant!" the garage owner feebly protested.

"I'm investigating crimes that were reported by you and two other people. As a police officer responding to those crimes, I'll look at whatever I choose." King hadn't raised his voice, but was sufficiently forceful that Farthing made no further objections.

"When I turned to the copy of the last receipt I noticed you had written across it, as it was signed by you, that the payment had been received."

"So what, nothing unusual about that."

"I agree, but what was important was the way it was written. Constable, your notebook and pen, please." Dyson passed it to her inspector. King scribbled on the first page and showed it to Farthing: 'PAYMeNT ReCeIVeD'.

"When you're writing in capital letters do you always show the 'e' in lower case? I'm sure it's not lost on you that the graffiti message and the bleach damage to Ms Croft's lawn also had the 'e' shown in lower case." No response from Farthing.

"Right. I'd now like to look inside your garage. We won't refit the door handle to the side door as it is evidence. You can put the Yale key in the lock, turn it and then hold it in that position, so it won't come out, and pull the door open using the key."

Farthing reluctantly took a bunch of keys from his trouser pocket and did as he was instructed. He stepped back to allow Dyson to enter the garage. She pulled on blue latex gloves before stepping inside. The uniformed officers moved closer to Farthing as they sensed the investigation was about to reach its climax. The four men waited in silence and after a few minutes the detective came out clutching a Tesco shopping bag with red drawstring handles. She opened it and held it in front of King without comment. He peered inside and saw a small paintbrush and a litre tin of black paint.

"I'll tell you where we are, Mr Farthing. We have enough evidence to charge you with criminal damage for defacing Ms Croft's lawn. If we can find evidence that you also set fire to Mr Grant's summerhouse, you'll be charged with that too. I believe you also defaced your own garage door; what I don't understand is why?"

He paused as Farthing was considering his options: denial or confession? King wanted to speed up the process and save himself and the judicial system time and money, but first he had to formally caution him, which he duly did and followed it with a 'get out of jail card' or in his case 'keep out of jail card'!

"If you make a full confession and plead guilty to the charge of criminal damage and arson I think any judge would look on that favourably and not impose an immediate custodial sentence. I can't charge you with defacing your own garage door, but could add a charge of wasting police time. If you plead not guilty, and are convicted, you may well go to prison." This unethical approach by the inspector was high risk because if Farthing chose the latter option, any defence lawyer would interpret it as coercion. Farthing paused and thought this might be a confession too far, but then remembered what King had said: "*I think any judge would look on that favourably and not impose an immediate custodial sentence.*"

"Okay, you're right I did torch Doug's summerhouse, which I now regret doing, and am deeply remorseful about putting bleach on Abby's lawn: you see I'm in love with her."

King mockingly added: "You have a funny way of showing it. So why do it then?"

"I was desperate for the planning application to be approved, but wanted Abby to think I agreed with her as she was strongly against it. If a secret ballot had been held, as I requested, when we voted on it, she wouldn't have known I was in favour of the development. By setting fire to Doug's summerhouse and defacing Abby's lawn I hoped they would change their view and other ditherers may too. I daubed my garage door to deflect attention away from myself. I also thought I could say that I was frightened to vote in favour because of the graffiti."

"Things are becoming clearer, but why were you so desperate for the planning application to be approved?"

"If it had been approved, the developers had promised to build a new community centre for the village. They couldn't build it on the site of the existing village hall as that's a listed building so couldn't just be knocked down. They offered me and my partner, Jim Preston, half a million pounds for our garage site, subject to getting planning permission. Approval would almost be guaranteed as our site is not listed, has a sizeable footprint, ample parking and is close to the centre of the village. Build Great Homes would redevelop the site and build a new centre as promised. Jim and I would never get a better offer. That's why I was keen to get the parish council to approve the outline plan for the executive homes."

With the full confession duly recorded, Farthing was handcuffed and led away to the waiting police car that would take him to Charles Cross Police Station in Plymouth where he would be interviewed under caution and formally charged.

*

King and Dyson returned to the station mid-afternoon and Sergeant Harris informed her inspector that Acting Superintendent Roberts wanted to see him immediately on his return. He knocked on the door and walked into his boss's office. Roberts did not offer a greeting.

"I know where you've been, inspector. Which bit of what I said to you – '*I think the shenanigans at Bolberry-on-Sea will have to wait*' – didn't you understand?"

"New evidence literally presented itself straight after our meeting, sir. I was confident we could charge Farthing with arson and criminal damage, which meant we could solve three crimes in the space of two hours. I thought that was a statistic you would appreciate, sir, and at the same time it would also reduce our increasing workload that you referred to in the meeting. I'm pleased to report that Farthing has made a full confession."

"If you countermand one of my orders it reflects badly on my authority."

King wanted to say, "What authority?", but settled for something less confrontational.

"I was responding to new evidence, sir, which shows we are a dynamic force not constrained by protocol. Given the new evidence, if I'd asked, I knew you would have approved my action."

"We'll leave the matter there, inspector." King took that as dismissal and left the room. Harris saw him come out and quietly enquired if everything was alright.

"The acting superintendent was very pleased we managed to solve three crimes in one afternoon, thus improving our arrest stats and saving the taxpayer a considerable sum of money as the accused has pleaded guilty."

His sergeant looked at him sideways. King, tongue firmly in cheek, gave an 'I wish!' smile and went to get a coffee.

THIRTY

The solicitor acting for Build Great Homes Limited had lodged the planning application with the district council relating to the executive homes development close to Bolberry-on-Sea, approximately four months previously. As the application was for twenty-five new dwellinghouses and fell in the 'major development' council category, it required statutory advertisement close to the site. The process to consider the planning application should have taken eight weeks, but that time had been doubled as an Environmental Impact Assessment was required.

South Hams District Council allows applications to be made online – via a planning portal – or by post accompanied by the appropriate fee. The fee for this particular application is £11,682 reflecting the scale of the proposed development and the additional work that would mean for the council planners; like for most organisations, time is money.

Minor planning applications are usually decided by a senior planning officer. No aspect of the application to build twenty-five executive homes was minor. In this case a planning officer was appointed to make a recommendation to the planning committee made up of elected councillors. The officer appointed to consider the Bolberry-on-Sea application was Mr Paul Armitage.

Karen White, the girlfriend of the murdered investigative journalist, worked in the planning department of the district council. It was less than a week since Dan Morris had been stabbed and thrown into Sutton Harbour. The council would have let her take longer bereavement leave in order to grieve, but she had decided that keeping busy was the best antidote to a broken heart.

She was one of Armitage's administrative assistants. Their role was to prepare all the documentation to support the planning officer's recommendation as well as the presentation brief for him to deliver to the planning committee, which comprised twelve councillors.

On the day of the planning meeting, the public gallery in the council chamber was full. Abigail Croft and Doug Grant were in the front row and Jim Preston in the back row; his disgraced partner, Mike Farthing, was not in the chamber. There were six applications to consider and the Bolberry-on-Sea application, to construct Burgh Island View, was last on the agenda. After the first five had been considered and voted on, most with the councillors unanimously in favour or unanimously against, the chairman decided the committee should take a short break. She may have judiciously sensed that the final application would not have unanimity; so it proved. Very few members of the public left during this break indicating their particular application of interest.

When invited to present his views to the councillors, Paul Armitage's presentation included a slide show comprising photographs of the proposed site, an artist's impression of the finished development and various plans of the houses themselves. Crucially he also included several slides of maps showing the juxtaposition of the development with the nearby caravan park. It was indeed a slick slideshow due in no small part to the presentation prepared by Karen White. She didn't have any input to the supporting script. Armitage began his well-rehearsed pitch.

"Madam chair, I would ask the committee to consider the application relating to twenty-five new houses at Bolberry-on-Sea, copies of which were recently passed to councillors in advance of this meeting. There is no doubt that councillors need to consider this application very carefully due to the proposed location of the development. Whenever the council has to consider applications with a coastal location, a very important part of the process is the Environmental Impact Assessment. Councillors will have received the EIA document and noted the main concern highlighted in the report was one of waste disposal."

He then showed a slide with a plan view of the location of the proposed development and the nearby local sewage treatment plant.

"Councillors will see the proximity of the sewage plant and will have noted the comment in the EIA that the plant has plenty of capacity to deal with an additional twenty-five homes.

"Let me move on to the view of the local parish council. I attended a site meeting with the councillors, an extraordinary meeting and the parish council meeting when the council voted on the application. There is no doubt the application aroused intense debate and the councillors were divided. Some were in favour as it would regenerate the village, particularly the local school that is under threat of closure, while others were concerned about lack of affordability for local people and that the new houses would become second homes. Also, doubts were raised over the impact on the environment and the view from the nearby coast path; as councillors know you cannot protect a view."

The smirk that accompanied this trite remark did not find favour with the objectors in the public gallery.

"The parish council narrowly voted against the application. Those in favour of approving the development put forward some very sound reasons.

"If I could digress for a moment, madam chair, I'd like to make another related observation. As the district councillors know, the village hall in Bolberry-on-Sea is owned by the South Hams District Council and is in need of extensive updating. New toilets are required and a disabled access in order to comply with Health and Safety regulations. The roof requires repair or replacement. The district council manager of building works has estimated the cost of all the remedial work to be in excess of £250,000. As owners and landlords that cost will fall to the district council and, ultimately, the taxpayer. The company that is applying to build the twenty-five new homes has agreed to build a brand new community centre for the village if the application is approved. This would save the district council a substantial amount of money. Also the new homes would annually raise approximately £80,000 in Council Tax."

It is not the job of planners to be impartial. Their job is to advise councillors on planning applications to enable them to make a considered judgement. There was little doubt what Armitage was implicitly recommending. Then he delivered the killer blow to any councillors with lingering doubts.

"I would remind councillors of the government's assessment of the number of new homes required annually across Devon to meet the housing shortage in the country. Our county's quota is 5,255 houses per year! We are encouraged as planners and councillors to approve developments unless there is a significant reason why we shouldn't."

He hadn't quite finished. Just in case some councillors were still dithering, he concluded his advice, which left them in no doubt as to his preference.

"It is true that there are some objections to this planning application based largely on not wanting to spoil the coast. I have advised you on the facts: no threat to the environment; the local primary school should have enough new children to remain viable; the district council will not have to pay the substantial cost of repairing the village hall. Finally, and perhaps the most compelling reason to approve the application, is the government assessment of housing needs in our county.

"Madam chair, my advice to this planning committee is that the application should be approved without modification." With that he sat down.

Karen White could not believe what she had just heard. When she prepared the slideshow she had envisaged an entirely different narrative to that delivered by Paul Armitage. Her slides would have supported a more even-handed account.

The chairwoman took back control of the meeting.

"Well, councillors, you have heard what Mr Armitage has advised. I would remind you that it is only his opinion as a planning officer. The decision on whether to approve the application before us is entirely for this planning committee. I would further remind you the parish council rejected the application albeit by the narrowest of margins. So, before we vote on the application I'd like to hear the views of councillors."

One councillor wanted to raise the point made by the planning officer, which in his words had been 'glossed over'. It was not the affordability point, but the new houses would become second homes thus reducing the benefit from the influx of permanent residents. He mentioned the St Ives neighbourhood plan. He informed the meeting that following a referendum of residents in the Cornish coastal town of St Ives, as a reaction to an ever-increasing number of new homes in their area being bought as second homes, a purchasing clause was inserted in the properties' transfer-of-sale documents restricting new houses to full-time residents only. This was also being adopted by other scenic coastal towns, including Mevagissey. He thought such a restriction could apply in this application.

Madam chair turned to Mr Armitage to seek his view as the adviser to the planning councillors.

"The point raised is true. Furthermore, the ban on outsiders buying second homes was challenged in the High Court and was judged to be lawful. However, two things I would say, madam chair: firstly, I am not aware that second home ownership is a problem in Bolberry-on-Sea. Most importantly, if that restriction was introduced in this application it would have to be applied to future planning applications, otherwise it would be discriminatory. Also, it could be counterproductive as no builder would want to build homes in the village with that restriction on sales. Reduced buyers would result in lower house prices, which some might welcome, but developers simply wouldn't build houses if the profit margin was too low; the village would stagnate."

Further points were raised and when they had been exhausted a vote was held by a show of hands: the application was approved by eight votes to four.

Madam chair announced: "The application is approved. I declare the meeting closed."

Abigail Croft and Doug Grant sat motionless staring into space shaking their heads.

Jim Preston left the public gallery with a big smile on his face.

THIRTY-ONE

U nusually King was sat at his desk in the Charles Cross Police Station in Plymouth when his landline phone rang. He answered it with just his surname. "Good morning, inspector."

He recognised her voice. "Good morning, Ms White. How can I help?"

"You said to let you know if I thought of anything else. It may be nothing, but I told you that Dan hated anything that was unlawful and was determined to expose it. It's well documented he had an acute dislike of the drug dealers. They caused untold misery not for the users for whom he had little sympathy, but he was more concerned about the victims of crimes who had their homes violated simply to get money to buy drugs to fuel the never-ending cycle of dependency. He reserved his absolute disgust for the drug barons. Those sinister people who arranged for the import and distribution and then sat back while the money rolled in."

King wondered where this diatribe was leading, but he wasn't about to interrupt as he knew there was a purpose in her call.

"Equally, he hated corruption, particularly when this involved already well-off people who, by deception or coercion or both, sought to gain additional wealth, usually at the expense of others. He believed there was no such thing as a victimless crime.

"Well, you may not know that I work for the South Hams District Council and in the evenings at home we talk…" she then corrected herself "… used to talk about our day, although Dan never opened up much because of the nature of his investigations. When they resulted in a prosecution he would be more forthcoming. Sorry, inspector, I'm rambling. Anyway, I remember something I told Dan. About a month ago we were chatting over dinner at home and I happened to mention something odd I'd seen that day. On a workday one lunchtime I went into town – that's Totnes – to have a chat and a bite to eat with a friend from work in the Royal Seven Stars Hotel.

"We sat in one corner of the bar and in the distance I noticed one of our planning officers, who I work quite closely with, come into the hotel bar. He didn't see us sat in the corner. He was with a tall man who was very well dressed, probably in his mid-fifties, carrying a small laptop case. I didn't think anything of it as our planners are always meeting with people to discuss planning applications. These informal meetings are usually held in Follaton House, which is the headquarters of the district council. There is nothing inappropriate about having meetings elsewhere, but what I thought was strange was the planner walked in without a briefcase or any files. I thought that if they were discussing a planning application he would at least be carrying a file with a copy of it inside. As it turned out they hadn't come in to eat and after a drink they left."

"So what was strange about that?" King asked.

"I said to Dan that when they left, the planner carried the case out not the tall man who had brought it in with him."

"What did Dan say?"

"He said perhaps he might have been returning his laptop to the planner if he'd left it in his car on a site visit. He did casually ask his name and then took an interest in the planning applications I was preparing; I had a few on the go at the time. He was always interested in what I was doing at work, but on this occasion I thought he asked me more about them than usual. I didn't think any more of it until now. It was the fact that Dan was so inquisitive when I had only casually mentioned what I had done at work that day. It may be nothing, inspector, but I thought I'd mention it."

"Thank you, Ms White. What's the name of the planner you saw in the Seven Stars that lunchtime?"

"He is Mr Armitage, Mr Paul Armitage."

"Would you recognise the other man?"

"I think I probably would as he was quite suave and, as I said, well over six feet tall. My friend, who was with me, I'm sure would recognise him as she said she fancied him."

"You said you had lunch with a friend from work; who is your friend?"

"Her name's Debbie Norris. She is in the planning department like me and is the same grade as Paul Armitage. She told me the following day that she had said to him about the laptop case and was it being returned by the man as he'd left it behind on a site visit? Mr Armitage told her that's exactly what happened. He'd grabbed his briefcase, but forgot his laptop. She said he seemed a bit prickly that she'd mentioned it."

King thanked her and rang off. He put the phone down and wandered into the meeting room where his detective team had been working on the tasks he had set them. He was sucking a sherbet lemon. Before he could tell them of the phone call from Karen White, they wanted to update him. His sergeant spoke.

"We've been working on Morris's laptop, mobile phone, diary and paper files as you asked, sir. We'd like to tell you what we've discovered."

"I'm all ears."

"I'll ask Alex to start as he was looking at Mr Morris's laptop."

"Thank you, sergeant. The laptop was decrypted by the Cyber Crime Unit. Morris evidently was very careful about what he committed to computer files. I think this was to protect his sources if the laptop fell into the wrong hands. There is very little information held on his hard drive. I suspect when he was working on an investigation on his laptop he downloaded the information onto a memory stick and then deleted the document. The more detailed documents were probably held on a stick or sticks and hidden in a secret place, possibly where he lived. I say that as his home is where he would have done much of this computer work. With Ms White's permission it might be worthwhile to get our forensic people to give the apartment a thorough search for the sticks, computer discs or anything else that might help the investigation.

"However, until we can do that, what I have found are two main folders and in each there are numbered lists of people or activities and that's all. That's why I suspect he has memory sticks hidden somewhere. Interestingly the two folders are titled; one is called 'DRUGS' and the other is called 'PLANNING'. The first is obvious, but I'm not sure what the second is referring to. Possibly his plans to expose the drug dealers or how he thought his investigation should proceed."

King's update was timely.

"I took a phone call earlier from Ms White, Alex. Now I think I have a good idea what the PLANNING folder refers to. Following the casual conversation with her – she works for the planning department – Morris had stumbled onto possible corruption in South Hams District Council. It sounds like a planner was receiving a back-hander, presumably for information or possibly for influencing the outcome of planning applications."

"That's interesting, sir. Obviously Morris was a very principled man. Even though he was pursuing one set of villains, he wasn't about to let another villain get away with fraud and deception.

"The numbered headings in the folder, which I assume relate to files on the memory stick or sticks, do give us some information. In the 'DRUGS' folder they read as follows:

1. Bristol connection
2. County Lines
3. Possible cuckoo nest
4. The Baron
5. The Church connection
6. The Drugs Store

"The 'PLANNING' folder is similarly numbered:

1. Build Great Homes Ltd
2. Bolberry-on-Sea application
3. Parish councillors
4. District councillors
5. District planners (particularly PA)
6. Seven Stars CCTV
7. Protect KW

"So, sir, I think these folders are just a reference point for him. The hard evidence is secreted elsewhere."

King sensed a breakthrough.

"In the meantime let me speak with Karen White to explain your hypothesis and get her permission to strip out her apartment. When I explain our theory I'm sure she will be only too happy to move out for a day or two. Let's move on to his mobile; Sam."

"Much like Alex reported, sir. Mr Morris was a very cagey man. The contact list on his phone consists of initial letters followed by the number. KW is obvious, while others are simply two-letter titles, which I assume are Christian and surnames; so, KW, PA, JG, DN and RB. I've got a printout from his network supplier and am working through the numbers and trying to identify the contacts. Some would appear to be so-called 'burner' phones. As you know, sir, drug users have immediate contact with dealers and these mobiles are very difficult to identify. They are pre-paid and are disposable; once used they are binned. I think Morris had some connection to drug informers, but relied on them contacting him, possibly to make a rendezvous. He could have been paying them for information. Obviously, because they used 'burners' we can't trace them.

"However, I have identified three people he rang at the council offices. He had many conversations with his girlfriend and phoned a few other numbers there. Anyway, I'll keep trying to identify who he was talking to apart from his girlfriend."

"Ring the numbers, Sam, and ask to whom you're speaking; apologise for a wrong number and hang up. Alex will be very interested in that 'conversation'. I don't want any of them spooked just yet."

"Thanks, Sam. That leaves you, Lucy."

"I agree with Alex and Sam, sir. He was a very careful man. He had to be as he was involved with some potentially dangerous people. His diary was similarly vague. In his paper files, I found a copy of the minutes of the Bolberry-on-Sea extraordinary parish council meeting to discuss the planning application lodged by Build Great Homes, the Bolberry-on-Sea church magazine – that covers several parishes –

a list of the South Hams District councillors from the council's website, and a copy of the annual financial statements from Companies House, Cardiff of Build Great Homes Limited. This also named all the directors of that company. BGH turned over £50 million in the last financial year and declared a profit of close to £7 million. That's all the paper files revealed."

King took out a sherbet lemon and the other detectives waited patiently.

"Good work, you three. The laptop folders give us a clue as to what Dan Morris was busy investigating. I agree with Alex that finding the memory stick or sticks will give us a lot more to go on. Get Forensics onto the search of the apartment, please, Alex, asap.

"Sam, ring that number and let Alex know if the PA in the folder is indeed Paul Armitage. See what you can dig up on him as I think he is the guy referred to in PLANNING number 5 item. Discreetly, Sam, as, remember, I don't want him spooked. If he's been up to no good, I'd like to catch him in the act if we can.

"Lucy, see if you can throw some light on the connection with the church. Apparently Morris seemed to think there was a link to drugs. I'll contact Karen White and tell her what we'd like to do. I'll give her time to pack a few things and then Forensics can go in. I'll also update Acting Superintendent Roberts on what we've discussed.

"From the information we have gleaned today, I think we need to review the *modus operandi* in Mr Morris's killing. It could be drugs related, but increasingly I'm thinking someone connected to property development wanted to shut him up!"

THIRTY-TWO

Plymouth is not particularly a multicultural society when compared to some other places in the UK; you will not see many black faces in the city. So when you combine a black face with a huge, muscular body it can turn heads. But when DC Hammond entered the Plymouth Pilgrim pub there weren't any heads to turn as it was just before noon and the place was empty. For those colleagues in the force that knew him, that day his oversized upper body seemed even bigger than usual.

The décor of the pub could be described as shabby or retro chic; the detective's view was not so fashionable, preferring an alternative description: grubby chic.

The landlord did not show any surprise as the giant approached his bar. He was not particularly welcoming and gave the impression that he treated all of his customers in the same monosyllabic manner. His attire fitted his demeanour: he was wearing slippers, jogging bottoms and a crumpled T-shirt that looked slept in. The stain on its front could have been gravy, brown sauce, discoloured ketchup or even blood. It was likely that poor personal hygiene would complete the slovenly landlord's ensemble. Fortunately for Hammond, the counter kept them far enough apart not to test his hypothesis.

He ordered a pint of lager and then sat down in a far corner of the pub and took out a copy of the *Western Morning News* from the pocket of his coat, which he kept on despite the warm, ambient temperature in the bar. His seat was chosen with care as from where he sat he could easily observe customers entering and leaving the pub, while his own position was unobtrusive.

As earlier surveillance had intimated, Gilmour came in almost exactly at noon, wearing his backpack back to front just as DC Baxter reported. He ordered a pint of beer and gave the landlord a £20 note, without getting any change; the money never made it as far as the till. He then disappeared from view into the poolroom at the rear of the bar.

The undercover cop thought that a 'blind eye' payment of over £200 a month was much more profitable than selling pints; he pretended to read on.

If there had been other customers in the pub they would have seen and heard him mumbling the occasional word apparently in response to something he had just read in his newspaper. However, he was not mumbling to himself, but into a small microphone discreetly protruding from the buttonhole in the lapel of his coat. This linked to Sergeant Harris's mobile phone and through the marvels of modern technology, namely voice recognition software, any spoken words appeared as text on her phone.

She then verbally relayed the message to the other officers in the van she was in and by walkie-talkie to colleagues in vans nearby.

"Testing," was the first message she'd received and quickly sent a reply to the sender's mobile; it duly pinged acknowledging receipt of the test message. Shortly afterwards testing gave way to reality reporting.

"Gilmour in," text message came up on her screen.

Other customers then started to enter the pub in quick succession. Men, always on their own, and their arrival was duly reported. The running commentary continued: "Number One in," followed by "Number Two in," and then, after a short pause, "Number Three in." All collected their pint from the dishevelled landlord before disappearing in the same manner as Gilmour and, like him, not to play pool.

As arranged by Inspector King, the plan was to arrest him in the pub along with any other associates while simultaneously raiding his house. The pub raid would trigger the house raid. He was about to give the prearranged signal when the bar door was flung open and four burly men strode purposefully into the pub in quick succession one after another, not stopping to collect a drink. His report to the listening sergeant raised the tension among the waiting officers, both in the van with Harris and in vans handily parked nearby.

"Number Four in, Number Five in, Number Six in, Number Seven in!" he hurriedly announced followed moments later by: "Number Three out, Number One out, Number Two out." (He had memorised their garb and order of departure, not that it mattered unduly, but did give the covert officers an ID before arresting them as they had viewed the arrivals from discreet CCTV.)

It seemed the early gathering had been ended unceremoniously as the early entrants trooped out one by one as soon as the other men arrived.

Harris, having seen the different directions the three men went through the two-way glass windows in the van, alerted the officers waiting nearby and all three men were duly arrested a street or two away and would later be charged with possession. Fortunately for the police, and unfortunately for them, Gilmour had had sufficient time to deal before being rudely interrupted.

The undercover cop took a swig of his lager, put his paper down and placed his glass on top of it to signify he would be returning. He stood up after saying, "Checking out back of pub," to his lapel.

The sleazy landlord glanced at him as he passed and then returned his attention to placing yet another bet on his mobile phone and losing more money he could ill afford to lose. He assumed the big guy was visiting the gents' toilet located down a corridor behind the poolroom. Hammond had expected to see five guys huddled around the pool table; the room was empty.

The door at the end of the corridor was marked 'TOILETS'. The right-hand wall had a window that was partially open and also a door leading to a courtyard at the back of the pub. The yard housed some rusty tables and chairs and was littered with cigarette butts. As he came level with the window he paused and glanced into the yard where he saw Gilmour, looking terrified, surrounded by the four men who had marched into the pub moments before, one holding a pool cue. Hammond caught the end of a one-sided conversation.

"… and you've had your hand in the till, Gilly!"

He had good cause to be frightened as a few seconds later the man on his left-hand side, semi-circular scar on his cheek, stepped forward and punched him on the side of his face. A cowardly attack delivered from Gilmour's blind side. He sank to his knees, clutching a likely broken jaw. One of the other men standing in front of the hapless druggie took a pace back as a footballer would when taking a free kick; in the courtyard the 'ball' was to be Gilmour's head.

The detective reacted quickly to what he had just witnessed and swiftly opened the door to the courtyard without actually stepping fully outside.

"STOP!" he shouted at the top of his voice that made his eavesdropping sergeant recoil. The 'footballer' froze as if someone had hit the pause button and four heads swivelled in his direction. By shouting he had achieved his objective as he would prefer to interview Gilmour at the police station rather than the local hospital. Taking advantage of this momentary 'freeze frame' the detective stepped fully into the courtyard and took a few paces to his left, so he had a wall directly behind him as he wasn't about to let the men surround him.

"This is none of your business, you nosey black

bastard; now fuck off unless you want some of the same!" Apparently, Scarface was also the leader of the quartet.

The unwanted attention of him entering the courtyard had angered the leader still further and he moved to confront the unwelcome intrusion; the other three men soon followed, forming a menacing semi-circle. Undaunted the detective didn't flinch.

"You're right, it was none of my business, but then you threatened me and racially abused me, so now it is." He then inclined his head towards the microphone and said: "Back up."

The men thought this was directed at them and he was telling them to move away, but those two words were the prearranged signal as the trigger for intervention by his colleagues.

As the burly detective had guessed, the leader was the first to attack him by throwing the self-same punch as he had at Gilmour. This time with the intention of hitting him full in the face; now he wasn't punching a timid, defenceless drug dealer; he was about to get his comeuppance.

At the very last second, when his clenched hand was close to connecting, Hammond moved his head slightly to one side and the fist smashed into the wall behind him. Simultaneously to taking evasive action he brought his knee up into the attacker's midriff forcing the air out of his lungs. The impact of the knee jerking into his body sent him flying backwards scattering a table and chairs; he lay gasping for air and, at the same time, clutching his damaged hand with his good hand.

Next, the man on the detective's right-hand side aimed a kick in the general direction of his groin, only for it to be parried by a solid left arm quickly followed by a right boot that connected with the man's scrotum. He screamed in agony and lay on the courtyard ground in the foetal position with his hands clutching his genitals.

Then the man with the pool cue saw his opportunity to attack while his colleague was being kicked. He held the cue by the thinner end and raised it above his head like a lumberjack chopping wood. Unfortunately for him the attack had been anticipated and a backward kick, like a horse would deliver, made a mess of his right knee and the cue fell harmlessly to the ground.

Amid the courtyard carnage it flashed through Hammond's mind just how many people had these men inflicted pain on down the years; it was now their turn to suffer.

But there was still one aggressor left standing and he wasn't about to beat a retreat.

He reached into his pocket and produced a flick knife, pushed the button, and the blade shot out. This happened while Hammond was shattering the knee of the erstwhile pool player. He was momentarily slightly off-balance and the last man grabbed his chance. He leapt forward and plunged the blade into the right side of the detective's body, sending him sprawling to the ground. The man, who was now towering over him, yanked his head back by his black curly hair intent on slitting his throat. His bravado, or desire to give him the final message of his fairly short life, probably saved it.

"This'll teach you to mess with The Baron's boys, you black bastard!"

He placed the glinting blade close to his left ear in readiness to drag it to his other ear.

"TASER, TASER!" Shouting reverberated around the courtyard, simultaneous to two small pairs of dart-like electrodes piercing through the air from two yellow guns, delivering high-voltage shocks to the knifeman, who in an instant dropped his weapon and was writhing on the ground as if having an epileptic fit. The officers, seeing the imminent stabbing of a colleague, weren't about to wait before firing on the remote possibility the knifeman would have second thoughts.

In the few seconds it had taken the man to spit out his message to the defenceless detective, officers had entered the courtyard from a back alley and also from the door off the corridor to the toilets. Police officers were now swarming over the pub.

Sergeant Harris had witnessed the stabbing and was quickly kneeling down in front of the apparently stricken detective as he lay on the ground.

"Alex, Alex, are you alright?"

He was motionless for a moment and then looked up.

"This stab vest is marvellous, sergeant." The addition of the vest to his other garb explained why he had seemed to his colleagues even bigger than usual.

He quickly jumped to his feet and helped the officers arrest the five men, including Gilmour who was still clutching his face. One ambulance was called for the man with the mangled knee. The man with the broken hand, despite it starting to swell, was handcuffed, the arresting officers showing no compassion for the thug. The man with the extremely tender testicles hobbled towards a waiting squad car.

Some were later charged with affray and causing actual bodily harm, while the man with the broken hand would also have the racially aggravated attack added to his charges. The knifeman would be charged with the more serious offence of attempted grievous bodily harm. The police also arrested the landlord for allowing his premises to be used to deal drugs; his last act before getting into another police car was to lock up the Plymouth Pilgrim pub, possibly for the last time.

Outside by the police van, the undercover detective constable spoke to his sergeant.

"Sorry, sergeant," Hammond sheepishly offered his apologies to Harris, "if I had called for back-up earlier, I may have been able to avoid the fracas."

"From what I could gather from listening in, after you went to check out what was happening, as soon as you saw the men in the courtyard you should have called us in. There again, I know you wanted to save Gilmour from a beating. The other thing, Alex, is that by taking on the four thugs you could have got yourself killed." This was as close as Harris got to an admonishment. "All I know is that the four men, Gilmour and any other druggies arrested at his house, face prosecution, so a good day's work."

"Point taken, sergeant. One other thing I remember is after he knifed me he said: 'That'll teach you to mess with The Baron's boys.' So, I assume their boss, and the one who ordered the attack on Gilmour, is nicknamed The Baron. We need to identify who he is if we really want to defeat, or at least disrupt, the drug scene in the city. We've netted a few of his people, so let's see if their mobiles give a clue as to his identity. I doubt they will be offering that information voluntarily. Of course, it's possible they don't even know his true identity."

THIRTY-THREE

The old-fashioned bronze weighing scales were in constant use in the back room of the terraced house in a suburb of Plymouth. One man was carefully sliding the white powder into the shallow gold-coloured dish that had an indentation on its lip to aid pouring. When the calibration needle attached to the central pivot showed the weight of the powder was equal to the weight in the other dish, the correct amount of cocaine had been weighed. The small sachet could be bought for £30. Of course, there are more modern electronic scales, but they could be manipulated. The dealers and users had more faith in what could ironically be called the 'Scales of Justice'. The powder was gently slipped into a small plastic bag with zipper and money exchanged for the precious package.

The raid on the Plymouth Pilgrim pub triggered the raid on John Gilmour's end-of-terrace house. Sergeant Harris and DC Hammond oversaw the pub raid and Inspectors King and Best plus other officers, including DC Dyson, attended the house. The difference between the two was stark. Hammond had gone undercover at the pub, while the latter was a full-on surprise attack launched simultaneously at the front and at the back of the property.

Ten officers executed a drugs warrant, smashing down the front and back doors in unison: five at the front and five at the rear. Other uniformed police were on standby in the next street should they be needed.

One man was intercepted on his way to the toilet, hurriedly carrying a sizeable plastic bag, which looked like half a kilogram of flour. He was on a disposal mission. In the ensuing struggle the contents were thrown into the air creating a mini white dust cloud in the room. This was not flour, but high-grade cocaine. The panicked drug dealer thought it was better to dispose of the high-value drug rather than face prison... again.

When the house had been secured the three detectives entered the property, already wearing blue latex gloves, as four men and a woman were led out in handcuffs to awaiting police vans that would take them to Charles Cross Police Station to be interviewed under caution and then processed as appropriate.

The unmistakeable smell of hashish hung in the air. This potent form of cannabis was the roll-up of choice for the people just arrested. A ray of sunlight penetrated the front window of the house and revealed some of the earlier cocaine cloud still hung in the air. What with that and the hashish smoke, King turned to his colleagues.

"We'll get high if we stay in here for too long."

The coffee table in the middle of the lounge was filled with drug paraphernalia and surrounded by dirty plates. In amongst the Coke cans, numerous empty takeaway meal cartons, pizza boxes and overflowing ashtrays, King found four cheap mobile phones.

"No doubt 'burners', Sam. Check them out now before any leads go cold." Dyson offered a separate evidence bag for each to her inspector. She then took the four bags, sat in a police car and systematically started punching buttons on each mobile in turn.

King took out his bag of sherbet lemons and offered one to his fellow inspector, but Jim Best declined the offer.

"Let's have a look to see what other incriminating evidence we can find, Jim. Mind you, you already have plenty with which to charge these low lifes. The 'burner' mobiles could prove fruitful. What I'm also interested in is anything that might lead us further up the chain. You know better than me, County Lines don't happen by chance. There is someone masterminding this whole operation. Somebody who controls it all from afar, possibly from Manchester or London. On the other hand, it could be someone who lives somewhere in Devon who has identified there are rich pickings to be had away from the tentacles of the Met Police. A coordinator who controls all the drugs coming into the area by whatever means; possibly by land, sea or air. A person making a fortune out of other people's misery. We need to catch that person to prevent our area becoming a pariah county."

Jim Best nodded in agreement and then suggested the rooms in the house for each to conduct an initial search; a further examination would be conducted later by more meticulous searchers.

It didn't take King long to locate several shrink-wrapped packages in a kitchen cupboard, poorly hidden behind cereal packets. He thought Gilmour had become over confident and should have at least put them under the floorboards.

"Richard, take a look at this!" Best called out from another room.

"I found these papers stuffed in the bedside cabinet of what I assume is Gilmour's bedroom. They are from Plymouth City Council showing payment of rent on the house for the last financial year. No arrears. They were sent to Gilmour as the occupier and I assume he has scrawled across the statement, 'PASS TO RON BATHE'. We already knew Gilmour was having his rent paid for him, but we still don't know if he is a willing participant or he's been cuckooed. Whether his landlord, Mr Bathe, is a friend or someone for Gilmour to fear."

King took out another sherbet lemon and began sucking as he thought.

"Is there anything that strikes you, Jim, when looking at the name Ron Bathe?"

"Not particularly. We've run checks on all the men with that name in Devon; there weren't many and they all check out. I also Googled 'Bathe' as a surname and apparently it relates to Anglo-Saxon habitation; way back the family lived in Bathe Barton in North Tawton in Devon."

"It's a lot simpler than that, Jim. I was thinking more of the letters that make up his name."

Inspector Best looked at what had been written on the statement.

"We know it's fictitious so it could be a pseudonym or maybe an anagram. 'Beth Nora' doesn't make sense and neither does 'Bea North'. Hang on, I get it now; the payments are made by someone calling himself The Baron."

"Exactly, but what does that tell us? Are we any the wiser? Well, knowing the nickname of Mr Big could be useful. Keep looking, Jim."

For his part King was searching an old sideboard in the lounge. In a buff folder that had been stuffed under some pornographic magazines, he found a single sheet of paper. Written on it, all in capital letters, were a month and an unintelligible list of numbers and letters:

MAR: DELIVER TO LP
3/3 AHRINGMOREEAMES
10/3 SPBOLBERRYCURTIS
17/3 SGMODBURYPRICE
24/3 SAAVETONGLAVERY
31/3 SJKINGSTONSTERLING

The experienced detective inspector was puzzled by the list. He took out his mobile and took a photograph of the sheet of paper before putting it back in the folder, then under the porno mags. After another half an hour he called out to his fellow inspector.

"Okay, Jim. We're done here. Let's leave it to your drugs team to sort out what's what. Let's check if DC Dyson has found anything on the mobiles."

Dyson was sat in an unmarked police car right out front of the raided house.

"Any joy, Sam?" her inspector enquired.

"Well, sir, on one phone is a message that read: 'LP, Usual place behind Eames this Sunday @ AH. Gilly.' A message on another phone read: 'LP, Usual place behind Curtis Sunday week @ SP.' Nothing I could see on the third one I looked at, but the last one appeared to be a demand for payment. It read: 'Tanner, you owe me a monkey. Deadline is Friday this week. You know where I'll be. Gilly.'"

King reached in his pocket for his sherbet lemon bag and popped one in his mouth.

"Five hundred quid is a tidy sum. I wonder how much 'coke' that bought? Let's digest this new info back at the station. Please ring Sergeant Harris, Sam, and set up a debrief meeting for two o'clock this afternoon. I'll invite AS Roberts. Jim, I'd like you there too if you can make it.

"I think what we've got from raiding Gilmour's house could prove very useful. All we have to do is work out what the messages on the mobiles mean and also the alphanumeric list I found in that folder. Answers on a postcard!"

THIRTY-FOUR

That afternoon following the raids on the Plymouth Pilgrim pub and Gilmour's house, Inspector King and his three detectives were in the main meeting room at Charles Cross Police Station. They had been joined by Acting Superintendent Roberts and Inspector Best from the Serious Organised Crime Agency. Although King wasn't the most senior officer present it was clear he was in charge of the meeting.

"There have been some significant developments on the crimes we discussed when we last met on Monday. I'll ask the various detectives involved to update the meeting."

Sergeant Harris then outlined the raid at the Plymouth Pilgrim pub, which had resulted in nine arrests for various offences including possession of a Class A drug, for the three users arrested as they left, and Gilmour charged with dealing the drug. She reported that he had also been charged with involvement with the ram-raid on Plymouth Albion Rugby Club as his DNA was found on a glass left at the scene and also some discarded chewing gum in his hiding place. She further reported that charges had been brought against four men for grievous bodily harm for the attacks on DC Hammond and Gilmour. The landlord of the pub had been charged with allowing his premises to be used for the sale of illegal drugs.

Harris said that Gilmour would be formally interviewed by both inspectors after the meeting. The sergeant paid tribute to DC Hammond as, due to his bravery, the pub raid had been a complete success. Roberts questioned the fact an officer had unnecessarily been placed in danger. King responded that if the raid had started earlier then four men would not have been charged with any offence. He also said that DC Hammond was wearing a stab vest, but acknowledged he could have been seriously wounded if the knifeman hadn't been tasered.

Roberts sat in silence.

King then asked Inspector Best to cover the raid on Gilmour's house. He confirmed that five people had been arrested and it was evident that Gilmour was a main dealer, judging by the amount of cocaine seized from his property. His team from SOCA were carrying out a thorough search of the house to try and establish how the drugs had come into the county. He also outlined the information they had from mobile phones found in the house and a list found in a folder that appeared to be about drug drops.

King moved the meeting on to the body on the beach case. DC Hammond informed the meeting that after identifying the body from Rolex watch records as being Mr Marco Coppola from Naples, the Italian police had now located his boat called *Marcass* in the marina. It already had a quantity of drugs on board, presumably the next consignment heading for the UK.

Hammond revealed that from historical records on the yacht's Global Positioning System it was confirmed it had sailed to the south coast of England the previous week. A map had been found on board showing the south coast and close to the shore, opposite Mothecombe near the River Erme estuary, written on the map, and marked with a cross, was '*Incontro con Cass alle 20.00 ore.*' The Italian police had kindly provided a translation: '*Meet with Cass at 20.00 hours.*' The detective commented that obviously this was some sort of rendezvous that was assumed to refer to the delivery of a consignment of drugs by that boat to be collected by Cass, whoever that was. He had checked the tide times on the day before the body was found. It was a full moon and therefore a high tide. Also the moon would provide sufficient light to help them to see to their business, without artificial illumination, if the cloud cover was kind; high tide was 19.42 that night. Hammond commented that it was assumed Mothecombe was chosen as a road leads down to the water's edge of a gently sloping beach. Transfer of drugs from the boat at high tide to a waiting vehicle would have been relatively straightforward.

King then informed the meeting that all his team were working to decipher the information they had from the earlier raids and the interview with Gilmour could prove fruitful.

Roberts seemed happy with the progress on the various cases, as well as closure of the Bolberry-on-Sea arson and criminal damage cases, and asked to be kept informed of any developments.

*

Inspectors King and Best moved from the meeting room and before they went to interview Gilmour they were told that the other four men arrested at the pub were giving 'no comment' interviews. The inspectors knew that he provided the best chance of gaining more information, which hopefully would lead them to the so-called Baron. Fortunately, Gilmour was the opposite of his 'no comment' associates and was ready to talk. He knew his defence was poor and the judge might mitigate his sentence if he cooperated with the police.

As they entered the room he sat nursing his swollen jaw. He was known to both detectives from previous drug-related convictions. The inspectors sat down opposite the hapless drug dealer; King was the first to speak.

"So, Gilly, it seems like you'll never learn. We've raided your place and got enough evidence to send you away for a lengthy term as this isn't your first offence, is it?"

"Okay, Mr King, you got me bang to rights, but if I come clean, will you put in a good word for me with the judge?"

"I will make sure that it is recorded that you cooperated fully with the investigation."

"Good enough. Truth is I was forced to use my place to trade and to get involved in the rugby club raid."

"Are you saying you were cuckooed?"

"Bloody right I was. That's exactly what I'm saying. About six months ago I had a visit from four heavies and they said they wanted to use my place as a base for trading in Plymouth. I had no choice, Mr King, as they said they would beat me up and smash up my place if I didn't agree."

"My detective at the Plymouth Pilgrim pub tells me you were attacked. What was all that about?"

"They accused me of not passing on drug money I owed them. I gotta eat, Mr King, and they were virtually taking all the money I collected. All they did was pay my rent, but that was for their own good."

"So, you did have your hand in the till?"

"I did keep back a few wraps to sell. Good-quality coke can sell for a ton a gram and I was desperate for some cash."

"Tell us about the rugby club raid."

"I owed them over a monkey for drugs I used for my own needs, but I couldn't muster fifty quid let alone 500. So I was told to meet this geezer at the Crowne Plaza Hotel on Plymouth Hoe one evening. He'd obviously been watching too many old movies as meeting him was just like *The Thomas Crown Affair*, one of my favourite movies. You seen it, Mr King? Bright light in my face and using a gizmo to change his voice. I was told not to disrespect The Baron or I'd regret it. I was instructed what to do in the rugby club and if it went well I'd be let off my debt. Well, I probably couldn't refuse even if I wanted to so I said I'd do it.

"I hid in the club, as instructed, and then used the code I'd been given to switch off the alarm. Two men I'd never seen before or since then ram-raided the place and I'm sure you know the rest."

"Chewing gum can make you thirsty, Gilly."

"I know, Mr King, I made a mistake."

"Well, two actually. Your DNA was on the gum and the glass we found at the scene. Can you tell us anything about the guy in the hotel room?"

"I could make out his silhouette that's all. Even though he was sat down I could tell he was quite a thickset bloke and obviously a tall guy with a full head of hair. Couldn't tell you what colour though."

"Does this mean anything to you?" King produced a printout he had taken from his mobile of the list they had found in Gilmour's house.

"Sorry, Mr King, sir. I've probably told you too much already. These are scary people I'm involved with and they don't forget. I don't want to say any more until I've got a brief."

With that King ended the interview. Outside of the room he said to Jim Best that they would have to work out what the list meant without Gilmour's help.

*

Back at his desk, something was nagging away at King's thoughts. He called across to DC Hammond to join him. Sherbet lemon time. The detective sat quietly by his boss's desk and waited.

"Have the forensic team had any joy with the search of Morris's apartment yet?"

"Not so far, sir. No trace of a computer disc or memory stick we'd hoped for and they've more or less finished their search." With his tongue King rolled his sweet from one side of his mouth to the other.

"Do you watch *Antiques Roadshow* on the telly, Alex?"

It seemed a bizarre question, but he said he'd occasionally watched it. He asked the inspector why he had asked him.

"You were there when we interviewed Karen White. Do you remember what she said when I asked her about the antique bureau in the corner of the room? Don't worry, Alex, that was rhetorical. I'll tell you what she said: '*He spent many hours sat at it with the drop-leaf front down and his laptop on it and plugged into the socket next to it.*'

"So if he spent most of his time sat at it, surely he would keep his memory sticks not far away. She also said: '*He did most of his work on his laptop, but did use the bureau for filing papers and other things he used. He liked all the little compartments.*' Liked all the little compartments," King repeated.

"I remember a similar bureau that was featured on the *Antiques Roadshow* a few years ago and that one had lots of little cubbyholes too. It also had a hidden compartment. You had to slide out a piece of veneer, that looked fixed, then press a button and a shallow drawer would pop out from what looked like a solid piece of wood that formed the lining on the inside of the bureau. Also, if after he'd finished on his laptop and had downloaded the files onto sticks, he's unlikely to hide them in another part of the house. He'd hide them close to where he was working, wouldn't he? Get your coat, Alex, and we'll take a look. You never know, we might get lucky."

THIRTY-FIVE

Jane Ferris had been fairly busy all day in the village stores and post office at Bolberry-on-Sea. She was looking forward to cashing up and then locking up. Her partner, Ted Bayliss, had gone upstairs, as they lived over the shop, to prepare their evening meal; it was his turn. The last customer had left ten minutes before so as the clock ticked inexorably to the top of the hour and closing time, she had done her final tasks for the day and was looking forward to putting her feet up with a glass of Pinot Grigio.

As she reached up to slide the bolt across at the top of the door as the first stage of locking the shop, the door opened. She was about to say, "Sorry, but we are closing," when it was forcibly pushed fully open and she fell back against the shop shelving. Several tins of beans and spaghetti hoops clattered to the floor.

The intruder, clad all in black and wearing a motorcycle crash helmet with the visor closed, barged in. He lunged at the shocked postmistress and with his left hand grabbed a fistful of her white blouse. In his other hand he was brandishing a double-barrelled sawn-off shotgun. He didn't speak, just roughly half dragged half pulled her to the door of the normally secure post office cubicle; his intention was clear. He threw her into the counter chair to free one of his hands and tried the money drawer; it was locked. He jabbed the gun into Ferris's stomach so hard the short barrels were consumed by her clothing and the flesh beneath.

She reached into her pocket and nervously took out a bunch of keys and fumbled to find the right one. After another bruising prod she shakily put the key into the lock and after two turns she pulled the drawer open. The robber opened the zipper on his tight-fitting hoodie, with elasticated waistband, and began stuffing high-value banknotes inside his now gaping clothing.

"Oh no you don't, you bastard!" Ted Bayliss, alerted by the falling tins, appeared in the doorway to the stairs wielding a frying pan, which he happened to have in his hand when alerted by the clattering cans.

With considerable force he smashed the pan over the head of the thief. If he hadn't been wearing a crash helmet, no doubt the blow would have had a different result. As it was the robber was only momentarily thrown off balance. Bayliss, seizing the opportunity, dropped the pan, grabbed the weapon and began grappling with the thief. They had both their hands on the gun, although there was only one finger on the trigger, the same finger that had been on it from the start. They twisted first one way and then the other as their scuffle was played out with upper body movement only, their feet being firmly planted on the floor.

One barrel exploded and in the cramped cubicle the report was deafening. Over a hundred small pellets spewed into the ceiling tiles that then rained down on the three like confetti.

The wrestling went on and Jane Ferris was trapped in the small room as the men barred her escape route. The thief was winning the tussle for the gun and both men were now in the main shop, having half fallen and half lurched out of the post office cubicle, their feet no longer anchored.

Suddenly the other barrel was discharged. The thief wrenched the weapon from Bayliss's grip and hit him in the face with the butt of the gun, before fleeing the scene with the blast still reverberating around the shop.

Bayliss lay dazed on the floor, briefly concussed by the blow to his face. Blood was seeping from a gash above his right eye. He wasn't sure how long he had lost consciousness; it was only a matter of a minute. Slumped with his back against the newspaper shelving in the main shop area he gradually returned to full consciousness.

As the sticky substance ran over his eyebrow and eyelid onto his cheek, he instinctively reached into his pocket and used his handkerchief to stem the flow and wipe the blood away from his eye.

"Jane, Jane, where are you?" he frantically called out, but he was met with silence. He looked at the open shop doorway and the darkness beyond. Dragging himself to his feet he stumbled to the post office cubicle entrance. He reached under the counter and pressed the panic alarm button that was linked directly to the police station in Kingsbridge.

Then the full horror of the robbery hit him. Lying motionless on the floor, was his partner. There was a large red patch on her white blouse, just over her left breast, that was getting bigger as he watched. In his confused state he wasn't sure whether to give first aid or ring for an ambulance; he hoped the police were already on their way. He ripped open her clothing and pressed his already bloodstained hanky over the wound and secured it in place by the left cup of her partly shredded bra. The close proximity of the blast to her body meant a higher concentration of pellets than if the gun had been fired from further away. At that moment Ted Bayliss didn't care: damage done.

He grabbed her mobile off the counter and with his bloodied index finger stabbed in the three figures on the keypad and blurted out what he wanted to the ambulance operator. As soon as she heard the word 'shot' she immediately contacted the police as well; as it was they were already over halfway to Bolberry-on-Sea.

When the first of the six police cars arrived at the village stores all sounds of gunshots had long ceased. An eerie calm awaited the armed officers as they surrounded the building and stealthily entered the shop. The first two moved quickly to the post office cubicle and looked in, guns at the ready.

Ted Bayliss was cradling his partner in his arms and her blood had partly transferred to the front of his shirt. The red patch on her blouse was no longer getting bigger. He looked up at the officers and, with rivulets of tears cutting a path through his own bloodied left cheek, just shook his head.

THIRTY-SIX

As what was called, in shorthand, 'the Farthing Case' had been successfully concluded, thus reducing the workload of Inspector King's team, Acting Superintendent Roberts had, rather grudgingly, allowed his team to investigate the murder of Jane Ferris. In fairness to the senior officer, he had realised that the team was already active in the Bolberry-on-Sea area due to the previous recent crimes. It was also a fact that his other detectives were stretched dealing with a burgeoning workload, which included people-smuggling at the local ferry port and boat thefts from Queen Anne's Battery, a prominent marina in the heart of Plymouth.

As with the Morris murder, King had his whole team on the case. Ted Bayliss had been taken to hospital by ambulance the previous evening to treat his head wound and also, sadly, post-traumatic stress or, in old parlance, shock.

As the detectives approached the village stores, they were faced with the familiar exclusion tape and people in white one-piece suits; those suits would always convey the gravity of what had happened.

They were briefed by a uniformed sergeant and then visited the scene of the murder. The broken shelves in the shop and goods liberally scattered on the floor gave evidence of the struggle, as did the blood-spattered post office security screen and floor. Jane Ferris's body was covered in a shroud. King reverently and slowly took one corner and lifted the cloth to reveal the true horror of what had happened the night before.

He asked Hammond and Dyson to knock on a few doors close to the village stores before checking with the hospital that Bayliss was fit to be interviewed. For their part, King and Harris had been informed that two people, although not witnesses to the attack, had come forward already and were able to give information that might be of help.

The first witness, who was cycling home on her way from work, said she heard two loud bangs and about ten seconds after them saw a figure running up a lane not far from the village stores, before it disappeared into the darkness. That's all she could offer, but at least it gave the possible route of escape. The other witness, who was walking his dog, also heard the gunshots and then soon after thought he heard a motorbike start up and roar off. The detectives thanked both for the information they had supplied and moved up the lane the woman had identified as the possible exit path for the murderer.

About seventy metres along it was a recessed entrance. Two tractor tracks were clearly visible leading to and from the field and in between them was the imprint of a tyre. This was narrower than the flanking tractor treads and larger than a bicycle. Harris alerted one of the forensic team working in the village stores and they quickly taped off the entrance and began taking photographs of the imprint.

*

Hammond and Dyson having drawn a blank on their enquiries back in Bolberry-on-Sea had now arrived at the hospital where Ted Bayliss had been kept in overnight. Dyson apologised for intruding on his grief. He was keen to assist the detectives in any way he could to help catch the person that had not only destroyed his partner's life, but his also. He was still clearly distressed, but determined to help. Handkerchief at the ready, he began his gruesome recollection: "I came downstairs after I heard some cans being knocked off a shelf. I was carrying a frying pan, which I was about to use to prepare our evening meal..." He paused as the events of the previous evening came flooding back.

"As I came into the shop, I saw this black-clad figure threatening Jane and I instinctively went for him. After I'd hit him over the head, I realised he was wearing a crash helmet, but he was shocked at the blow and it gave me enough time to grab the gun he was carrying. He had hold of the stock, if that's what you call it, and his finger was on the trigger guard, while I had one hand between his two and my other on the short barrel." He went on to explain the struggle and the gun discharging.

Hammond asked an important question: "The robber, presumably a man judging by his strength, was wearing black including black gloves?"

"Yes, definitely a man. He was wearing gloves, black I think, and the trigger finger of the glove on his right hand had been cut off."

"Did you notice anything else about what he was wearing? Any distinguishing marks or features?"

Bayliss thought for a moment: "Yes, two things come to mind. His hoodie was unzipped when I arrived and he was stuffing money into it. He was wearing a T-shirt underneath it and that was black too, but had a yellow logo on the front. It looked like a headdress. You know like an American Indian would wear. It was bright yellow. The other thing I remember is his helmet. It was black, but had the word 'SHARP' written on the front. At least I think it was SHARP. I assume it's the maker's mark."

A doctor then appeared with a look that meant the interview was over.

"Thank you, Mr Bayliss. You've been very helpful. We'll keep you informed of any developments. Once again, please accept our condolences for your loss."

That expression of sympathy was too much to bear for the distraught postmaster and he began sobbing. The detectives left and headed back to the main police station as they knew their inspector wanted his team to update each other.

*

"Okay. What have we got on the Ferris murder?" King wasn't in the mood to waste time as he looked at his two junior detectives.

Hammond replied: "Well, sir, Mr Bayliss was obviously traumatised, but very keen to help. He gave us some very important information about the robber. Firstly, he's sure he was male and, secondly, under his black hoodie had a black T-shirt on, which had a yellow headdress on the front like some sort of logo. As you know, sir, I spent some time in Exeter and often went to Sandy Park, the home of the Exeter Chiefs. They play their home fixtures in black most of the time and the yellow headdress is the rugby club logo.

"Thirdly, he said the crash helmet he was wearing had the word 'SHARP' written on it, possibly a maker's mark. I've checked out crash helmet manufacturers and we think he probably saw 'SHARK'."

Dyson looked up from taking personal notes of what was being said and wondered to herself where she had seen that before.

She was shaken out of her thoughts as King gave his report on the investigation in the village.

"It would appear that the assailant came to the robbery on a motorbike because, as we've heard, he was wearing a crash helmet. At first we kept an open mind as other robbers have used a helmet simply to disguise their identity. However, one witness, not to the actual murder, who was out walking their dog, heard the gunshots and a short while later heard a motorbike start up and roar off. We later found the imprint of what looks like a motorcycle in a field gateway fairly close to the village stores."

King noticed a puzzled look on the face of his detective.

"Something worrying you, Sam?" he asked with his palms up.

"Sir, you know on the day we arrested Farthing at his home, we had gone to his garage first? I seem to recall there was a motorbike parked outside in one of the bays with a black helmet on the seat. I think there was some white lettering on the front. It may be a coincidence, but may be worth checking out?"

King summed up: "Thanks, Sam. So, we want a biker who follows rugby. Alex, please get a print from Forensics of the tyre tread we found close to the village stores and you and Sam pay a visit to Farthing's and Preston's garage; take two uniformed officers with you. If the bike is there and you get a match, arrest the owner of the bike and bring him in for questioning. Check out the helmet too. I have a hunch to follow at Karen White's apartment and Lucy will come with me."

Sergeant Harris's day suddenly got better. King was always happy to work with his sergeant, but on this occasion his main reason for pairing Hammond with Dyson was that he wanted his burly detective constable on hand at the garage as arrests can sometimes turn ugly.

"Let me know how you get on. I hope we are not following false optimism on these cases. We could draw a blank on both, but you never know, if my hunch is right, we could be closing in on two murderers in the same day!"

THIRTY-SEVEN

Sandra Coppola had left her boss – and rumoured partner – finishing an appointment at the Making Waves hair salon as she had offered to make an Italian dish for their dinner that evening. She walked to Dawn Proud's house in the middle of Bolberry-on-Sea and began preparation for *patate al forno* (Italian oven-roasted potatoes). She was serving it with charred lemon chicken *piccata*.

As was her way of doing things in the kitchen, she took a week-old copy of the *Western Morning News* from the pile of papers in the recycle bin, opened it and began peeling potatoes ready for slicing into wedges that would form layers on top of the dish. Having prepared all that were needed, she was about to wrap up the peelings and put them in the bin, when she glanced down as something had caught her eye. Sweeping the peelings away with the back of her hand she read:

BODY FOUND ON DEVON BEACH IDENTIFIED

She gasped and clutched her mouth with her hand.

She slumped onto a kitchen stool and snatched the paper for a closer look, the peelings falling into her lap. The article's heading was somewhat misleading as it didn't actually name the dead man; it didn't have to. She instinctively knew the article referred to her brother, Marco. It was either him or Fabio Gallo, but she just sensed it was Marco.

Although it didn't name the man, it gave enough information for Sandra Coppola to be in no doubt. It named the boat as the *Marcass*, registered in Naples, and the man's body was assumed to have fallen from it after suffering a blow to the back of his head. She thought that explained why he hadn't been in touch all week. The short report finished by commenting that the Italian police in Naples were investigating.

She started sobbing and then the questions started to flood her thoughts: Why had he fallen overboard? Who had hit him on the back of the head? Fabio? Surely not her brother's girlfriend, Isabella! Which of the other two people on board could have done that to him? Why hadn't one of the others contacted her?

She knew she had to return to Naples to find answers to all those questions and she had to go back now. Leaving her meal preparations, including potato peelings scattered all over the kitchen floor, she went upstairs to pack, but not before ordering a taxi. In a matter of minutes she had gathered her essential belongings and hoped Dawn Proud would not be home before her taxi came. She knew it would be there in about another ten minutes; too many unanswered questions and too many lies told, which she would just not be able to explain. She had also grown very fond of her and leaving in the manner she planned would be too painful for both of them.

Still wiping tears from her eyes she took out a pad and pencil from the kitchen drawer and scribbled a note. She knew she couldn't tell her partner the real reason for her hasty departure as, if she did, and it was passed on, she may be stopped at customs. The taxi duly arrived and, never to return, Sandra Coppola got in with her suitcase.

The hairdresser returned a little later than planned as the last appointment took longer than expected. She was surprised when the front door wasn't on the latch. She used her key and shouted breezily, "I'm home," her greeting only to be met with silence. When she went into the kitchen she was confronted by potato peelings scattered on the floor and a note pinned to the cork notice board. Had her girlfriend been abducted as she had obviously left in a hurry? Was this a ransom note?

She removed the pin and saw the note was in Italian, which she couldn't translate:

Cara Dawn, sono tornata in Italia. Mi dispiace ma ho dovuto andare di fretta e non potevo dire addio. Ricorderò sempre il nostro tempo insieme. Ti prego, perdonami. Adoro Sandra

Feeling slightly panicky she quickly booted her computer and Googled 'Translation Italian to

English' and feverishly typed in the Italian and got an immediate response:

Dear Dawn, I have gone back to Italy. Sorry but I had to go in a hurry and I couldn't say goodbye. I will always remember our time together. Please forgive me. Love Sandra

That night Dawn Proud was the second woman to cry in that kitchen.

*

Sergeant Harris had contacted Karen White who had now returned to her apartment after staying with a friend for one night. It had been thoroughly searched, but the searchers could find no trace of computer discs or memory sticks. She confirmed she was home and Harris said she and her inspector would be with her in ten minutes. King was following one of his hunches that may or may not prove fruitful.

"Hello again, Ms White, and thank you for letting us disturb you again. I'm sorry to say the search of your apartment yesterday did not reveal what we had hoped, namely some computer discs or memory sticks that Mr Morris may have hidden. However, I would like to have another look at his bureau if you don't mind. If he was going to hide something, I think it would be close to where he actually worked on his laptop. I seem to remember you said he worked mainly at his bureau?" She nodded her agreement.

A Devon Deception

"We think he downloaded his work onto a disc or stick, but he wouldn't just pop it into one of the drawers. Do you happen to know if the bureau has any secret compartments?"

"No, inspector, I'm sorry I don't. I've seen him using memory sticks, but don't know where he kept them. He could be quite secretive."

"Do you mind if we have another look?"

"No, please help yourselves."

With that Harris began removing the drawers from the bottom of the bureau. She wasn't interested in what was in them. Other searchers would have closely examined the content. She then dropped down the folding leaf, revealing smaller drawers, which she also removed and stood back to allow her boss to follow his hunch.

There was no veneer for King to slide to reveal a button on this bureau as he'd seen done on the *Antiques Roadshow*. He sat on the chair in front of the piece of furniture and took out a sherbet lemon. He began to ponder. It went through his mind that if needs be he would have the bureau systematically dismantled, but that was a last resort.

Eventually, with Harris and Ms White looking over his shoulder, he leaned forward and closely inspected the drop-down flap. This was a reasonably thick piece of wood; it would have to be as it had to bear the weight of any writer who would no doubt lean their upper body weight on it. Ingeniously, as the flap was lowered, two arms made of rectangular pieces of wood came out to support it. When it was shut the arms were synchronised to retract into the main body of the bureau. King moved it up and down several times and watched from underneath as the arms moved in and out. He reasoned that no one ever saw the top edge of the arms as, when extended, they were always covered by the flap. Perhaps an ideal hiding place? He didn't want to hold the arms and force it up as that could damage the linked mechanism. Indeed, the force may have been so great that it may not have been possible to have it up and the arms out.

He then looked at both sides of the bureau, taking particular interest in the area near where the arms came out. On the right-hand side he noticed there was a small, darker part of wood that could easily have been mistaken for a knot or defect. It was circular and the size of a pencil end. It appeared to have ballpoint marks over and around it.

"Pen, please, Lucy."

King then leaned around the side and pushed the end of the ballpoint against the small defect, which moved no more than a millimetre inwards and then sprang back out when King withdrew the pen; nothing else happened. He looked perplexed, but repeated the ballpoint pressure. This time, whilst keeping the pen firmly pressed against the small blemish he lifted the bureau flap and shut it; the arms stayed out.

"Very ingenious. The small point on the side, when depressed, deactivates the mechanism that operates the arms allowing the flap to be raised without the arms retracting. Then when I lower it again, the mechanism resets itself." He then demonstrated what he meant and he was right, the flap was again synchronised with the two arms. Having proved his point, he then once again pushed the disguised button on the side and closed it; the arms stayed out.

On close inspection of the arm on the right side, he gently applied pressure to the top edge and it flicked up along half its length, which was about fifteen centimetres; it was hinged. When King pressed the top edge again it clicked back into place. Further pressure and, once again, it flicked up. As he opened the thin rectangular piece of wood on its hinge, the contents of the small compartment were revealed.

"Abracadabra!" he said as he took out three memory sticks and placed them on the palm of his hand. Each was marked with a letter from an indelible pen.

"Three sixty-four-gigabyte memory sticks," he triumphantly announced. "One marked with capital letters 'DD', another marked, but with a single 'D' only, and the last with a 'P'. I'll wager the one marked solely with 'D' relates to the work Mr Morris did on his first drugs investigation and the 'DD' relates to his investigation of drugs in Devon, the so-called County Lines."

Harris asked: "What about the other stick, sir, which has a 'P' marked on it?"

"I wouldn't be at all surprised, Lucy, if that stands for 'Planning'."

THIRTY-EIGHT

Closely followed by a police 4x4 in full blue and yellow livery, DCs Hammond and Dyson arrived at the Farthing/Preston-owned garage in their unmarked car. Once again there were very few cars parked outside awaiting attention. This time Farthing had seen them arrive and came out to meet, not greet, the detectives.

"For crying out loud, what now? I thought I'd done all I could to cooperate with you."

Hammond spoke: "We are here on a different matter today, sir."

"What matter?"

"We would like to inspect the two motorbikes parked outside."

"Why?"

"We believe one may have been used to commit a crime."

"What crime?"

"We would like to inspect them if you have no objection. Who do they belong to?"

"The nearest one is Jim Preston's, my partner, and the other one is Lucas Peverell's, he works part time for us doing the books."

DC Dyson took out a print from an envelope she was carrying and walked over to where the first motorbike was leaning on its stand; DC Hammond joined her. They compared the tread with the image they were holding and had a brief discussion. Both shook their head and moved on to the second bike. After a few minutes Dyson addressed Farthing who had stayed in the same place, while the detectives deliberated.

"We suspect this is the motorbike that was used to commit a crime, sir. Who did you say owns it?"

"I do. What's the problem?" Jim Preston, the mechanic, had emerged from the service area of the garage puffing on a cigar. Dyson recognised him, but still asked his name for the benefit of Hammond.

"And you are, sir?"

"Jim Preston. I am part-owner of this garage."

"You said you own this motorbike, sir. Would you mind showing us the crash helmet you wear?"

Preston grudgingly trooped back into the building and came back out carrying a black helmet, which he passed to Dyson. She looked at it, as did Hammond, and they could see the word 'SHARK' in white letters on the front. Both detectives thought not quite 'SHARP' as Bayliss had reported, but near enough.

"Where were you last night around six o'clock?"

"Let's see. I think I left here before then, so I went to the village. Why what's the problem?"

"The problem is we suspect that this motorcycle was used on the raid of the post office in the village last night. Mr Preston, I am arresting you for the murder of Jane Ferris last evening at the village stores in Bolberry-on-Sea." She completed the arresting statement and Preston was not a happy man. He squared up to the diminutive detective, but as Hammond stepped forward, he knew he was no match for him and quickly realised resistance was futile; he resorted to a verbal attack.

"What the bloody hell are you on about? I never went near the village stores yesterday. I remember I left work just after five thirty on foot as I was going to the pub. I left my bike locked up here." Dyson beckoned the two uniformed officers and they handcuffed him. As he was led away he shouted over his shoulder: "What a way to treat a vet!" He was put in their car and taken to the Charles Cross Police Station.

Farthing was left open-mouthed and Dyson asked him not to touch the bike or helmet. They would be collected later as evidence.

*

There was little doubt in Inspector King's mind that all the various investigations his team were dealing with were reaching a critical juncture. Yet there was still a lot to do in order to apprehend the villains and have watertight evidence against each and every one of them.

Now Preston had been arrested for the murder of Jane Ferris, he wanted his detectives to concentrate on the information they had seized from the drug raids and the memory sticks found at Dan Morris's apartment.

They all met in the conference room at the police station. Before the meeting, King had asked Dyson to fix an enlarged version of the sheet of paper found in the folder in Gilmour's house, downloaded from his mobile, to the display board. They formed a semi-circle around it and he asked them to look at what was on the sheet in silence for a moment and consider what it meant. He took out a sherbet lemon:

MAR: DELIVER TO LP
3/3   AHRINGMOREEAMES
10/3 SPBOLBERRYCURTIS
17/3 SGMODBURYPRICE
24/3 SAAVETONGLAVERY
31/3 SJKINGSTONSTERLING

Hammond was first to speak: "I think, sir, it seems that it's a delivery schedule for March. All the dates are a Sunday."

Harris joined in: "We know Dan Morris had done some research on churches in the area as he had the church magazine in the papers we found at his apartment."

Dyson added: "I remember that the Reverend Brown looks after five parish churches, although he bases himself in Bolberry-on-Sea where he lives."

King asked Dyson to Google Ringmore church and see what came up. Forefinger jabbing on the screen she gave her reply.

"It says, sir, 'Welcome to All Hallows, Ringmore.'"

"So AH stands for All Hallows. Let me guess, if

you Google Kingston church in Devon you'll find it's dedicated to Saint John, Saint Joseph or Saint James?" More jabbing and she answered his question: "You're right, sir, Saint James."

"And Aveton Gifford could be Saint Andrew?"

"Right again, sir."

"So, we now know the date and the location presumably of a drugs drop. What about the names? Do you think Eames and the others are the people collecting the stuff?"

Harris looked quizzical and then put forward her view.

"As you say, sir, we know the date and location, but not the specific place the drugs are left. They wouldn't be left in the church, would they? Someone might be suspicious of the comings and goings. Also most churches are locked on non-service days to prevent the theft of altar crosses and other valuables.

"So, I think the names could relate to graves. I don't mean the drugs have been buried, rather more likely put behind the headstones. I also think the hiding places would be well away from the church itself in a more remote part of the graveyard, possibly close to the boundary of the church grounds, or at least where people couldn't walk behind to see what was hidden."

Just then there was a knock on the door and the desk sergeant asked to speak with Inspector King. After a few minutes he rejoined the meeting and told his detectives the solicitor for Preston was alleging his client had a perfectly good alibi, from two witnesses, for the time Jane Ferris was murdered.

He insisted they were checked out and the charges against his client dropped and that he be released immediately, on bail if necessary.

"Okay. Sam and Alex get the alibi names off the legal rep and, as I assume the witnesses to Preston's whereabouts live in Bolberry-on-Sea, go and interview them. If you're satisfied as to the validity of the alibis, call Lucy and we'll release Preston. He can stay inside 'til then.

"Also, while you're out that way, check if there is a gravestone in Bolberry churchyard dedicated to 'Curtis'. You'll be passing close to Kingston as well so check for a gravestone for 'Sterling'. On your way there pick up two bunches of cheap flowers and only one of you go into the churchyard armed with a bunch, so you look like a grieving friend or relative of a deceased. We don't want to spook the person who might be collecting the drugs. Obviously, if you find a stash, don't remove them. We'll stake out the place and catch the collector red-handed. Judging by the pick-up date set for Kingston next Sunday, that's the most likely place you'll find drugs. Any questions?

"Lucy, you and I will have a look at what's on the memory sticks."

*

DCs Hammond and Dyson did as they were told and bought two bunches of cheap flowers from a supermarket en route. Although Kingston came before Bolberry-on-Sea, they decided to interview the alibi witnesses first, as Preston's solicitor was getting very agitated. Then they'd look at the graveyard for 'Curtis' in the village, before trying to find the resting place of 'Sterling' at St James's church in Kingston on their way back.

*

It had been alleged that Preston was drinking in the Duke of Cornwall pub at six o'clock the previous evening, the time of the murder. The witnesses were the landlord, Dave Smith, and Doug Grant, who had called in on his way home from work. Hammond would speak to Dave Smith and Dyson to Doug Grant as she had already been to his place investigating the arson of his summerhouse.

"So, Mr Smith, what time did Mr Preston come into your pub last evening?"

"It was just before six o'clock, as I remember serving him his usual pint. I know the time as I had the telly on in the bar and the news was just starting."

"You're sure that it was Mr Preston and about the time are you, sir?"

"Listen, I'd swear on my mother's grave if she was dead!"

"This is a very serious matter, Mr Smith. It's no time for flippancy."

"Sorry, sergeant." Smith duly admonished deliberately inflated Hammond's rank and accompanied it with a salute. Hammond was unimpressed.

"Can you confirm Mr Doug Grant was also in the bar at that time?"

"I can as we chatted about Farthing's misdemeanours. I served him just before I served Jim."

Meanwhile Dyson was, for the second time, ringing the doorbell on Doug Grant's front door. He, too, confirmed that Preston was in the pub by six o'clock the previous evening.

When both detectives were back together and exchanged information, Dyson rang her sergeant and Preston was released on bail pending further enquiries. However, before he was freed, he was asked by King, if he wasn't riding his motorbike the previous evening, who else would have had access to it? He said the keys were hung up in the office and his helmet was on top of the cabinet. He added that his partner couldn't ride a motorbike.

King thought if not Preston or Farthing then who? In any event, a potentially closed case was still very much alive.

After duly contacting the police station to trigger Preston's release, the detectives parked a hundred metres or so from the Bolberry-on-Sea church. Hammond took the first bunch of flowers. He entered the churchyard and casually walked around its perimeter. In one corner he stopped and looked at various headstones. He looked down at an overgrown grave dedicated to Anna Curtis; something didn't fit. She had died over a hundred years ago and yet there were half a dozen red roses stood in the moss-covered vase on the grave. On further inspection, he looked behind the stone and found nothing, though he thought it would make a good hiding place. He placed his flowers on a recently deceased child's grave and walked back to the car.

At Kingston church it was Dyson's turn to carry out the grieving charade. It took her over ten minutes, but she eventually came across the grave of Ava Sterling, tucked away in a distant corner of the churchyard. What attracted her to it were the half a dozen red roses on it, stood in a vase just like at the other grave in Bolberry-on-Sea. Placing her flowers on an adjacent grave of a more recently deceased person – so as not to unduly arouse the suspicion of the drugs collector – she casually looked behind the headstone; to her surprise and delight she found a shrink-wrapped package about the size of a margarine tub. As instructed she didn't touch it and walked away in the same nonchalant manner as her arrival.

When reporting her find to Hammond, he thought it wise to check with their boss.

King reasoned that it was impractical to keep a remote churchyard under surveillance in the hope the drugs would be collected and the collector arrested. He also thought that the news of Gilmour's arrest and detention might have spooked the collector. On balance he told Dyson to collect the package and bring it back with them. He would arrange for it to be handed to Inspector Best.

*

Fifteen minutes after the detectives had left the churchyard, a scrambler motorcycle quietly arrived in the church carpark. The black-clad figure was also interested in Ava Sterling's resting place. He stopped and stooped to arrange the roses on her grave and remove an imaginary weed from the side of the headstone. He then coolly walked away from the grave back to his bike. He was angry and perplexed in equal measure; the package he had come to collect had gone!

THIRTY-NINE

I n a marina in the Italian port of Naples, Fabio Gallo was on board the ketch *Marcass* about to leave port bound for the south coast of Devon. This trip would take several days and he had done it many times before, usually accompanied by his unmarried twin sister, Isabella, and her boyfriend, Marco Coppola. It was Coppola's boat; Fabio Gallo was the hired help.

The last voyage had initially been very successful until disaster had struck in the form of the boat owner falling overboard close to the coast. Gallo's sister was distraught at the time, but it was business as usual now or some people would not have been happy. The tragic event had happened over a fortnight before and another consignment had to be delivered. This time the crew would be two people only: Gallo and his sister. That wouldn't be easy, but with help on their arrival at the collection point, on a high tide, it would make the trip viable.

Under cover of darkness the night before departure, the *Marcass* had her cargo stored on board. The cabin area looked completely normal, but the void below decks was crammed with shrink-wrapped packages.

The twins were preparing to leave port under cover of darkness and both were in the cabin sharing a bottle of grappa. They were well paid for these trips and were living the high life on the back of the white powder. They had planned to leave the 'shin' of the Italian 'leg' in an hour. The weather report across the Tyrrhenian Sea was favourable. Isabella had grieved the loss of her boyfriend and was now ready for the next trip. Little did they know that this was the last grappa they would drink for a very long time. The calmness in the marina was about to be shattered.

"*Polizia armata! Non muoverti! Non muoverti!*"

Boots could be heard over the deck above and the cabin door was smashed open.

The first thing to enter the cabin was the barrel of a sub-machine gun. The twins had been told not to move and that had been followed by another instruction.

"*Mani sulla testa! Mani sulla testa!*"

They did as they had been told and put their hands on their head and were unceremoniously stood upright and then their arms forced down and behind their backs. Their hands were secured by wrist ties and they were escorted to two waiting vans; one in each. Their criminal lives were over.

The boat was impounded and at first light would be moved to a part of the marina used by the police. It wouldn't take long for them to locate the contraband.

*

I

Flight NA364 from Exeter Airport landed at Naples International Airport on time and the passengers were soon collecting their luggage from the carousel. Sandra Coppola left the terminal building and headed for the taxi rank; she never made it. Five Carabinieri surrounded her, two with pistols drawn, one took her case, while the others grabbed an arm each and frogmarched her to a waiting police van.

*

Chief Commissioner Borrelli in Naples sent an email to the chief constable of Devon and Cornwall Police in the knowledge that it would be passed to those directly involved in the investigation of the specific drug trafficking linked to the *Marcass*. Chief Superintendent Harper passed it to Acting Superintendent Roberts and he called King to his office.

"There's been a development on the case of the body on the beach. The Italian police have arrested three people and their chief has sent an email to the chief constable. I've copied it for you, inspector, so I'm hoping that's one case we can consider closed, save for what happened to the drugs the boat brought in. Anyway, well done to you and your team for identifying Coppola from his watch."

King was slightly shocked that he was receiving praise from his nemesis.

"Thank you, sir, I'll pass that on to DC Hammond."

The chief of police in Naples had written a narrative changing the various interviews from the first person to the third person and had provided an overview in English. King thought that was a nice touch fully warranted due to the information supplied by his team. The chief wrote in the *sans serif* font favoured by Italians:

"We were alerted to the possible link between some of our citizens and drug smuggling. I believe this was as a result of a body being washed up on a UK beach. Your investigation from very little evidence - an expensive watch - was excellent.

From the name we were given we traced the boat that was used in the smuggling. This was located in a port marina and two people were arrested initially and then a woman returning to Naples from the UK. The man and the woman are twins and the man wanted to cooperate with the investigation."

King knew that 'cooperate' was a euphemism for some sort of plea bargain. Reading between the lines of the impressive report written in English by the chief, he wondered if a bargain had been struck in exchange for a reduced prison term, no doubt for both of the twins. The inspector also suspected that they would be given a new identity when released; you don't cheat on the Mafia. He knew they may not be safe in prison as that criminal organisation has many tentacles that infiltrate many places.

He read on:

"In interview the full story was revealed. Sandra Coppola went to Devon to act as a guide to her brother. She befriended a woman, believed to be a local hairdresser, and used her car to look at the best beaches in your county called Devon, to unload large quantities of drugs from their boat. A shallow estuary was favoured. The boat was named after the brother and his sister. The brother, Marco, and the sister's real name, Cassandra, hence *Marcass*.

They worked out that leaving Naples when they planned would mean arrival after dark at the nominated Devon beach several days later. Cassandra Coppola had identified Mothecombe beach as the drop point on a high tide and moonlit night, so, hopefully, if no clouds, they could offload their cargo without the need for torches. The *Marcass* towed a small flat-bottomed dinghy, which could be used to get the drug packets to the shore. That part worked well as Miss Coppola was there to meet them and helped them transfer the drug packages to her borrowed car. Gallo said she would then take the drugs to a farmhouse near a place called Two Bridges, which she found using sat nav on her mobile. Two trips were necessary due to the quantity of packages and the size of the car. The second was the most difficult as the tide had started to recede.

On their way back, travelling under sail to avoid noise from the engine, Mr Coppola, maybe aroused by the successful drug drop and drinking from a bottle of grappa, wanted to make love to his girlfriend, Isabella Gallo, while her brother, Fabio, steered the boat towards the Straits of

Gibraltar. Mr Gallo said that Mr Coppola came on board some minutes later, naked and carrying his mobile. He knelt on the fixed bench in the well of the boat, rather than sitting on it, facing out to sea and began to make a call. A sudden gust of wind shifted the main sail violently from starboard to port causing the metal boom at the bottom of the sail to whip across the boat. It hit the back of Mr Coppola's head and knocked him into the sea together with his mobile. Both Mr Gallo and his sister frantically searched with torches, but saw no sign of him in the water. Isabella Gallo wanted to get in the dinghy, but the brother said it was too dangerous as the sea was getting rougher. They could not risk a distress call as they would have been asked to explain the purpose of their voyage. After searching for an hour, Mr Gallo decided to continue their journey. Isabella wanted to inform Cassandra Coppola of what had happened, but all her contact details were on her lover's mobile lost in the sea.

The Gallo twins are due in court shortly following their admissions. Cassandra Coppola has pleaded not guilty and her trial will take place in six weeks.

Thank you once again for your cooperation. Chief Commissioner Borrelli."

Commenting on the healthy state of Anglo-Italian relations, King shared the informative and congratulatory email with his team. He asked DC Dyson if, once again, she would visit Bolberry-on-Sea and break the news to Dawn Proud. Not an easy task to tell someone that their erstwhile tenant was in fact part of a drug gang who had used Proud's car to transport a large quantity of drugs. She later confirmed to the visibly upset hairdresser that Coppola was under arrest in Naples and awaiting trial. To add insult to injury, Ms Proud's car would be impounded, while Forensics carried out an inspection for evidence of drugs; this would help the Italian prosecutor's case.

King also asked his detective to speak with the Reverend Robert Brown as there appeared to be a clear link with drug supply and his parish churches. He asked her to ask if he'd seen anything suspicious at any of them over the last few weeks within the grounds of his churches.

The inspector took out a sherbet lemon and reflected on the communication from the commissioner. From all the information contained in the email, one sentence stood out:

"Gallo said she would then take the drugs to a farmhouse near a place called Two Bridges."

It was clear that Cassandra Coppola was not about to divulge the actual location of the drugs store as that would seal her guilt. King knew that was the best lead they had in identifying where a huge quantity of drugs were stored before being spread around the county.

From a bookcase in the detective's office, he reached for an Ordnance Survey Explorer map of Devon showing Dartmoor National Park. He spread out the detailed map and there, right in the middle, close to the River Dart, was the isolated village of Two Bridges. What did 'near a place called Two Bridges' mean? He decided on a two-mile radius from the prominent landmark of the only hotel in the village.

He reasoned that any storage place, required to house such large quantities of drugs, would require large outbuildings. He also knew the best way to identify a possible store was from the air. He contacted the Unmanned Aerial Systems Team to provide an 'eye in the sky' over Two Bridges. When the covert aerial surveillance was completed by a drone, he and his team, with advice from Inspector Jim Best, could watch the footage and see if they could close in on one of the most insidious crimes to ever impact upon the county of Devon.

FORTY

While King, Harris and Hammond worked feverishly on the memory sticks, DC Dyson was on her way, yet again, to Bolberry-on-Sea to see Dawn Proud and the Reverend Brown. Making Waves hair salon was closed as the owner was too upset to work. Dyson had arranged to see her at her shop and was duly let in without having to ring the out-of-hours door bell.

The detective explained that Sandra Coppola, full name Cassandra Coppola, had come to Devon to identify a beach where drugs could be delivered from her native Italy by her brother, who had subsequently drowned off the coast at Hope Cove. She must have found out about his death from a phone call or media source and fled back to Italy. Dyson finished her update by telling the disbelieving hairdresser that she had been arrested by the Italian police, charged with drug trafficking and had pleaded not guilty. Two other associates had also been arrested and had pleaded guilty. Dyson informed her Miss Coppola was being held in Poggioreale prison in downtown Naples and was due to stand trial in six weeks' time.

She was also told she may be called as a witness, not an accessory, by the Italian police. The detective hoped this wouldn't require her going to Naples, rather making a written statement. The hairdresser took the news stoically, but as soon as the detective left, she broke down.

*

Dyson had also arranged to see the Reverend Brown at St Paul's church in the village. She told him that it was suspected the church graveyards at all five churches in his diocese were being used to hide drugs for collection by a dealer. The reverend was horrified that a house of God, as he put it, could be used in such a way.

"From the information we have received it would appear that the drugs are left behind specific headstones in the five churchyards on successive Sundays to be collected later that day. Have you noticed anything suspicious or seen anyone you don't recognise loitering in the vicinity of any church property recently?"

"I'm sorry, but I can't say I have, detective. I spend most of my time inside the churches. I'll ask my curate."

With that he shouted the name 'Lucas' and when the curate joined them from the vestry, the reverend introduced Lucas Peverell. Dyson summarised her previous question.

"Come to think of it, I have seen someone here and over at All Hallows in Ringmore. It was a tall man wearing a flat cap, you know a tweedy thing, brown cavalry twill trousers, a waxed coat and green wellies. At the Ringmore church, the car park is right opposite and I saw him drive off in an expensive car; I think it was a black Range Rover." He could have been describing a prominent village figure; all that was missing was the name. As Dyson hadn't actually seen the colonel, she was none the wiser.

"And when was this, Mr Peverell?"

"I think it was the first Sunday in the month whatever date that was. I was on duty at a service taken by the reverend."

"The third of March?"

"Yeah, that must have been the time. Exeter Chiefs were playing at Sandy Park that Sunday and I couldn't go. I wish they wouldn't play on Sundays."

"That's a remarkable memory you have, Mr Peverell, to remember what he was wearing in so much detail from so long ago." Dyson had said it more in disbelief than a plaudit.

"Thank you." Peverell took it as praise.

"And you said you also saw the man here in Bolberry-on-Sea? The same man?"

"Same bloke. I think that was about a week later."

"What was the man doing when you saw him?"

"He was carrying a bunch of flowers and seemed to be wandering around looking at the headstones."

"And what were you doing at the time you saw this man?"

"We hold services throughout Sundays at the different churches in the diocese and I help the reverend as I've mentioned already. I was popping to the village stores here in Bolberry to get some milk as we have a coffee after our first service."

Dyson noted his observations and wasn't sure if the village stores opened on a Sunday. She thanked him for the information then headed back to the police station.

*

The other detectives were printing out the documents held on the memory sticks marked 'DD' and 'P' having discounted the 'D' stick as it didn't relate to the current investigations. Sergeant Harris was working on 'DD' and DC Hammond on the 'P' stick. King was looking over the printed copies of what Morris had written on both and it made for very interesting reading.

The investigative journalist had amassed anecdotal evidence and had diligently recorded what he had been told and what he suspected. His information came from unnamed drug user sources.

The intelligence on County Lines he had recorded was that the supply was being controlled from Manchester and that vast quantities were stored ready for distribution somewhere on Dartmoor. The information didn't come cheaply or without risk. Not only to the person passing on the details for cash, but to Morris himself, as he found to his cost when his car was rammed. He had assumed that the Dartmoor location, if true, had two key benefits: seclusion and easy access to the cities, towns and villages around Devon.

It transpired he had correctly identified Gilmour's house as a main drugs distribution point in Plymouth and he had also pinpointed another house on the other side of the city. King made a note to pass that information to Inspector Jim Best so that place could be raided too, skipping the surveillance process. Apart from the Plymouth Pilgrim pub, he had personally witnessed two other pubs in the city where drugs were being openly traded.

From his narrative it became clear he had gone undercover at one place, masquerading as a user. This was a high-risk strategy as, had he been discovered as an impostor, the consequences would have been terminal. From one file it became apparent that Morris had also found out that drugs were coming into Devon by light aircraft from the north of Spain and by boat, delivered under cover of darkness to isolated coves around the south coast. He suspected from Italy, but had, it seemed, not yet adequately researched that potential avenue.

Tellingly the most recent document he had prepared, judging by the date, began to cast doubt that the drug dealers were responsible for the attempt on his life. Increasingly, his other investigation concerning corruption at the local district council was gaining greater prominence. The people involved with that dishonesty, like the drug pushers, also had a lot to lose if their scam was uncovered. The more he read, the more King admired the journalist as he had gleaned enough from speaking with his girlfriend, Karen White, to know his motivation wasn't money;

this was a one-man crusade against wrongdoing in society.

What the inspector wanted more than anything else from Morris's investigation was a direct link to the so-called Baron and also to the drugs stash. The video footage from the drone would be available that afternoon and he had arranged a viewing for his team at two o'clock in the main conference room.

When Dyson arrived back, King reviewed what she had found in relation to the drugs investigation at the church and Dawn Proud's reaction to the news of Sandra Coppola's subterfuge. She reported the disclosure to Proud and the conversations she had with the Reverend Brown and his curate. Mr Peverell said he had witnessed a very dapper man lurking around the churchyards of some of the churches in the diocese on Sundays and provided a very detailed description of the man.

King thanked Dyson and then deferred to Harris and Hammond on the fact-finding over the alleged corruption. They reported what they had read, alternating on giving the information they had discovered.

It appeared from his files that Morris's inquisitive instincts on possible corruption within the planning department of the district council had been piqued, inadvertently, by his girlfriend on a how-was-your-day catch up chat over dinner one evening a few months before. Morris referred to their chat on a Microsoft Word document in his files. He had downloaded from the district council website, minutes of three planning meetings held over the last year. He thought number four would be the application lodged by Build Great Homes Limited relating to the development of twenty-five executive homes near Bolberry-on-Sea.

The three he had obtained were all similar in nature to the Bolberry application in that they were all developments of twenty to forty executive homes overlooking the sea that would fetch a premium when sold. They were in Salcombe, Noss Mayo and Dartmouth. Harris and Hammond were aware of the last site as they had visited it in relation to the clifftop ramming, Hammond having expertly discovered the vehicle, but not who was driving it that night.

The journalist had identified that there were certain similarities between the three planning applications and he had documented his findings. All three applications were made by Build Great Homes. All three were objected to at parish council level. All three had been 'sponsored' by Mr Paul Armitage. All three had eventually been approved by the district councillors. Armitage had skilfully dismissed many of the objections and commended the positive aspects. On every occasion in the chamber, he reminded councillors that they were under pressure from central government to allow developments due to the chronic housing shortage. The councillors knew their place in the overall order of governance.

For his part, Morris had linked the rendezvous his girlfriend had seen in the Seven Stars Hotel, when a laptop case had changed hands, with skulduggery. He figured it was payment for services rendered and had documented his suspicions.

After his tragic murder, Karen White had phoned Inspector King and told him that her friend Debbie Norris had unintentionally alerted Armitage to the fact they had witnessed the handover. Before then there was no link to an investigative journalist; that was about to change.

What Morris didn't know was a few months before, when he came to collect his girlfriend from the council offices where she worked, as her car was being serviced, he was being watched. Armitage's office faced the front of the building so he could see who was arriving and leaving. As usual that afternoon he was gazing out of the window rather than working and he saw a car pull into one of the bays reserved for visitors. He didn't think anything of it until the man stepped from his car and headed for reception. He had seen that man before. He then noticed Morris and Karen White come out of the building together and get into his car.

Armitage had then casually strolled up to Debbie Norris's desk and said he had noticed Karen didn't have her car today and wondered if she needed a lift home.

Norris said she had a lift from her boyfriend and added that his working hours were very flexible as he was a freelance investigative journalist.

Armitage was taken aback, but kept his composure. He remembered the first time he had noticed Morris was at the enquiries counter at the council offices. The second occasion was when he sat in the public gallery during a council planning meeting. The last time, which was after his profession had been divulged, was at the extraordinary parish council meeting held towards the end of the previous month at Bolberry-on-Sea when the BGH planning application was discussed.

When Armitage had recognised Morris at the meeting that night in Bolberry-on-Sea village hall, he had texted his accomplice, alerting him to the presence of the journalist. He had already told his associate of his concerns when he had first suspected he was on their case. Did he but know it, but the accomplice was also present at the meeting, sat at the back, with his mobile on silent but vibrate for incoming calls. This presented the perfect opportunity to eliminate the interfering busybody.

Although King and his team were unaware that Armitage had been alerted that his corruption was under scrutiny and about to be exposed, they had enough information from Morris's files to make an arrest.

"Lucy, I'd like you to do something." King addressed his sergeant. "Make discreet enquiries at the district council offices; I suggest you ask to speak to the head of HR. Their team will have access to pay records. Find out who Armitage has his bank account with for salary payments and contact the bank. Ask for a copy of the transactions on any account he holds with them. I'm particularly interested in payments into any account."

*

Early morning turned into late morning and copies of bank statements had been emailed to Sergeant

Harris. The other three detective colleagues were still working through Morris's data. King took the printed copies of the bank statements; he knew what he was looking for. Sherbet lemon time. It took him several minutes as they had all the transactions over the last year. He eventually came to a special saver account. Before he began to work his way through the numerous deposits and withdrawals, he had jotted down on a piece of paper three dates. He took them from Morris's records. They were the dates when the three district council planning meetings had been held when the particular applications of interest were approved, thanks to Armitage's support.

Looking at the bank statements, King looked for large deposits soon after those dates. Sure enough, within five working days of all three, £10,000 had been paid into his saver account... in cash.

King looked at his watch. "Sam and Alex, if you could look at the drone footage, with Inspector Best, and try and identify a likely location for a drugs store. It won't be obvious; will no doubt be well protected; probably have large outbuildings; and, above all, will be very isolated. These villains don't like neighbours.

"Lucy, you and I will pay a visit to the district council offices. If Armitage is not on a late lunch or a site visit, he should be at work. Let's go and confront him with some of the findings. It'll be very interesting to see how this smoothtalker justifies his inflated bank balance."

FORTY-ONE

King and Harris arrived at the district council offices, supported by two uniformed officers, and parked at the front of the main building in the visitors' car park. As ever, Paul Armitage had one eye on his work and the other on arrivals and departures; he was nosey by nature. By the time the detectives had entered reception he had grabbed his jacket off the back of his chair and was heading down the back staircase to the staff car park behind the offices.

He had been on tenterhooks ever since he suspected he was the subject of Morris's unwanted attention. Even the news that the investigative journalist had been murdered did not stop him worrying; in fact it heightened his tension. Journalists kept a record of their work and his dishonesty might soon be exposed.

As the detectives were being shown to his office – with uniformed officers closely following – he was already on his way to his home in Totnes a few miles away. He reckoned he had about a maximum of fifteen minutes to gather a few things and be away before the police arrived at his house. He hurriedly packed a small suitcase with his passport, some toiletries, underwear and several changes of clothes. He was back in his car in a little over ten minutes. He was heading for Dartmouth, a journey of fourteen miles that would take him less than half an hour. He was heading, in his mind, to sanctuary.

He arrived undetected at the luxury apartment overlooking the Dartmouth Marina and quickly garaged his car. As he closed the front door he was slightly out of breath and sweating. He reached for his mobile and jabbed 'Contacts'. He selected the person he wanted to call and jabbed the green phone icon.

"Baron," came the swift reply.

"I've been rumbled. The police were at my workplace less than an hour ago and I've escaped to your apartment in Dartmouth. I'm pretty sure I wasn't followed and I've garaged my car. I packed a few things including my passport. What shall I do now?"

"I am flying down later, so I'll meet you at the farm at about six o'clock. Leave your car and take the Range Rover; the keys are hanging up in the kitchen cupboard on the right as you enter the kitchen. Wait until it's dark as they will be on the lookout for you." 'The Baron' was advising him what to do more out of self-preservation than any allegiance to this weak individual. With that he rang off and Armitage poured himself a large whiskey.

Back at the council offices it was obvious he had left in a hurry as he hadn't even switched off his computer and the coffee on his desk was still fairly hot.

King obtained his home address from the council's HR department and also issued an APW (All Ports Warning), which alerted all ports, airports and international railway stations of a suspect's name, description and that he was wanted for questioning. The Automatic Number Plate Recognition system was also updated with the registration of his car.

When the detectives arrived at his home address and gained entry, it was obvious he had left in a hurry. A cursory inspection of his house did not reveal any incriminating evidence. It was noted that the space in his concertina file headed 'PASSPORT' was empty.

*

At Charles Cross Police Station, four detectives were closely studying footage taken earlier that day from a police drone that had flown over Two Bridges and the surrounding locality. Detective Inspector Best and Detective Constables Dyson, Hammond and Baxter were viewing the images, which had been projected onto a screen, being viewed in conjunction with an Ordnance Survey map of the area; DC Ken Baxter was operating the images and Hammond the map.

They were looking for an isolated large house, probably with outbuildings, that was secure. This last prerequisite was difficult to differentiate as most large houses had substantial security, for one thing to keep out various animals that roamed the National Park.

Best asked DC Baxter to stop the footage now and again if he thought he had detected a likely place. When a possible place was found, Hammond identified the property using the coordinates shown on the screen with the map.

"That is Dartmoor Rise House and certainly seems to tick all our boxes."

Inspector Best wasn't so sure. It just didn't seem to him like a drugs store. He should know as he worked day in and day out with illegal substances and hiding places.

"Let's not discount that place, but keep looking."

Over the next twenty minutes, three more possible locations were identified. As the footage rolled on, the viewers began to consider going back to the possible sightings they had already identified.

Then they came to Bracken Hill Farm. Once again Best asked for a freeze frame.

"That's the place we're looking for, I'm sure of it!"

This eureka moment was timely as just then King and Harris entered the room. The others had already been informed of Armitage's disappearance.

Best updated them on their aerial search and the properties they had earmarked as potential locations for the drugs store. The others looked quizzically at him when he was unequivocal that Bracken Hill Farm was the place they were seeking; all the other detectives then peered more closely at the frozen image.

Hammond offered: "Why do you think it's this place, sir? Solar panels? Wind turbine? Vehicles out front?"

"None of those, detective, as additional energy devices are commonplace on Dartmoor to supplement other energy supplies."

"Worn perimeter path?" King offered.

"That's one, Richard. If you look next to the hedge that marks the boundary, you can see a path has been worn all the way around. Just like you would get in the cage of a big cat at a zoo. I'm not suggesting the track here has been made by a lion, but probably a dog or dogs are being used to patrol the garden, which to me looks more like a secure compound.

"There are two other things I think look rather suspicious; first the gates to the property. Ken, please zoom in on the entrance gates. I'd call them substantial and totally unnecessary for a normal property. Note the CCTV camera you can just see on a pole close to the right-hand gate pillar. The occupiers are overly keen to protect something in that house."

"And what's the last thing that worries you, Jim?" King asked his fellow inspector.

"Go back to the footage showing the front of the house, please, Ken. Freeze it there. If you look at the bottom of the screen, what do you see?"

King offered: "Something bright orange. A windsock?"

"Exactly. Presumably the occupier uses a helicopter to get to and from his property. The size of the compound and unevenness of the ground wouldn't support a runway for an aircraft, so the sock must be for a helicopter. A pilot would need to know wind direction and wind speed when landing and taking off. The surprising thing is there's no obvious helipad! I'm speculating, but that may be part of the deception of this property. It's pretending to be something it's not. A drugs store masquerading as just a private house – granted an unwelcoming private house – trying to be unobtrusive."

The examination of the flyover continued and previous possible places reviewed and discounted. Best was adamant; this was the place they were searching for and, such was his insistence, he convinced the others.

King had seen enough: "Well done, Jim. So, Bracken Hill Farm is the probable place where the drugs are being distributed from across the whole of our county; even the name is a misnomer and further deceit. I doubt anything has been farmed there for years, except maybe cannabis!"

Little did he know his words would turn out to be a very accurate assessment.

FORTY-TWO

Having identified the probable drugs store close to Two Bridges, the inspectors, King and Best, set out their reasons why they thought they had correctly identified it to an attentive Acting Superintendent Roberts. He may have had his interpersonal failings, but he wasn't stupid. He knew any progress on the drugs scourge would impress the chief superintendent and the chief constable. His inspectors made a compelling case for a planned raid on Bracken Hill Farm. They stressed that time was of the essence before the main protagonists were spooked.

Roberts involved his boss in the decision to mount a full-blown raid on the so-called farmhouse and it was duly authorised around lunchtime to take place later that day. Authorisation was a necessary process. Planning such an event was essential as to undertake a raid against potentially desperate people was life-endangering. The planning was intense and the decision was made that it would be carried out that evening under cover of darkness at precisely 18.30 hours.

*

'The Baron' was pleased when Morris was no longer a thorn in the side of his planning interference; he had much to lose if either of his lucrative operations was exposed. He had been instrumental in it happening: first the warning-off attack, which hadn't deterred the tenacious journalist, and then his murder. However, in hindsight, his murder had alerted the police to his criminal activities, which were coming under increasing scrutiny. Deciding he had to personally intervene in the situation he and his cohorts were now facing, he began to make plans; he hoped they were more than damage limitation.

It was late afternoon when he switched on the ignition of his Bell 505 helicopter and took off from his palatial mansion, 'Baron's Retreat', at Rossmill Lane in Altrincham, Manchester – with its private helipad – heading for Bracken Hill Farm.

*

The briefing for the raid on the farmhouse was held mid-afternoon and took an hour, involving over twenty officers, some of whom would be armed. All of King's team would be involved and Roberts also insisted on being part of the raiding party. He said he wanted to give his boss a first-hand account of the successful outcome, which was one interpretation; glory-seeking was another.

*

With the raid scheduled for later that day, after the briefing King wanted his detectives using the time while they were waiting for it to begin to pursue their other investigations; he knew there was still much more work to do.

Progressing the scrutiny of the evidence relating to the Jane Ferris and Dan Morris murders was a priority. King and his team, along with Inspector Best and DC Baxter, were in the main office of the police station. Richard King was in determined mood.

"Right, let's start with the Morris murder. We know he had upset the drug gang and he was also gathering evidence about possible corruption in the planning department of the district council. The first was well documented by him and the second seems to be confirmed as Armitage has, in colloquial terms, done a runner. The ramming of Morris's car is linked to Build Great Homes as it was the company vehicle that was used. There is also the more than coincidental discovery of a military button at a crime scene in Bolberry-on-Sea with the other clutched in his hand when he was attacked in Sutton Harbour."

Dyson wanted to speak: "Sir, when I arrested Preston he shouted something about what a way to treat a vet! I didn't pay it much heed at the time, but when you mentioned military, I think by the word 'vet' he meant 'veteran', as in ex-member of the armed forces. When we got back from interviewing Mr Grant – we found the first button on his drive – I checked out the motto on it. You were right, sir, about the military link. I translated the French motto into English: 'Evil be to him that evil thinks'. It's used on the badge of the Royal Engineers."

"Good work, Sam. Could you go and make enquiries of the people that deal with pensions for the armed services and check on Preston. Find out his regiment."

With that Dyson left the meeting.

"While we wait for Sam to check that out, let's focus on the murder of Jane Ferris. We arrested Preston as we think his motorbike was used to commit the crime, but he had an alibi. We know Farthing hasn't got a motorcycle licence, which doesn't mean he can't ride a motorbike, but who else had access to Preston's bike? I can think of at least three others: the Garner lads, who tried to intimidate us when Sam and I were in their dad's field where the houses are planned; there's also Lucas Peverell. He rides a motorbike that he uses to get around the various churches he helps out in as the curate."

Dyson rejoined the meeting and Hammond spoke: "When I went with DC Dyson to arrest Preston there were two motorbikes outside; one belonged to Preston and the other to Peverell. Farthing said that Peverell works at the garage part time. I read Preston's statement, when he was arrested, and he said he had left his motorbike locked in the garage and walked to the pub. I assume as the curate is an employee he has keys to the place. There was nothing stopping him from riding his own bike to the garage, swapping bikes and robbing the post office. The cheeky devil could even have used Preston's helmet!"

"If I could add something, sir." Dyson had heard the bike swap account. "When we interviewed Mr Bayliss, the postmaster, he told us that apart from remembering the logo on the helmet the robber was wearing, he also saw his T-shirt. As he stuffed money into his open hoodie he saw a logo that Alex later identified as being Exeter Chiefs rugby club logo. When I spoke to Peverell, he told me he was a fan and moaned he couldn't go to see his team as they were playing on a Sunday. He was prevented from watching his team due to his ecclesiastical duties."

Inspector Best had sat listening to the exchanges and joined in: "It's looking increasingly likely he has become our main suspect as our robber and murderer. If I could add one other thing: as you know, I'm particularly concerned with the drug investigations and have been looking at the piece of paper Inspector King found at Gilmour's house when we raided it, showing drug drops at churches in the area. I particularly remember the top line."

On his mobile phone, he then produced a copy of the list and showed it to his colleagues:
MAR: DELIVER TO LP

"I think the LP referred to is Lucas Peverell. He's the link with the church that Dan Morris was trying to establish. Due to his role in the diocese he was above suspicion; it was the perfect deception. Who would suspect him any more than they would the Reverend Brown? We didn't and yet all the time he's been collecting drugs, presumably delivered from Bracken Hill Farm, and selling them to all the villages where he helps out at the five churches. He may even have been supplying Gilmour."

Dyson picked up the thread from Inspector Best: "When I interviewed him, he provided a detailed description of someone he said he'd seen hanging around the churchyards. I was surprised at the time he could recall so vividly the man he'd allegedly seen. I now think that was a complete red herring. There was no man and it was Peverell that was collecting from behind designated headstones and then distributing the drugs.

"One other thing that didn't ring true, sir, was when I asked him when he'd seen this man he said it was when he popped to the village stores in Bolberry-on-Sea on that Sunday to get milk for coffee for him and the reverend; I checked and the village stores don't open on a Sunday until after Easter."

Best completed the circumstantial circle.

"No doubt on a day off from his curate duties and garage work, he would head to Bracken Hill Farm on his scrambler with the money he collected, minus his cut."

King was mindful to avoid too much speculation as he knew it was too easy to make the facts fit the fanciful theories. However, he thought the narrative was quite compelling.

"We've got time before the raid to have a word with the curate. Sam and Alex, take a quick trip out and bring him in for questioning, that's if you can find him."

"Before we do that, sir, I've got the information you wanted on Preston. I checked with the armed forces pensions people and their records show that James

Terence Preston was indeed in receipt of a pension from his time serving in the Falklands among other campaigns. His regiment was the Royal Engineers."

"Thanks, Sam. You two get after Peverell and Lucy and I will pursue Preston. Although we're going to the same place, let's travel in separate cars as your man could be in any one of the five parishes. I'll update AS Roberts before we leave."

Turning to his fellow inspector he added: "Jim, I'll make sure we're back by five o'clock at the latest, so we can be properly prepared for the raid at six thirty."

With that King asked his sergeant to get the car ready and arrange for two uniformed officers to go with them, while he spoke with his boss.

After ten minutes he joined her in the car: "AS Roberts is somewhat uneasy about us acting on circumstantial evidence and he's right to be apprehensive. I told him we are just making progress on an investigation; making good use of the time before the raid later on. If I'd told him what we really think, that we're going to nail Peverell and Preston, he might have started talking about search warrants. That could have taken ages. If these two are the villains as we suspect, they've been living on borrowed time; that time is about to end."

FORTY-THREE

Two Bridges is a remote location at the very centre of the Dartmoor National Park. It boasts a delightful three-star hotel, aptly called the Two Bridges Hotel, but little else. About a mile from the hotel down a single-track lane stood an isolated farmhouse.

The long drive leading to it was gated, but not with the archetypal five-bar gate; this entrance was much more substantial. It was set about halfway along the 200-metre-long approach to the house. Hinged on solid gate posts were steel mesh electronic gates. The entrance to the lane, immediately off the main through road, had an infrared motion detector; when the beam was interrupted by movement, an alarm would sound in the farmhouse. The occupants didn't like surprise visitors; truth be told, they didn't like any visitors, save for those doing business.

Fixed to one post was a key-opened letter box; fixed to the other a sinister sign that read: 'BEWARE. DOBERMANS RUNNING FREE'. These were not pets. The reputation of this breed as being quick, fearless and intelligent made them ideal guard dogs, which is exactly what they were. Their masters didn't use their birth names; they had renamed them Lean and Mean; both were both. They were to Bracken Hill Farm what the hound was to the Baskervilles.

Each dog was fitted with a shock collar that was remotely controlled. These devices could deliver a shock as a way of keeping them under control. Much like Pavlov's dog, when the Russian physiologist discovered a learning procedure for dogs; when he rang a bell, his dog knew he was about to be fed. When the Dobermans received a shock, delivered remotely, they knew they had to be obedient and not attack. Evidently the occupants valued their privacy. Everything about the entrance to the farm was deliberately unwelcoming.

The high Berberis hedge completely surrounded the house and formed a natural compound. This dense, thorny, evergreen shrub, forming a two-metre-high barrier, would deter even the most determined trespasser. The occupiers would have preferred a two-metre-high chain link fence, topped with razor wire, but that would have drawn unwanted attention. A rabbit occasionally, with some difficulty, weaved its way through the base of the hedge into the garden ground only to be ripped apart by the Dobermans. So frequent were the dog patrols and general vigilance, they had worn a muddy path all around the inside of the compound, as detected by Inspector Best from the aerial view provided by the drone.

In the far corner was a solid wooden door, barely visible through the overgrown hedge, which provided the only other exit from the property and that could only be opened from inside the compound.

The long pot-holed drive eventually led to an apparently dilapidated farmhouse with two equally ramshackle barns. A small garden shed was used to kennel the two dogs and sturdy chains with leather collars formed their leashes; these were seldom used. They were fed once a day and the only training they had received was not to attack the occupants and 'The Baron', who was a regular visitor.

Two nearly new Land Rover Discovery vehicles, both black in colour, and a big black Nissan Navara car stood close to the front of the main buildings.

The interior of the farmhouse was in complete contrast to the exterior. The front door, with its flaking paint, led to a shabby hall, which belied the rest of the house's interior. It gave way to a palatial lounge with three expensive Stressless chairs handmade in Norway – arranged around a sixty-inch TV. The room was untidy, but, at the same time, opulent. The kitchen had every labour-saving gadget ever invented and there was no expense spared in the rest of the house either.

The other thing that was unusual about it was what was propped up just inside the front door. Two loaded twelve-bore shotguns rested on their butts on either side of the door. The arsenal was completed by two handguns, one kept in a drawer in the kitchen and the other in a bedroom upstairs.

No farm animals roamed free in the surrounding fields and certainly not in the dog-patrolled confines of the farmhouse grounds. All was not as it seemed at

Bracken Hill Farm; referring to it as a farm was a gross misnomer. Its outward appearance was carefully designed to deceive the casual observer. A more apt title would have been 'depot' or 'supply store'. It was ideally situated in the middle of Dartmoor to serve its customers in towns and villages on and around the moor as King had earlier asserted.

Three people controlled every aspect of the 'farm': the distribution of drugs, the collection of money owing, the CCTV, the dogs and the 'greenhouse'.

Two brothers and a woman, Nick and Wayne Brody and Evelyn Whitaker, lived in the isolated farmhouse and they were very well paid for their labours. They received cocaine from wherever 'The Baron' had sourced it: delivered by boat to isolated coves, by aircraft landing at remote airfields, by lorries from the nearby ferry port of Plymouth or delivered in a helicopter by the man himself.

Each had their designated drug drop, which took them to all parts of Devon, usually two or three times a week depending on demand. They rotated the places they delivered to so as not to be recognised as regular visitors. In different places they had different methods of leaving their high-value packages.

Not wanting to be seen handing them over, they devised many surreptitious ways. The chosen way for the tame curate was to use headstones in churches around the South Hams. When the drugs had been delivered, half a dozen red roses were placed on the chosen grave. The graves used were chosen because they were on the perimeter of the graveyard. Also, they were unlikely to have any walk-by mourners, because the deceased were decades old. Ideally, an unused vase would be available in front of the headstones; this was so the red roses could be stood erect to make it easier for the person collecting the drugs to identify the location. If there was no vase, that was easily remedied by taking an unused one from an adjacent equally age-old grave. This was because the choice of grave sometimes varied; predictability could make people suspicious. On collection, checking the name of the person buried against his list, the curate would move the roses to another more recent burial mound.

The tenants seldom saw their employer, but they were very aware of his power. Neither did they know his name, only his nickname. 'The Baron' gave them their orders and controlled the supply chain. They were very well paid, lived rent free and did what they were told to do. They knew better than to cheat him, knowing that if they did, the punishment would be swift and brutal.

The entrance to the bigger of the two barns was by way of two huge doors, which looked big enough to accommodate a double-decker bus. The inside of this building was devoid of farm equipment or stored animal feed. All it housed was a big flatbed trailer with towbar, measuring four metres wide and eight metres long, with no side panels. A white cross, like a Swiss flag, each arm a metre wide, was painted on the bed of the trailer, rather than the standard H seen on most helipads. On each corner it had a halogen light facing directly up and these were all linked to a single connector near the towbar that could be plugged into the electric supply of the towing vehicle.

The smaller barn didn't appear to be used for any farm-related tasks either as it too was virtually empty, save for a quad bike in one corner, two brooms resting against the back wall and, in the other corner, what looked like discarded shrink wrap. The concrete floor was lightly strewn with straw, placed there simply to disguise its true use; the deception was complete. This was the so-called 'greenhouse', which they all tended. A two-metre-square wooden trap door, with iron pull ring, when opened revealed a wooden staircase leading down to a vast underground cellar. Hidden under the shabby barn, the cellar was crammed with over 500 cannabis plants at various stages of growth, from cuttings to middling on to mature plants ready for processing and selling. The underground hot house consumed vast amounts of electricity to give the plants the best chance to accelerate growth. The 'gardeners' knew that problems with growing cannabis are many and that's why the plants demand regular attention. Nutrient deficiencies need to be addressed; overwatering can stunt growth; too high humidity is not good; poor air circulation damages development. All these things and more can have a devastating impact on two things: turnover and profit.

The farmhouse had an outbuilding joined onto its rear with three sides comprising full-length louvre panels. On any particular morning when a light covering of snow could be seen on the roof of the farmhouse and barns, no snow would settle on the roof of the attached outbuilding. Not only was there no snow on the roof, there was none on the ground for two metres surrounding it. The hot air flowing from the louvres would probably have melted ice!

The brothers and Whitaker had been alerted to the next visit by 'The Baron'. He would be landing at about five thirty that evening and they knew to make preparations. This involved connecting the Nissan to the flatbed trailer, connecting the electrical supply – that would power the improvised landing lights – and be ready to have it in place just before landing. A spotlight on the back of the Nissan would illuminate the bed of the trailer and the windsock. The halogen up-lights would guide the pilot to the landing zone.

They were well rehearsed and well prepared for that particular visitor. They had been told to expect other visitors that evening.

FORTY-FOUR

DC Sam Dyson was yet again on her way to Bolberry-on-Sea to make her second arrest. Although they had good cause to arrest Preston for the murder of postmistress Jane Ferris, his alibi meant he couldn't have committed the crime and had been released.

This time she and DC Hammond were on the track of Lucas Peverell. All was not as it seemed with Mr Peverell. He was now suspected of the murder of Jane Ferris and was also implicated in the distribution of drugs around South Devon.

He wasn't at his flat in the village. St Paul's church, understandably, was locked as it was mid-afternoon. Next they tried the vicarage and the Reverend Brown was home. The detectives were short on time as they had to be back at the police station in Plymouth in a little over an hour to prepare for the raid.

"Good afternoon, reverend." There was a sense of urgency in Dyson's tone of voice. "We are looking for Lucas Peverell. Do you know where he is? We've checked his home address and he's not there."

"Lucas? Why do you need to see Lucas?"

"We are following a lead in two investigations and we think he might be able to help us."

"Sorry, I'm not sure where he went. He left about an hour ago on his motorbike."

Hammond didn't want a completely wasted journey, so asked if he would mind opening the church. The reverend was perplexed, but readily agreed. He walked the short distance to the church rather quicker than normal as he sensed the detectives were in a hurry. They weren't entirely sure what they were looking for, but were content to spend half an hour searching the church, hoping to find some sort of incriminating evidence. The last half hour was needed to inspect the graveyard at this church and one other.

"Is the vestry through here, reverend?" Hammond asked and the vicar nodded. Ever since the detectives told him they were looking for his curate, he was speechless.

"Where does the curate change? Which are his vestments?"

When pointed out, his area was no more than an open-fronted cupboard, which Hammond duly searched. He didn't find anything and didn't expect to as Peverell would have been much more careful than to hide something in such an obvious place. He and Dyson then searched the rest of the vestry as the Reverend Brown looked on, sat in a nearby pew in obvious dismay. Next the detectives searched the sanctuary where the altar stood as the centrepiece. The reverend became uneasy and asked them to respect the sanctity of the church.

Taking great care not to disturb anything on the

altar, Dyson squeezed behind it and gently parted the white, embroidered cloth at the back. She couldn't see anything in the dark void under the sacred table and was about to straighten the cloth to how she'd found it, when Hammond passed his mobile to her with the torch app switched on. She gratefully took it and, once more, reverently parted the cloth. Now illuminated, the first thing she saw was cobwebs; the second thing was a shoebox tucked into the far corner under the altar. She had to kneel and stretch to retrieve it. Brushing the cobwebs from her arm she took it into the nave of the church paying due respect to the sanctuary.

She handed Hammond his mobile and placed the box on a pew seat, close to where the reverend was sitting. She reached into her pocket and took out two blue latex gloves. She then took off the lid, and to the vicar's astonishment, revealed a rolled wad of £20 notes, neatly held in place by an elastic band. Also in the box were several small plastic packets of white powder. She first took out the banknotes and guessed they amounted to several hundred pounds. Then she lifted a single packet to her nose and said the only word that had been spoken between the three of them for some time: "Cocaine."

Hammond rang Sergeant Harris who had now arrived at Preston's place with Inspector King, not far from the church where the detectives were explaining to a bereft vicar that his curate, in all probability, was corrupt. They spared him the specifics of drug dealing and murder.

*

The inspector and sergeant had first gone to Farthing's garage and having bcen told Preston was not at work, drove to his home. As they arrived at his address, Sergeant Harris told her boss of the find at St Paul's church and he was delighted; less so that Peverell was nowhere to be seen.

The miserable mechanic's house looked deserted and, after ringing the doorbell, they walked around it in different directions and peered through the windows as they went. They both arrived at the back door at the same time. King was not about to be thwarted: he felt sure that Preston was a murderer.

"You know, sergeant, we really should return to the station and apply to a judge for a search warrant. Then we wait at his or her convenience to justify why we want to search this house. That will take hours, certainly, if not days."

With that he turned to face the door and with the flat of his shoe and considerable force kicked it open.

"Some owners are really careless, leaving their houses unlocked, don't you think? Once we've established he's not here, you search downstairs and I'll take upstairs. We can't take too long as we need to be back at the station to get ready for the raid."

The place smelled of cigars and a full ashtray of cigar butts meant the smell wasn't going to go away. After about ten minutes Harris had found a pair of boots and was studying them when her boss shouted: "Lucy!" She rightly interpreted his call as, "Come up." She took the boots with her. When she entered the bedroom, King was standing in front of a wardrobe with both its doors open.

"Look what I've found; gloves, please, Lucy." She was already wearing latex gloves that she had put on as soon as she entered the house. She put the boots on the floor and handed two gloves to her inspector.

Neatly folded in the bottom of the tall cupboard was what looked like a British Army coat. He took a spare hanger from the rail, lifted the heavy, woollen greatcoat and hung it on a sturdy coat hook on the back of the bedroom door.

"Just as I thought, sergeant, two buttons missing. Well we know where they are: both in an evidence bag back at the station. Let's see what else we can find."

With that he opened the front of the coat, but saw nothing untoward. In the large outside pocket on the right-hand side of the coat he pulled out a key fob and held it up. "If I'm not mistaken, this is the duplicate key to a black Ford Ranger car."

He then paused as he remembered what pathologist Gleeson had written in his autopsy report: *"He confirmed the weapon used was a narrow-bladed implement, rather like a stiletto, not a flat-bladed knife; deduced from the puncture wound. It had penetrated the victim's ribcage just below his right nipple up to a depth of approximately fifteen centimetres, or six inches, possibly suggesting the attacker was left-handed."* He looked at his sergeant then put his hand in the large left-hand pocket of the coat and pulled out a rag. He placed it on top of a chest of drawers and carefully unfolded it to reveal a bloodstained screwdriver.

"If I'm not mistaken, Lucy, this is the weapon that ended Dan Morris's life."

There was a short pause as the enormity of the find slowly sank in. Harris wanted to reveal her find too, although it was no match for the potential murder weapon.

"I found these boots downstairs, sir, and the tread pattern looks very similar to the boot print that was found at Sutton Harbour where Mr Morris was murdered. I'll check it out."

King asked Harris to call Forensics and also some uniformed officers as the house would have to be secured as an evidence scene.

"Good work, Lucy. Right, let's get back and see what's been going on at Bracken Hill Farm."

FORTY-FIVE

Paul Armitage lived alone in Totnes. His wife had left him two years before and there was now no one to curb his excesses. He had worked for the district council for many years, starting as an administrator, and after studying was sufficiently qualified to move into the arm of the council that dealt with planning. He rose through the ranks and eventually was promoted to the role of planning officer. With his new-found status he began to realise his position was not without influence.

Around that time, with his higher salary, he began investing in high-risk stocks and shares. Initially his dividends were substantial and he reinvested the money he made. Risk can bring reward, but it can also bring heartbreak. His broker had advised him to consolidate his money and invest heavily in a fast-growing company in China. Initially the returns were excellent and the share price rocketed.

Sometimes companies expand too quickly and if their bubble bursts it happens in a matter of hours not days. The company had overstretched itself and its share price fluctuated over a matter of months before collapsing. Investors had very little time to sell their shares to at least recoup some value from their investment. Armitage's financial adviser was otherwise engaged when the Chinese company crashed and he lost everything.

In his job he was constantly meeting property developers who legitimately sought his advice before they submitted a planning application, to gauge what building was likely to be approved. There was little point in them spending a considerable sum of money on an application that was unlikely to find favour with the councillors on the planning committee.

He had regular contact with property developers and they often had lunch together, usually to discuss a proposed planning application. The council rules on Gifts and Hospitality applied to either over the value of £50; the lunches the planning officer consumed never exceeded that amount.

There was one developer in particular who he seemed to meet quite often, and in casual conversation over lunch and too much wine, Armitage told him of his disastrous investment. The developer was sorry to hear the sad tale and, in future, offered to pay him for his professional opinion on planning applications in the area covered by the district council. He didn't want to waste money on applications, that could cost over £10,000 to lodge, that were then refused. Armitage saw the justification of accepting money for his advice as freelance work and readily agreed to what the developer was suggesting. He had conflict-of-interest thoughts, but they were quickly dismissed as to him this was

legitimately separate work, albeit arranged by a simple verbal contract. He overlooked the fact the council paid him a salary to do that work.

His professional opinion proved to be very lucrative and when applications he presented to councillors, that happened to have been lodged by his developer friend, were accepted, he received £10,000, tax free. He tried hard to persuade his moral compass that the arrangement was definitely freelance work and a legitimate arrangement; deep down he knew it was corruption.

So, when he suspected an investigative journalist was taking a keen interest in his planning activities, he sensed it was only a matter of time before he would come under scrutiny. He informed his developer friend of his concerns and was told not to worry as he would deal with it. When he realised how Morris had been dealt with, he was even more worried than before.

When he saw the police arrive at the council offices, he knew they'd caught up with him and he wasn't going to wait to find out how much they knew. He left in a hurry and then updated his developer friend. After stopping to collect a few things from his home, he drove to a luxury apartment in Dartmouth. He was then instructed to take the owner's hardly used Range Rover and head for Two Bridges.

*

Lucas Peverell attended Exeter University where he began taking drugs. He started on ecstasy and amphetamines and progressed to cocaine. He studied theology and achieved his Bachelor of Arts in the prescribed three years. His degree gave him curate status, but he knew that to become a fully ordained vicar could take as long as eight years. He didn't want to wait that long and in the end for what? After all that time he wasn't impressed with a vicar's salary of less than £20,000 a year. Possibly because of the money or maybe his drug taking, his vocation and a career in the church became a sham. As a drug user he had contacts and he thought being connected to the church was a very convenient cover for a dealer; whoever would think a curate was trading illegal substances?

His profitable pastime was well ordered and helping the Reverend Brown in five churches was perfect as it gave him good reason to be travelling around the parishes.

He had graveyard drug drops carefully planned from the Two Bridges drugs store, to coincide with his church duties. He could even secrete the drugs he was selling in the churches; who would look in those holy places? He met his clients in local pubs, church halls, bus stops and, occasionally, on sacred ground.

Even with his curate's salary, garage pay and drug money – the latter amounting to more than the first two combined – he still wasn't satisfied. He wanted to save enough money to live abroad on the Costa del Sol.

He was friendly with the Garner sons from Ringmore Farm and they would often go scrambling around the beaches and dunes on their part of the coast. When Peverell was in a barn on the farm, drinking cider with the brothers, he spotted an old twelve-bore shotgun propped up in the corner. The Garner boys said it was for shooting rats. After he had left, following the heavy drinking session, he sneaked back to the barn and stole the gun and hid it under a bench in the storeroom at his workplace. Sometime later he took advantage of the owners' absence and retrieved the gun.

Gripping it in a vice, he used a hacksaw to shorten it to a third of its original length. He wanted it to threaten any of his clients who were in arrears or, if necessary, for self-protection.

One day when he popped into the local post office in Bolberry-on-Sea, he noticed how lax the security was, with the door to the post office cubicle just left open while the postmistress attended to a village store customer. He decided there were easy pickings to be had and he needed to boost his savings.

He left work at his garage one evening around five o'clock and then returned half an hour later when the place was deserted. He had a plan. He walked to the garage from his flat and opened the roller shutter door into the main workshop area. He knew Preston had left his motorbike and helmet there and he was going to use them both: the bike as a means of getting to and away from the village stores and the helmet for disguise. He grabbed the gun from its hiding place as he thought that would encourage a swift handover of money at the post office.

Just before six o'clock that evening he entered the village stores. Everything was going well as the frightened postmistress had opened the money drawer; then the postmaster appeared from upstairs.

While they were wrestling for control of the gun it went off twice and it was only in the morning he found out that Jane Ferris was dead. He reasoned that if that stupid bastard Bayliss hadn't fought back, he would have been off with the money and she'd still be alive. It wasn't his fault she was dead.

For Peverell, life went on as normal until he went to collect a drug drop at the church in Kingston from behind a grave with its six red roses identifier: the package wasn't there.

He needed to understand why it hadn't been delivered, or if it had, who had taken it? There was also an element of self-preservation, as if there weren't answers to those two questions, the finger of suspicion might be pointed at him. He made contact using his mobile phone as he was more worried about the missing drugs than the call being traced. Wayne Brody from the farm wanted a face-to-face meeting with the dealer as he had dropped off the drugs at the Kingston church. Brody was already suspicious that this was a scam as he had hidden the drugs particularly well behind the grave. It was almost impossible for anyone to know they were there except Peverell. For his part, the curate wanted to meet as he could more easily, if required, stress his innocence. He rode his motorbike out of the village heading for Bracken Hill Farm.

*

Jim Preston was never a happy man and things were about to get worse in his life.

He had served in the Royal Engineers during his service days, mainly repairing and maintaining army vehicles. Active service took him to the Falklands during the war in 1982 and a few other skirmishes. When he left the army, his pension wasn't great and, like many in his regiment, he made a smooth transition to civilian life by becoming a mechanic.

When his mother died he used his part of her legacy – split between him and his estranged sister – to buy a half-share in the local garage where he worked. At the time, the owner had a cash flow problem and when he offered Mike Farthing the money in exchange for shared ownership, he was happy to take it. Preston knew he got the best of the deal and it was better than the money earning meagre interest in his bank.

He lived alone in his run-down cottage and was beginning to consider retirement. Perversely he fancied spending his last years in the very place that he had defended: the Falkland Islands and, as he often used to say, "Not the bloody Malvinas!" But he roughly calculated that his pension, plus his half-share in the garage, wasn't enough to sustain him in his dotage. He'd have to work longer and save more, neither of which pleased him.

That's why when a director of Build Great Homes offered him and his partner half a million pounds for their garage site, he could see himself escaping from the inspection pit in the garage to the endless space of the Falkland Islands.

There was just one snag: the offer was dependent on the developers getting planning permission for the field at Ringmore Farm. If that was granted, then their garage would be the site of the new community centre as the developers had promised to build a replacement for the crumbling village hall.

When Farthing and Preston were alerted by a director of BGH that some parish councillors were against the development, they colluded and realised they had to influence the outcome. They decided to target only two parish councillors as they knew some were already in favour. They reasoned that if they could persuade at least two who were against it to change their minds that would be enough to get the planning application approved.

The garage owners came up with ideas that would scare the councillors and coax them to change their voting intentions. Farthing agreed to target Ms Abigail Croft and Preston wanted to target Doug Grant as: "the bastard had complained about some work I did on his car!"

They agreed it should be done on the same night to add impact. Farthing set off after midnight with his bleach bottles and the mechanic with his lighter and petrol can. Before Farthing left, he had an idea that would deflect attention from him and daubed his own garage door. Unfortunately for him he had been careless and his ruse had been rumbled by the police. As it was his fault their plan had been exposed, he confessed to the lawn bleaching and the arson of the summerhouse, even though his partner had done the latter deed. Neither did he name him as an accomplice.

At the time, the mechanic delighted in the blaze, but cursed the loss of a coat button as he clambered his stocky frame over the locked five-bar gate into Grant's garden. He had searched for it, but in the darkness, and not wishing to use the torch on his mobile, he gave it up as lost.

When the developer saw them both some days later, he expressed some concern about an investigative journalist snooping around, falsely claiming he was an environmentalist who was trying to stop any developments on the coast. He identified the person threatening their deal and suggested he should be warned off.

Just to really focus their attention, he upped his offer for their garage site by an extra £50,000.

The director thought that the journalist would attend the extraordinary meeting in Bolberry-on-Sea, where the planning application relating to Burgh Island View would be discussed, before the actual vote later in the month. He arranged to meet Preston at the BGH building site in Dartmouth before the parish council meeting. The director gestured to him to put his motorbike in the show home garage. He then gave him the duplicate key to the company's Ford Ranger and also the show home garage. He told him what car the journalist would be driving and suggested he needed to be warned off. If he was successful, not only would it increase the chances for the sale of the garage site, he'd also personally get an additional reward of £10,000.

Preston was also at the extraordinary meeting and left shortly before the end, parking in a secluded spot where he could see all the cars leaving the village hall car park. He followed Morris looking for an opportunity, without any other cars about, to run him off the road. He couldn't believe his luck when the journalist turned into the road leading to Oceans Restaurant on Bolberry Down. He duly followed him and rammed his car, watching it disappear over the cliff. The only thing that went wrong was the number plate of the Ranger was broken. *No worries*, he thought, *I can get that fixed*.

He rang one of his few mates and told him he needed a damaged plate replaced and he'd give him £100 if he could do it that night. With that fixed, he drove back to the Dartmouth site and duly locked the Ranger in the garage of the show house, put the keys in his pocket and left on his motorbike.

He was livid when he found out that Morris had not only survived the ramming, but was still snooping. He worked out he'd get £250,000 for the garage site – when he had paid a fraction of that to Farthing for his half-share –, £25,000 as a half-share of the bonus and £10,000 if he could get rid of the nosey journalist. That sum would set him up nicely in a cottage at Port Stanley. He found out, from covert observation, that Morris was partial to a pub crawl every Friday night so he followed him. When he delayed his journey home by having his nightcap in Kitty O'Hanlons and was staggering home without anyone about, Preston seized the moment. He earned his bounty when Dan Morris drowned in Sutton Harbour.

The one thing that irritated him was being arrested for something he hadn't done. He knew he'd been set up by Peverell who had borrowed his motorbike and helmet without asking. He would have to pay for that at some point in the future. He could wait for his revenge, but not for his blood money and the director told him to be at Bracken Hill Farm just after six o'clock to collect.

*

It wasn't such a coincidence that Armitage, Peverell and Preston were all heading for the farm that evening as they all had business with 'The Baron'; for two of them it would be their last ever deal.

FORTY-SIX

It was dusk as the movement sensor at the junction of the farm lane – which led to Bracken Hill Farm – and the main road, alerted the occupants in the farmhouse of an impending arrival. They recognised the Range Rover and remotely opened the steel mesh electronically controlled gates. As Armitage approached, he was eventually recognised and as the dogs were tracking his progress, Nick Brody pressed the button on the other remote control, to signal through the dogs' shock collars not to attack. Wayne Brody left the house and directed him to park towards the side of the building as the part in front of the barn with huge doors was needed for another visitor.

Next to arrive was Jim Preston, who had driven there rather than use his motorbike. Exactly the same procedures as for Armitage's arrival were followed and he, too, was directed to park away from the barn.

Both Armitage and Preston offered the same reason for their attendance at the 'headquarters' of the drug operation across Devon.

"I've arranged to see 'The Baron'."

Evelyn Whitaker made them coffee and they both sat scanning their mobiles without engaging in conversation.

It was time for the brothers to prepare for their main visitor. Wayne Brody opened the barn doors, while his brother started the Nissan. He gradually reversed the huge vehicle towards the barn and his brother, using hand signals, coaxed him closer to the trailer's tow bar. He fastened the coupling and connected the electrics before standing clear to allow the Nissan to gradually pull the landing platform clear of the barn.

Just then the sensor announced the arrival of another visitor; this time it was a scrambler motorbike. Whitaker recognised Peverell and opened the gates. She also pressed the shock collar button to ensure Lean and Mean didn't attack him. He didn't enter the farmhouse, rather choosing to watch the distant light of the helicopter grow bigger as it made its approach. The preparations for the arrival of the main man continued as he radioed ahead that he was approaching the farm.

Dusk had given way to darkness.

All of a sudden, the front of the barn was lit up by a spotlight fixed on the back of the Nissan and also one attached high up on the front of the barn, above the doors. The peripheral light also illuminated the windsock that showed a strong wind. As further help to the pilot, the halogen uplights on each corner of the trailer pierced the blackness of the sky. He expertly landed on the white cross on the trailer. The positioning of it ensured the rotor blades would not foul on nearby buildings or vegetation. If it had been daytime, the helicopter would have been reversed into the barn so as not to arouse interest, but as it was dark there was no need for such caution. Unlike other occasions, the motor wasn't switched off, rather left in idle mode with the rotor blades barely turning. This visit was obviously going to be fleeting. However, all the lights around the barn were quickly switched off leaving only the light from the porch to cast a dull glow across the scene.

'The Baron' carefully stepped down from the trailer carrying a laptop computer case. The Dobermans didn't need any shock treatment for this visitor as he was known and liked by the dogs. As usual they were each given a chewy artificial dog bone they had eagerly anticipated. (Pavlov's theory in action.)

As Nick and Wayne Brody approached 'The Baron' there was no friendly greeting.

"Two packages in the back. Usual quantity." He never came empty-handed.

With that he strode into the farmhouse as if he owned the place, which he did. Peverell followed closely behind. When Preston saw him, the curate tensed, but both knew better than to cause a scene in front of the drugs boss.

"Right, let's deal with Paul first. In a moment I'll fly you to Manchester Airport and my private jet will then fly you to Malaga Airport in Southern Spain. There you'll be collected by one of my men and taken to my villa in Nerja. We'll then decide what to do next.

"Jim, good work on the journalist. Here's your money." With that he handed Preston the laptop case containing 500 £20 notes in ten bundles.

"Now, Peverell, I understand some drugs have gone missing!"

"The last drug drop, sir, at the church in Kingston, it wasn't there when I went to collect it. So, I've come to ask Nick, as I think he does the drops on my patch, what happened?"

'The Baron' turned to Nick Brody and obviously wanted an explanation.

"I did the drop as planned. I used Ava Sterling's grave and placed the red roses in the vase as usual. The package was very well hidden behind the headstone. Nobody would have seen it if casually walking by. Someone would have had to know to look there to find it."

"One of you is lying." 'The Baron' menacingly spoke through gritted teeth adding, "And I don't like liars!"

Just then the sensor on the entrance to the lane beeped and all heads in the farmhouse swivelled to look at the CCTV images. Although only using sidelights, several vehicles could be seen approaching the farmhouse in convoy.

"Paul, get in the chopper!" the boss ordered and Armitage willingly accepted the command. Grabbing his case he ran outside towards the helicopter, with its engine idling on the trailer, and the Dobermans in pursuit. The shock collar remote was no longer being operated.

He thought he'd made it! His right foot was inside

the cabin and he was about to pull himself up, but before he could get his left foot inside, Lean sank his teeth into his ankle. He squealed and began kicking out, which was just sufficient to momentarily break the dog's grip and it fell back and rolled off the edge of the trailer.

"Jim and Peverell, you'll have to take your chances." Turning to the Brody brothers and Whitaker he said, "As for you other three, I'll get you a good defence lawyer." With that he ran to the improvised helipad before they had a chance to complain.

The convoy hadn't quite reached the entrance gates, but it was only a matter of time. Preston saw his chance and moved closer to the curate.

"You tried to stitch me up, you bastard!" With that he punched Peverell full in the face and poleaxed him. As he put his hand over his broken nose, blood began oozing between his fingers. "I'm taking your bike just as you took mine." He searched his pockets and, finding no keys, assumed they had been left in the ignition of the scrambler. He grabbed his 'blood money' and made for the front door leaving the curate moaning on the floor.

Fortunately for him, Lean and Mean were distracted and were barking at Armitage who was now safely in the helicopter, although he was nursing a very sore ankle.

The rotor blades moved from idling to near full rotational speed as Preston ran from the house and kick-started the scrambler into life. He knew exactly where he was heading and hoped the police hadn't covered that particular escape route. The dogs saw him and took off in angry pursuit. He got to the partially hidden door, dismounted and, with some difficulty, opened it sufficiently wide to get him and the bike through. The door slammed shut behind him as the dogs leapt ferociously at it.

The lead police Land Rover Defender had reached the steel mesh gates and wasn't about to wait for the remote control to be activated. Engaging four-wheel drive, the driver accelerated and the gates burst open.

The helicopter had nearly reached the maximum revs that it needed to get airborne. 'The Baron' knew he still had just enough time to escape the clutches of the now rapidly advancing police.

Peverell emerged from the house and in the gloom saw the back light of his motorbike shining brightly as it braked before exiting through the back gate. He foolishly started to run after him and when he got halfway there, realising his mistake too late, he turned to run back to the house. Mean jumped on his back and as he flattened him, Lean was quick to pounce on the defenceless curate. His motorbike leathers offered some protection from the bites, but not much. He curled into the foetal position for protection. The dogs remorselessly bit any part of his body they could get their teeth into, with his legs being the most vulnerable.

The brothers and Whitaker were busy trying to destroy what drugs they could by flushing them down the toilet, a task made all the more difficult by the recently arrived packages. Flight or fight? The former was not an option due to their own efforts to make the compound secure; it wouldn't be easy to escape. They decided to fight.

Each grabbing a shotgun, the men ran up the stairs and stood at windows overlooking the front of the farmhouse. They could see the helicopter just about to take off. Whitaker went to the kitchen and took the handgun out of the drawer.

Armed police were now walking behind the Land Rover Defender, while other police vehicles followed, still in convoy.

Wayne Brody smashed a window with the butt of the shotgun and fired at the advancing police before ducking back behind a curtain. Just a few seconds later, he decided to fire the other cartridge, but before he could pull the trigger he was hit in the chest by four bullets delivered by two police marksmen. The last thing he saw were the red laser dots on the front of his shirt, before his chest exploded.

The helicopter was now gradually lifting into the air and the armed officers were ordered not to fire. It was one thing to kill when threatened, but quite another to kill simply if someone was avoiding capture.

'The Baron' had taken off from the trailer a hundred times before, but never under so much pressure and, without the improvised landing lights, without any light.

The chopper rose at an acute angle away from the ground, instead of straight up, which was caused solely by the pilot's lack of spatial awareness due to the darkness. The tail rotor clipped the wind turbine and both the helicopter and the turbine lost a blade as they were snapped off in the collision. The helicopter kept rising, but the main body now started spinning out of control in the opposite direction to the main rotor arms. The tail rotor was designed to hold the aircraft steady, but with that gone, it began spinning faster, completely disorientating the pilot. It just cleared the compound's hedge and appeared to be gaining in altitude, but that was only because the ground fell away. It spun faster and faster and with one defiant surge skywards it then plummeted to the ground in a ball of flames.

The people still involved in the drama unfolding in the house never even noticed the fireball illuminating the night sky from behind the hedge.

The brother that was still alive came out of the front door with his arms raised and was ordered, twice, to lie face down on the gravel drive and not to move. He was then cuffed and unceremoniously carried face down to a waiting police van. When you'd done wrong, you lost the right to be treated in a dignified manner.

Peverell was still being mauled and as police marksmen got closer to the melee of man and dogs, both Lean and Mean simultaneously decided to launch a new attack on the approaching officers. Each chose their own prey and eagerly leapt towards their next victims; both were dead before they hit the ground. The Dangerous Dogs Act apparently didn't apply on the moor; neither did the Animal Welfare Act 2006. These dogs had started life as puppies and had been turned into killers. They had to be killed, all because they had been conditioned – just like

Pavlov's dog – and human greed had made their behaviour unacceptable.

The marksmen didn't approach Peverell and remained vigilant not knowing if the scene had been secured. An officer in the police convoy had already summoned the other emergency services and knew that one ambulance wouldn't be enough.

The catastrophic events, which lasted only a matter of minutes yet seemed longer, appeared to be over as armed police entered the farmhouse.

Inspectors King and Best stood with King's boss and were keeping well out of the way at the side of the building. They knew there was nothing that could be done for whoever was in the helicopter.

Peverell was receiving emergency first aid from officers, whilst waiting for an ambulance, and was unconscious. Such were the number of bites and blood loss, survival looked unlikely.

One of the people in the house was presumed dead, while the other was under arrest. That summed up for the senior detectives what they had just witnessed that evening – not quite. Best moved cautiously from the side to the front of the farmhouse leaving the other two detectives reflecting on successfully identifying and neutralising the drugs store.

They were stood next to some double doors that opened outwards, and which were at a forty-five-degree angle to the ground; this is where the coal would have been delivered in the past, straight into the cellar.

All of a sudden the doors burst open like a jack-in-the-box and in the half-light the detectives could make out a woman emerging. She was carrying a gun: Evelyn Whitaker was on a revenge mission. King saw her first as he was slightly in front of his temporary boss.

"You've ruined everything, you bastards, everything!" She raised the weapon about to fire at King, who became transfixed, from almost point blank range. In that split second he thought to himself that this was where his life would end.

He never knew what prompted Acting Superintendent Roberts to do what he did next. The bullet had barely left the gun's muzzle, when Roberts aggressively pushed King to the ground and made a grab for the weapon; he was too late and was hit twice full in the chest.

Roberts recoiled on top of King – his back on King's front – and blood oozed from the exit wound onto the inspector's shirt.

As they lay on the ground, two shots rang out and the woman was jerked back into the cellar. The marksmen had witnessed the shooting, but were just too late to prevent it.

Police now swarmed over the compound and the whole place was bathed in light from headlights and from switches flicked on by an armed officer by the front door.

Further activity to secure the site found the back exit and the senior officers realised that their planning hadn't been as thorough as it should have been.

The police helicopter could now be heard overhead. It had been held back from the start of the raid so as not to spook the occupants of the farmhouse.

If it had been a few minutes earlier, it may have been in time to track Preston escaping across the moor. He knew what he was going to do and even now was turning from his northerly direction to find a road to take him back towards Plymouth and Millbay Docks.

Several ambulances eventually arrived and crews began to work feverishly on Peverell and Roberts. The brother, shot on the upstairs landing, and the woman in the cellar, were pronounced dead at the scene; the death toll so far was two.

Other police and medics, assisted by a fire engine that had now arrived, were gathered around the scene of the helicopter crash; the death toll rose to four.

Medics were feverishly working on the acting superintendent having carefully lifted his body off the inspector; the bullets had penetrated the left ventricle of his heart; the death toll rose again.

King's detective team had been at the back of the police convoy, leaving the initial assault to be carried out by trained armed officers. They now joined their colleagues as the farmhouse was declared safe.

When Sergeant Harris saw her inspector, sat on a nearby garden bench, with what looked like blood on the front of his coat she was visibly shocked and upset. She sat beside him and took one of his hands in hers. He was shivering. She'd never seen him so vulnerable.

"Are you alright, Richard?"

He looked at her with tears in his eyes: "Why? Why? Why did he do that? He saved my life!" He was in shock and Harris moved her arm, placed it around his shoulders, and pulled him close.

FORTY-SEVEN

Forensics later confirmed Preston's guilt and an APW was eventually issued, warning all ports to be on the lookout for him; it came just too late to prevent his escape. The damning evidence against him comprised: the greatcoat, the missing buttons, the duplicate set of keys (of the car used in the ramming), the screwdriver murder weapon and the bloodied boot print found at the scene of Morris's murder.

Preston, who had started his getaway from the farm heading north, knew he needed to be travelling south. He gambled that the police would not follow him in their helicopter, which could be seen hovering in the distance, as they were unaware of his presence at Bracken Hill Farm.

Still on the open moor, and managing to cross the Blackbrook River, he skirted the Great Mis Tor that loomed above him in the darkness, eventually joining the road at Merrivale and heading for Tavistock. Once there, he took the main A386 to Plymouth and on to the ferry terminal at Millbay Docks. He was in good time for the eight o'clock sailing.

When in sight of the ferry, he dismounted. Not wishing to leave Peverell's scrambler where it could be found, thus alerting the police to his ferry escape, he decided to get rid of it. Now walking and pushing the bike, he reached the dockside and, after checking there was no one about, gently pushed it into the water.

He then bought a one-way ticket to Roscoff in France, as a foot passenger, and ambled aboard, heading straight for the restaurant and bar. Once there and after several pints of beer, fish and chips was his chosen meal; it was to be his last. When needing to pay for the drinks and the meal, he undid the zip of the computer case with its strap across his chest, given to him by 'The Baron', and fumbled in the bag. Taking out one of the flat-packed bundles of £20 notes – there were ten packs in all, each containing fifty notes – he slipped two out to pay for what he'd eaten and drunk and put the bundle back with the others. By the time he'd finished his meal and paid, the ferry had sailed across Plymouth Sound and was well on its way across the Channel. His clumsy handling when getting the money out to pay in his slightly inebriated state hadn't gone unnoticed.

Declining the use of a cabin, he planned to use one of the many reclining seats to pass the five hours the crossing would take, but before his nap he wanted one last smoke. There were only a few designated areas on the ferry where smoking was allowed and, rather unsteadily, he followed the 'SMOKERS THIS WAY' sign. Lighting his Hamlet cigar he began to plan for his arrival in Roscoff and beyond. His £10,000 bounty would smooth his passage, wherever that led. First he would need a backpack, some clothes and toiletries.

Puffing on his cigar in splendid isolation as the only smoker on that part of the open deck, his musings were suddenly rudely interrupted.

"Got a light, mate?"

Two other smokers had joined him and as he reached into his pocket for his lighter, without warning, the man who had asked him for a light punched him in the face and the other kicked him in the groin. Before he knew what was happening the strap on his computer case, still across his chest, was roughly pulled over his head and the two men were lifting him up. With a final heave they threw him over the side into the water thirty metres below.

If Karen White had seen what had just happened and compared the similarity between his demise and that of her boyfriend, Dan Morris, no doubt she would have uttered one word: "Justice!"

*

Lucas Peverell eventually regained consciousness and was immediately arrested. It was three days after he had been attacked and two skin graft operations had been carried out; more would follow. His wounds would heal and the scars would be a constant reminder of that fateful night; his mental scars would never heal.

*

The next morning after the raid, Bracken Hill Farm was a hive of activity. The bodies of Wayne Brody and Evelyn Whitaker had been removed as had the dead dogs. Drugs officers had found the 'greenhouse' and were busy cataloguing and removing the cannabis to a van. Several trips would be required due to the sheer number of plants. The huge amount of cocaine was also recorded.

One of the rotor blades, snapped off by the helicopter, lay on the ground at the foot of the wind turbine mast. The blade from the rear of the chopper, that had been severed in the collision, was found well away from the crash site. The landing trailer remained where it had been parked, as did the Nissan.

Air Accident Investigation Branch officers were sifting through the wreckage just outside the compound. The remains of two bodies were recovered, neither of which had been strapped into their seats when the crash happened. The identity of both occupants was later established from dental records. One was confirmed as Mr Paul Armitage from Totnes. The other was initially identified from his pilot certificate, authorising him to fly, which was filed at Manchester Airport. This contained information about him, including his name and address:
MR GEORGE LAWSON, 'BARON'S RETREAT',
ROSSMILL LANE, ALTRINCHAM, GREATER
MANCHESTER.

*

In due course, the operation at Bracken Hill Farm

was reviewed. It was difficult to regard it as a wholly successful mission as reconnaissance had not identified the door in the back hedge of the compound; judging by the fresh tracks, it appeared someone had escaped on a motorbike. The most damning indictment was the loss of life, including a police officer, as the site had not been properly secured.

*

The death of Acting Superintendent Roberts made the headlines in the national and local press. The circumstances in which he died made it doubly poignant; he sacrificed his life to save the life of a fellow police officer.

The fact that a sophisticated and widespread drugs operation across Devon had eventually been thwarted also filled many column inches. George Lawson was not posthumously vilified in the immediate press coverage, but when the full facts were known, his previous reputation as a self-made multi-millionaire was left in tatters.

*

Chief Superintendent Harper gave a number of press conferences, always leading with the sad death of the well-respected acting superintendent. Inspector King, whose life he had saved, was also mentioned, but more as a footnote; Richard King would have been more than happy if his role hadn't been mentioned at all. Harper went on to comment about the damage that had been inflicted on the so-called County Lines gang and the loss of its mastermind. King, whilst taking note of the disruption caused to drug dealing in the county, knew that void would soon be filled by another criminal.

*

The day after the raid, the inspector addressed his team in the conference room at the police station in Plymouth. He opened the informal gathering by paying his own tribute to his dead boss. Any rancour he felt towards him – having had good cause to dislike him – remained hidden and he was very grateful to him for his selfless act.

"Over the last few weeks we have had a number of crimes to solve and there was a common thread between them: they all had deception at their core. Despicable people pretending to be something they weren't. That is very difficult for us, as police officers, to detect.

"Following the recent criminal activities, and particularly the events of yesterday, when my life was threatened, Chief Superintendent Harper thinks I should take a short break. Thank you all for your support and hard work."

Although he was only bidding them a temporary farewell, as the detectives left, DCs Hammond and Dyson each shook his hand. Sergeant Harris was the last to leave the room and she looked troubled. King sensed her anxiety.

"What's up, Lucy?"

In the aftermath of the exposure of the drug and planning corruption criminals, Lucy Harris was in reflective mood. She felt compelled to share with her boss what she perceived as a personal failing.

"I was thinking about one particular aspect of the planning corruption case, sir. I interviewed Mr Simpson and I was told…" She paused and reached for her notebook and read out: *"George Lawson acquires building plots for the company and seeks planning permission, while Simon Webber deals with sales and I am responsible for getting the houses built."*

"So you see, sir, it should have been obvious to me that Lawson was corrupt as he was the one who dealt with planning. If I had pursued him, we might have prevented all the deaths and brought an earlier end to all his criminal activities."

"Hindsight is a wonderful thing, Lucy. As detectives our job is to get to the truth. When people are being deceitful, it is a very difficult, if not an impossible, task in the first instance to sort out the good from the bad: those that are being truthful and the people that are lying to us. When we know the truth, looking back some fact or other can seem obvious.

"At the time you interviewed the directors of Build Great Homes we were unaware of any planning corruption. It was only later when Karen White rang me and told me she had inadvertently set her partner off on a possible corruption trail at her place of work. Initially we made a natural assumption that his murder was linked to illegal drugs.

"In any investigation, when the truth is finally

exposed, of course we should review what we did. That's how we learn as detectives, and, yes, we sometimes make mistakes. In some cases, looking back, perhaps we could have been quicker to spot the bad people. As I recall, at the time, we were following a number of leads and maybe that was one that slipped past us, not just you. I told you before, Lucy, we are not the bad people here."

Reassured she eventually followed her colleagues' lead and offered her hand to the inspector. He refused it and instead hugged her. On this occasion there was no senior officer to interrupt them. They parted and Richard King uttered three words that for Lucy Harris might have been made in heaven: "Dinner tomorrow night?"

EPILOGUE

Bolberry-on-Sea: In view of the interference by Paul Armitage in the planning application process to build twenty-five executive homes in the village, its approval was revoked. This pleased and annoyed the residents in equal numbers.

The village primary school closed at the end of that summer term as there were not enough children for the education authority to warrant employing a teacher and an assistant.

The district council had to spend over £50,000 to make the Grade II listed village hall safe, watertight and compliant with Health & Safety regulations. The promised new community centre was never built.

The garage site owned by Farthing and Preston was put up for sale at an asking price of just £175,000, well below what they would have received from Build Great Homes.

The village post office and stores was closed for six months and eventually reopened with new owners.

For the hairdressing salon, Making Waves, and butcher's, Pleased to Meat You, it was business as usual.

The Duke of Cornwall had lost some of its customers through death or departure, but strangely continued to flourish. The events that had happened seemed to bring the village closer together and residents were more inclined to meet each other socially.

Marco Coppola: If the Italian boat owner from Naples had lived, he would have been convicted as a drugs runner. As it was, he was knocked into the sea by the sail boom from his boat and he suffered an ignominious end, eventually being washed onto the shore at Hope Cove. His body was subsequently repatriated and only a handful of mourners attended his belated funeral.

Cassandra Coppola: Marco's sister was arrested when she returned to Italy and pleaded not guilty to a number of drug-related offences. She was found guilty and sentenced to ten years in prison.

Fabio Gallo: The person who helped Marco Coppola deliver drugs to the UK on the ketch *Marcass* pleaded guilty to the charge of drug trafficking. In view of his plea, and for cooperating with the police, his ten-year prison sentence was reduced to seven years. In case of any reprisals from the Mafia, he served his sentence at a prison in the north of Italy, well away from Naples.

Isabella Gallo: Fabio Gallo's sister also pleaded guilty to helping transport illegal drugs and received a prison term of five years.

Colonel Davenport: The colonel continued as chairman of the parish council. The substantial dividends from his stocks and shares, plus his army pension, meant that financially he remained comfortably placed.

The council was only in the second year of its four-year term and there were now three vacancies: the disgraced Mike Farthing (who resigned before he was removed because of his criminal activities), Ted Bayliss (who just stopped attending meetings) and, of course, Jane Ferris. The colonel decided to fill just one post by co-option rather than election and he approached Maria Harkness, the butcher's wife, and she agreed to stand. Her name was advertised for the statutory four-week period and, as there were no objections, she joined the council.

Any planning applications that the councillors now consider always bring back painful memories of the infamous application that proved so divisive and led, directly or indirectly, to so many deaths.

Dawn Proud: The hairdresser eventually recovered from the loss of her Italian partner and, after a short break, following Cassandra Coppola's sudden departure, continued with her Making Waves business. She became friendly with Abigail Croft and they began spending more and more time together.

Abigail Croft: It eventually became clear why she never responded wholeheartedly to Mike Farthing's advances: she was gay. She had high hopes that her new relationship with the hairdresser might develop into something beyond mere friendship.

Until the two words were consumed by new grass, her lawn remained a painful reminder of what had happened in the normally tranquil village. Her own memory of the events would not be so easily covered.

Dave Smith: The landlord of the Duke of Cornwall, although disappointed the planning application had been revoked, remained his chirpy self. After all, he hadn't actually lost business just not gained any. The few customers he had lost, namely Peverell, Preston and Farthing, were replaced by other villagers with a social and sociable conscience.

Doug Grant popped into the Duke one late afternoon on his way back from his game of golf and Dave Smith served him. As usual, he was ready for a chat as there weren't many other customers in at that time.

"I went to a faith healing seminar this morning, Doug."

"That's interesting. What was it like, Dave?"

"Bloody awful. Even the guy in the wheelchair got up and walked out!"

The Reverend Brown: The vicar hadn't any idea that his curate was a drug dealer or that he was using his church duties as a cover for his sins. Neither did he suspect the various churches were being used to hide drugs and money. A shoebox, containing both, was found at other churches in the diocese, always under the altar. Because of this sacrilege it was hard for the reverend to forgive Lucas Peverell, but due to his devout belief he did.

Gavin Harkness: The local butcher continued to sell locally sourced meat and make disparaging remarks about veganism.

Maria Harkness: Gavin Harkness's wife – who to some extent had for many years lived in the shadow of her husband – became a prominent member of the parish council after being nominated by its chairman. Her elevation brought a new dynamic to the marital relationship. She remained very supportive of her husband, but vegan pasties are now sold in the Pleased to Meat You shop. She convinced him they were good for business and she was right. She only ate one when he was out!

Ted Bayliss: The technical term for what Ted Bayliss suffered was post-traumatic stress; the colloquial term, in his particular case, was a broken heart. The postmaster never fully recover from the loss of his partner, Jane Ferris. He never opened the village stores or post office after that fateful night. On the first anniversary of her murder, he committed suicide.

Jane Ferris: The whole of Bolberry-on-Sea village turned out for the funeral of Jane Ferris, the murdered postmistress. The Reverend Brown conducted the service and gave the eulogy. "Sadly missed" is often said at funerals; in her case it was undoubtedly true.

Mike Farthing: The part-owner of the garage was treated as a social pariah in the village. Due to his selfish scheming in order to manipulate the parish council vote on the planning application made by Build Great Homes, he lost three things: his seat on the council, his friends and his business. No one wanted to use his services or buy his petrol after his antics were made public. He later admitted that it was Preston who set fire to Doug Grant's summerhouse, although before his confession, King had already worked that out from the button on the drive.

He did face three charges made by the Crown Prosecution Service: criminal damage (to Abigail Croft's lawn); wasting police time (after he daubed his own garage door); and, most worryingly for him, accessory to murder. He pleaded guilty to the first two charges and not guilty to the third.

At his trial, the prosecution alleged that he colluded with Preston to carry out the murder of Dan Morris as he stood to gain if the journalist was silenced. Farthing denied any involvement and said his partner acted alone. This was true, even though the £10,000 for the contract killing was never revealed in the court case as only Lawson and Preston knew of the arrangement.

The jury found Farthing not guilty of being an accessory to murder by a majority verdict. He was sentenced to two years in prison, suspended for two years, and ordered by the presiding judge to complete one hundred hours of community service for the crimes he had admitted.

Preston's body was eventually found and his half-share of the garage, although he died intestate, passed to his estranged sister. The proceeds of sale for the garage were split equally between her and Farthing.

He sold the 1967 Aston Martin DB 6 – inherited from his father – he kept in his garage at home, for less than the asking price and only received £85,000 for the garage site as his half-share. He later moved to Southern Spain to live out his days, but not until he had completed his community service punishment. He still pines for his unrequited love, Abigail Croft. She made it clear to him when he called to see her that the chances of reconciliation were below zero!

Doug Grant: After his dream turned into a nightmare, Doug Grant eventually fulfilled his bucket list task and walked a tightrope. This feat was performed at the River Dart Country Park, between Exeter and Plymouth. It didn't matter to him that the steel rope was only ten metres off the ground and that he was wearing a security harness attached to an overhead rope!

Scott Osbourne: The teacher still cycles to work each day, a journey that takes him forty-five minutes. With the closure of the local primary school, he now supplements his income giving private tuition to some children in the village.

Kirsten Massey: The local artist continued to paint and sell her work to support herself. In conversation with Abigail Croft, over coffee and biscuits after a parish council meeting, she was asked if she was still painting seascapes?

"Yes, but I've considerably diversified as I needed a new challenge in my art. I wanted to combine the sea and the human form. I took my inspiration from Lluis Ribas, the Spanish artist. He paints scantily clad women in the surf. I also wanted to sell more canvases as I need the money. A gallery in Kingsbridge sells my paintings."

When asked by Croft if the scantily clad women had increased sales, Massey looked at her and simply said: "What do you think?" Croft took that as a yes.

Jim Preston: No one witnessed Preston being unceremoniously thrown overboard, so he was not reported missing. His body was eventually washed ashore at a place called Trouville-sur-Mer, between Cherbourg and Le Havre on the coast of Northern France. Identification was easy for the French police as he had his passport in a plastic wallet and zipped pocket in the coat he was still wearing when he was deposited on the beach. After several months, his body was repatriated. Preston and Coppola: one body into the country and one body out.

The full horror of his crimes was eventually revealed. Somewhat reluctantly, the Reverend Brown agreed to his burial at St Paul's in the village. His compassion was strained to its absolute limit as he conducted the short burial service. The church was eerily empty as his coffin was taken to the grave. Not even his sister attended the service.

Joe Garner: Farmer Garner was a bitter man when the approved planning application for development of one of his fields was revoked. He decided to buy Farthing's garage, but in a spiteful act, offered him a figure well below its market value. As he was the only buyer, and as Farthing was very keen to sell, the offer was reluctantly accepted.

The gun that Peverell used to kill Jane Ferris was eventually found by police, concealed in the Bolberry Garage, and was traced to Garner. He knew it had been stolen from his barn, but hadn't reported it as his licence had expired. To add insult to injury, he was fined £500 and £250 costs for being in possession of an unlicensed firearm.

Wayne and Buzz Garner: Garner senior gifted the garage site to his boys, Wayne and Buzz. They set up a motorcycle service and repair shop called Garner Bikes and, rather surprisingly, they eventually turned it into a thriving enterprise. They no longer ride their scrambler bikes recklessly through the village as it's not good for business.

Dan Morris: Dan Morris's role in exposing the drug gangs in Bristol and Plymouth, together with uncovering corruption in the district planning process, did not go unnoticed. He was posthumously awarded the British Empire Medal for meritorious service worthy of recognition by the Crown. Her Majesty the Queen presented his medal to Karen White at Buckingham Palace.

Morris was cremated at Efford Crematorium in

Plymouth and over 200 mourners attended, including Inspector King and his team.

Karen White: Karen White moved out of the apartment she shared with Dan Morris as it held too many painful memories of their time together. She is still friendly with Debbie Norris, her work colleague, and they go for the occasional lunchtime drink, but no longer use the Seven Stars Hotel where they witnessed first-hand the deception of Paul Armitage.

Debbie Norris: When Debbie Norris found out that she had unintentionally alerted Paul Armitage to the fact Karen White's partner was an investigative journalist, she was mortified. Her friend was quick not to attach any blame to her for what was an innocent observation. She knew that sooner or later the paths of her boyfriend and Armitage were bound to have crossed.

Simon Webber: Simon Webber was completely unaware of Lawson's criminal activity within their Build Great Homes building company. BGH Limited traded with just two directors and continued to be very successful, building high-class executive homes on legitimately acquired sites.

Len Simpson: Len Simpson told the truth when he said at police interview that he was out walking his two dogs, Layla and Oakleigh, on Slapton Sands beach on the night Dan Morris was run off the road. His lovely wife, Marion, when asked by the police to confirm that the dogs were tired – as a way of corroborating his alibi that evening – assured them that when she returned from her library meeting all three were worn out!

After Lawson's death, Simpson and Webber jointly took on the job of acquiring building plots for the company, including the planning permission element. Len Simpson continued his responsibility for getting the houses built and Simon Webber took care of sales.

George Lawson: After his death it was revealed that Lawson acquired nearly all his wealth from criminal activity. He ran a drugs cartel from Manchester, which he extended into Devon when he bought his apartment in Dartmouth. He owned three properties: 'Baron's Retreat' in Manchester was his main residence, a huge villa in Nerja, near Malaga, in Southern Spain was his second, and the Dartmouth apartment was his third (although that cost him over a million pounds). He started out as a legitimate developer and formed Build Great Homes after befriending Webber and Simpson on the course at the Thurlestone Golf Club where they were all members.

He was responsible for the robbery at Plymouth Albion Rugby Club. He carried out the 'Thomas Crown'-style interview with Gilmour at the aptly named Crowne Plaza Hotel in Plymouth. The character, portrayed in the original film by Steve McQueen, was a multi-millionaire who organised raids on banks simply for the thrill of planning their execution, not for the money. In fact the money in the safe at the rugby club to Lawson was chicken feed. He arranged the raid out of the thrill portrayed in his favourite film and a misplaced desire for retribution. Lawson was a vice-president of PARFC and the committee had denied him the opportunity to become president – a prestigious appointment. He wasn't used to being turned down, so he plotted his revenge, setting up the robbery, carried out by the brothers from Bracken Hill Farm, with Gilmour's help. He said to himself: "I'll teach the bastards for stopping me from becoming president. See how they like losing fifteen grand!"

The brothers cut open the safe with an oxy acetylene cutting torch, taking care not to ignite the bank notes inside. It was then hidden under a tarpaulin in one of the barns at Bracken Hill Farm.

Lawson was paying cash for Armitage's help in securing planning approval for lucrative development sites around the South Devon coast. The cash was usually handed over in the Royal Seven Stars Hotel in Totnes. One such payment had been witnessed by Karen White and Debbie Norris; indirectly that led to the death of the journalist.

Following a detailed investigation, carried out by the National Crime Agency, into Lawson's criminal activities, a judge ordered that his estate had to forfeit over £20 million under the Proceeds of Crime Act 2002. This sum included the sale of 'Baron's Retreat', his villa in Nerja and his apartment in Dartmouth.

Greg Carter: The opportunity of illicit sex for the site manager at the Build Great Homes Dartmouth building site reduced as houses were sold off. His assignation with one of the sales women was confirmed and he was discounted from any involvement with the car-ramming crime.

Paul Armitage: Armitage epitomised the axiom: *'Power tends to corrupt, and absolute power corrupts absolutely.'* In his early days working for the district council, he was absolutely honest. He became a key figure in the planning application process and later, as money became scarce, persuaded himself he was a freelance consultant; his moral degradation was complete.

Although he was disgraced, many attended his funeral and his eulogy covered the period before he succumbed to temptation.

Lucas Peverell: Peverell's recovery from being attacked by two Dobermans was slow and painful. When fit to stand trial, he appeared before a judge at Exeter Crown Court on charges of drug dealing and the murder of Jane Ferris. He pleaded guilty to the drug dealing charge, but, on the advice of his lawyer, not guilty to murder, arguing that she was shot while his client was wrestling with Mr Bayliss, the postmaster. After discussions between the judge and the defence and prosecution lawyers, the charge was reduced to manslaughter, which Peverell accepted.

He was eventually sentenced to life in prison with a minimum of fifteen years to be served before he could be considered for parole.

Soon after he began his sentence, he renounced his criminal activity and turned back to the church seeking absolution.

John 'Gilly' Gilmour: Gilmour was convicted of dealing in Class A drugs, which carries a longer prison term than selling Classes B and C. He was sentenced to seven years in prison reduced to five years on appeal as his defence lawyer argued he had been 'cuckooed'.

Chief Superintendent Harper: The chief superintendent gave the eulogy at AS Roberts' funeral and, naturally, spoke highly of the deceased officer. That wasn't the time or place to comment on what had happened at Bracken Hill Farm or the success of the police operation. However, at the end of the service, and while close family attended the burial, he took King's arm and led him a discreet distance from the other mourners. He knew the cases the inspector and his team had been dealing with and just how close he had personally come to being badly injured or even killed. After complimenting him, using his first name, on the successful conclusion of the various investigations, Harper instructed the indomitable detective to take a period of paid leave and he would arrange several sessions with a trained counsellor. His boss made it quite clear he would only be allowed back to his job on the counsellor's recommendation. King wasn't at all happy with the enforced break, but didn't argue.

Acting Superintendent Roberts: AS Roberts posthumously received the Queen's Police Medal as it was acknowledged he selflessly saved the life of another police officer.

Inspector Jim Best: Inspector Best continued to track down drug dealers in South Devon; there was a never-ending supply. King thanked him and DC Baxter for all the good advice and help they gave in closing down Lawson's drugs empire.

Detective Constable Alex Hammond: Apart from developing quickly as a detective, Alex Hammond was earning a reputation for criminal detection. This was exemplified in him identifying the Naples connection from the Rolex watch worn by Marco Coppola.

His undercover work also earned him high praise. However, his crowning glory was his work on the number plate fragment that eventually helped uncover the drugs trade across Devon and the corruption of the planning process.

Detective Constable Sam Dyson: DC Dyson benefited greatly from working with Inspector King. She appreciated the development and also being given specific tasks to complete on her own as her many visits to Bolberry-on-Sea testified.

Sergeant Lucy Harris: Sergeant Harris wasn't happy with her own reaction when told by her inspector that she wouldn't be working with him. She should have been more professional and mature, but love can do that to you.

After the events at Bracken Hill Farm, that concluded many of the current investigations, she resolved to put in a transfer request to another team, possibly working for Inspector Best. She couldn't continue to torture her emotions by having close day-to-day contact with Richard King; she knew she was slowly falling in love with him.

Detective Inspector Richard King: The inspector had mixed emotions about his erstwhile boss. When he was alive they had a mutual dislike for each other and yet he had, probably, saved his life. He found that dichotomy hard to rationalise. He came to terms with his imposed sabbatical, realising he probably was suffering from mild post-traumatic stress; his counsellor's rating was somewhat higher than mild.

*

In his absence, King's team had completed all the necessary reports on the cases they had recently dealt with and also any paperwork required by the Crown Prosecution Service.

After several weeks, one Monday morning the inspector walked into the main office at the central police station after being assessed as fit for duty. Dyson and Hammond greeted him like he'd been away for longer. They were both delighted that their mentor was back at work; he shook their hands and was touched by their welcome.

For Harris, the familiarity of a dinner date and a beach walk together during his leave, both ending in a hug rather than a kiss, seemed a distant dream. She too offered her hand, which he took in both of his and they both smiled a knowing smile.

As so often happens at these moments, something or someone would return them to reality. Inspector Best came into the room and, after saying it was good to see Richard King's return, he quickly got back to business.

"I've had a report about a rigid inflatable being abandoned on Slapton Sands. The size of this RIB would comfortably seat about a dozen adults; over twenty lifejackets were found strewn in and around the beached boat.

"The report was passed to me as it was thought it might be drugs related. I think this cargo was human, so it's probably one for you and your team, Richard. I'm still clearing up after the recent drug busts at Two Bridges we completed thanks to you and your team. Are you happy to take this one on?"

"No problem, Jim, leave it with us." With that, Best left the room.

King took out a sherbet lemon and the other three detectives simultaneously smiled. They waited as he read the report and then passed it to his sergeant.

"Well, I think we could all do with some sea air. Let's head for Slapton Sands and see what's happened there. At least we don't seem to have a body on the beach... yet!"

To be continued...